Stone Over Water

By the same author

ELVIS IS DEAD

Stone Over Water

CARL MACDOUGALL

Secker & Warburg
LONDON

First published in Great Britain 1989 by
Martin Secker & Warburg Limited
Michelin House, 81 Fulham Road,
London SW3 6RB

British Library Cataloguing in Publication Data

MacDougall, Carl
 Stone over water
 I. Title
 823'.914 [F]

 ISBN 0 436 27078 1

The author gratefully acknowledges financial assistance from
the Scottish Arts Council (bursary) and the Royal Bank of
Scotland (overdraft).

Parts of this book have appeared, in one form or another, in
Chapman and the *Scottish Review*.

Typeset by Deltatype Ltd, Ellesmere Port
Printed in Great Britain

For Kirsty

A double minded man is unstable in all his ways.

James 1:8

It has, I suppose, something to do with the light. But in the evening in June in Scotland – then is the time to see. For it is daylight, yet it is not day, and there is a quality in it which I cannot describe, it is so clear, as if every object was a reflection of itself.

Margaret Oliphant, *The Library Window*

Though it be broken –
Broken again – still it's there,
The moon on the water.

Chosu

Part One

GROUCHO: The party in the first part will be known as the
party in the first part.

A Night At The Opera

One

I am, sirs, a foundling who was given three separate accounts of my birth and background, the first told by Mr Bickerstaffe, headmaster of Greenbank House. On my eleventh birthday he handed me an envelope.

'Well, lad,' he said in the growlish voice he used to address us, 'Well, lad' was a verbal tic; it was a way of entering speech, a time-filler, a pause for recollection, or all four at once in the same sentence. It was always a harbinger of doom; messages flowed from it.

'You have been fortunate,' he continued, 'insofar as you have been chosen for adoption by a stable, God-fearing, working-class family. Count your blessings, lad. They know all about you. Nothing has been omitted, so why they have chosen you I cannot guess. I am also going to tell you what I know of your background so that you'll always be grateful to Greenbank as the place which gave you a start in life.'

He removed his spectacles and polished the lenses with the front of his shirt. 'The wife chose you,' he said, pushing the shirt down in his trousers. 'It has to do with the colour of your eyes. I cannot explain it further because I do not understand it myself. Never mind, we cannot understand everything this life brings us. A blue-eyed boy she wanted and a blue-eyed boy she's got.

'Now; this envelope contains all you possess in the world, or rather all you brought here which is of any use to you today.' And from his desk he produced an ordinary 9x4-inch manilla, buff-coloured envelope. 'We know its contents because it is our policy to check on the possessions and as much as we can of the backgrounds of our unfortunates. God help us, the mothers who send their sturdy sons here would

3

have us believe the earth was as flat as their imaginations; every single story culled from the pages of cheap, romantic fiction.

'These are the facts as we know them. Your mother was stabbed by a coloured sailor during a brawl in a public house. You were three months old when this incident occurred; you were brought here and have been with us ever since. The argument was apparently over a watch and ring which the sailor claimed your mother had stolen some time during the previous evening when he was in her company and much the worse for wear.

'She apparently wasted the last of her oxygen composing the enclosed drivel for your benefit. The note was dictated to a nurse by your mother before she died. The photograph is either of your mother or your grandmother, we do not know. It could also be a friend or another relation of your mother's; in fact, it could be anyone. The sailor got two years, but, alas, not his watch and ring. They were not recovered.

'I am sure you will agree that God has answered your prayers and given you a fine opportunity to better yourself. I hope you will take it. We neither want to see nor hear from you again, so off you go and eat your lunch up, every drop. And wait in the hall till your new family arrives. That will be all.'

'Thank you, sir.'

'Boy!' he shouted as I turned to go.

'Yes, sir?'

'Haven't you forgotten something?'

I saluted him.

'That's better,' said Mr Bickerstaffe. 'You're not away yet. Ungrateful wretch.'

The second account was in the envelope Mr Bickerstaffe gave me. It was supposedly composed by my natural mother and left with a photograph of a small, dumpy woman squinting into the sun. The note said: 'My darling. Never forget this. Your father was an Arabian prince who saw me dance in *Swan Lake*. He fell in love and courted me for six months by sending

4

a dozen red roses to my hotel suite every day. You were conceived on the night he left for his homeland where a cruel insurrection threatened the peace of his kingdom. We made love violently and passionately: the earth moved and stars fell. Your father wept when we parted, and wrote every day. He left this watch and ring which now I leave to you. I have been a sorry soul, alone in this world since he was ambushed and died a hero's death. "A prince among men," *The Times* called him. My darling. I love you as I love my dream of him.'

I happened.

That's what the woman I used to call Mother told me. 'You didn't come from anywhere, dear,' she said. 'You just happened.'

'Is that true?' asked the wall-eyed Wellington. All nameless foundlings were called after British heroes.

'Is what true?'

'Is it true you're leaving?'

We were having lunch. I looked at my plate and nodded.

'Then give us your tatties.'

It was a school custom. Anyone leaving Greenbank House gave his last meal to those who remained. The mince was divided between Churchill and Drake, Peel and Disraeli took the mashed turnip, Wellington and Wolfe the potatoes.

After lunch the matron, Miss Frore, ordered me to strip in the dormitory. I was given a cold bath and the block of yellow soap we used on bath-nights. My scalp was scrubbed with carbolic and I was dried with a hard, wet towel that smelled of unrinsed soap. Then I was dressed in clean clothes.

'These are the last of our clothes you'll be wearing,' said Miss Frore. 'And I suppose you'll be as ungrateful as the others. No one ever comes back to see us.'

I told her Mr Bickerstaffe said I wasn't to come back.

'You are mistaken,' she said. 'Very wrong. And it's naughty of you to say such things about poor Mr Bickerstaffe who works so hard for all our sakes. Now, say you're sorry and finish dressing.'

5

I sat in the hall wearing a navy-blue gaberdine raincoat, grey shirt, grey socks and black hobnailed boots. I could see my face in the mirror opposite; pale, my hair short and straight at the front.

Our history master and registrar, Mr Nettles crossed the hall. He looked at me, paused as though to speak, then passed on to the office where I heard someone laugh. On the way back he seemed surprised to see me.

'What class should you be in?' he asked.

'Please, sir. I'm leaving.'

'That's a new one,' he said. 'Come with me.'

Mr Nettles marched me to the dormitory. 'Put on your normal school outfit and come to my room immediately,' he said.

'Please, sir. I don't have a normal school outfit.'

'Why not?'

'Please, sir. Miss Frore took it.'

'And why would Miss Frore want to remove your normal school outfit?'

'Please, sir. Because I'm leaving.'

'Are you going to persist with this nonsense?'

'Please, sir. I don't know, sir.'

'Insolence.'

He ordered me to wait in the dormitory where I sat on the edge of the bed.

'Of all the ungrateful disgusting ill-mannered naughty boys with impure thoughts you are the worst, definitely the worst.' Miss Frore stood by the doorway, her arms outstretched with a pile of bed-linen supporting her chin. 'What are you doing here?' she asked. 'Don't you want to go to your nice new home. Wouldn't you like a mother and father to care for you, to comfort you and help to rid your mind of sin.'

'Yes, miss.'

'Then why are you hiding here?'

'Mr Nettles brought me.'

'Nonsense,' she said, dropping the sheets. 'Now look at what you've made me do.'

She gathered the linen and placed it on the bed beside me, then turned to the window and patted her hair. 'Dearie me; hurry along now or you'll have me all upset.'

She looked at her hand, bent and straightened her forefinger, turned to me and ran the second joint of her right forefinger down my cheek. I watched the fluff rise spontaneously from the floor beneath the bed, and heard approaching steps along the corridor.

Miss Frore turned suddenly and tucked away a loose strand of hair. Mr Nettles stood at the doorway with a short blue dress across his arm. 'Ah,' he said when he saw Miss Frore and I together.

'What a pretty dress,' Miss Frore said, staring out the window.

'Belongs to my niece.'

'Really.'

'Yes. I was just about to find some brown paper to parcel it so's I can send it to her for her birthday which is next week.'

'We'd better be going,' said Miss Frore. 'Say goodbye to Mr Nettles.'

'Goodbye, Mr Nettles.'

'And may I ask where young Lochinvar is off to?'

'He's leaving.'

Mr Nettles looked at me and shook his head. 'A word of advice,' he said. 'You'll find life much easier if you learn to lie a little. Not too much; too much is never a good thing, but some is all right.'

I saluted him and he smiled. He held the dress against my chest, shook his head, turned and left us.

Miss Frore smiled as we walked together, along the corridor, towards the stairway for the last time.

Mr Bickerstaffe was waiting in the hall with a small man I now find difficult to describe. His suits were grey, his collars white and starched. He wore dark ties and his shoes were polished like glass. He'd melt the polish, spit on the leather, then pour the liquid across the toecaps. When his shoes were set in a dull paste, he'd rub the leather with a series of rags, finishing the job with a clean yellow cloth specially kept for the final polish and which he hand-washed twice a week. He'd admire himself in the shoe-shine. His face was pale, his eyes strong and clear.

There is something misleading rather than dishonest in that portrait. It cannot be my impression of him as he stood with Mr Bickerstaffe by the door of Greenbank House, but rather a composite of the thoughts, experiences and flawed memories I gathered over the years, a long look backwards down the tunnel of my life.

'Well, lad,' said Mr Bickerstaffe. 'This is your father.'

'Hello,' said my father.

I saluted him.

'We'd best be getting along now,' he said.

Miss Frore dabbed her eyes with the corner of a bedsheet. My father took my hand, nodded to Bickerstaffe then led me to the doorway. He held it open and I felt the wind on my face, warm and wistful as it brushed through my hair.

'Bet you're glad to get out of there,' she said.

We walked across the gravel towards a pale blue Austin Cambridge. I had never been in a car and surprised myself by smiling involuntarily. I did not look back.

'In you get,' said Dad as he held the door open.

And in the car was Mum. My mother, taller than my father, of the same complexion, with a taste for floral dresses, sensible shoes, woollen cardigans and a string of pearls. She cried when she saw me. 'Hello,' she said.

'That's your mother,' said Dad. 'Give her a kiss.'

I kissed my mother and she held me tightly all the way home.

Two

Friday, February 8:
And that's enough of that. If I stop now I may be able to snatch a half-hour read by the fire. Otherwise I see tedium stretching into infinity.

When nothing's happening on the creative front it's best to count your losses, to snuggle up with a good book or get off to the kip, otherwise the mind compensates by being creative elsewhere. Sure as gun's iron, if I am working on my little project and find, as Hemingway said, that the words won't fit, and if I ponder the matter further by staring at The White Bull That Is The Paper With No Words On It, my mind begins to frisk in fields where it ought not to be grazing.

When I wrote that piece about my natural mother, or what Bickerstaffe told me about her, I was at a loss as to where the story should go or what I should do. I knew the way the story went because I had lived it and had further sworn to be truthful in recording events as they actually happened, which must be some sort of throwback to my inveterate diarism; but, as I progressed, the difficulty was what I should leave out. While pondering how things would look if I left out one bit that might be important, I also found myself inventing little scenarios – the kind of conversation you have with yourself after a humiliation. In short, I was fictionalising, making things up, telling lies. I then found myself thinking about Helen and our recent holiday, and, before I knew it, my time was up and it was bedtime. I must point out that our two weeks in Minorca were blissfully warm and companionable, restful and exactly what we both needed (see entries *July 19 – August 4*) though I do recall a mild susurration over whether or not the postcard to Strachan should come from both of us.

9

This is merely to show the curious way my mind works. Perhaps it's simpler to say that, if work is going badly, I chuck it.

So my habits are decided. At 8 p.m., after dinner, I go to my room, there to struggle with The White Bull, etc. Helen thinks I am working on stuff from the bank.

The fact is that I enjoy a good read and, like many another, feel there are few stories to rival my own for sheer fascination and general interest. I also decided to continue with The Diary. It has become too much of a habit, is too deeply ingrained for me to break the practice cold turkey. So The Book is as well as, rather than instead of, for, so far as I can tell, each fulfils a separate function.

You could say I've been Troubled. Troubled is a bit strong and even Disturbed is tainted with melodrama, so let's just say that I have lately been Concerned, but only insofar as Concerned means Interested; perish the thought of Involved or Guilty.

Everyone has a time when life treats them well, when it seems as if eternity has blessed you, when the mysteries of the universe are at your command, when you've got existence by the short and curlies; a time when what you don't know isn't worth knowing, when youth is immortal and what is happening is for the very first time, when all else is epilogue. So I conceived a book of recollections set in the time from which my other times flowed, the river from which the rest of my life has been a tributary.

My time began when Cameron got drunk to celebrate the big event, 'the end of thirteen years of Tory misrule'; Thursday, 15 October 1964, the same day as Nikita Khrushchev was deposed in Moscow. China exploded its first atomic bomb on Friday, 16 October and on 18 October Lyndon Baines Johnson, who became American President the day Aldous Huxley died, said: 'It has been an eventful week in the affairs of the world. It is not the first such week; nor will it be the last. For the world has changed many times in the last twenty years. Great leaders have come and gone. Old enemies have become new friends. Danger has taken the place of danger.' And later that year, on 3 November, Johnson was re-elected President after a landslide victory over Senator Barry Goldwater. That night I was in a café, now demolished, fourteen years old and waiting for my first love who had promised the house would be clear; all in all a memorable wee night, a TV set, black and white with a wonky vertical hold, blinking in the corner.

Goethe is supposed to have said, 'I am history,' which may seem a trifle gross until we consider how we help to shape, determine and retain the great events of our time. In which case, he might have said, 'I am memory,' but that is not enough since someone, and in some cases something, even time itself, can add to or subtract from, can alter or eliminate, our memories. Holding these truths to be self-evident, he could have said, 'I am time,' since we carry our own time with us and time has many dimensions. Maybe he knew time was relative.

Enough philosophy. I'm knackered. A ham sandwich, a glass of hot milk and bed. I was going to end my entry there, then read what I'd written. But attempting cohesion, if not actual sense, let me say this promising period ended around the time that Neil Armstrong and his machinery landed on the moon; Sunday, 20 July 1969. I know what I was doing then as well. I was watching television, live from the moon.

I don't know what went wrong; indeed I cannot state with any certainty that something, or a combination of deliberately unspecific, ill-defined things, actually did go wrong. Simpler to say there were changes I hardly noticed, matters which no longer were what they once had been; a bit like the alterations which assail us on our fortieth birthday, except we expect that one, the great non-event.

Or maybe that's the way I see it now. For some time I have been unable to distinguish between then and now. I still see myself as I was then. I haven't changed all that much, a few grey hairs, laughter-lines and hardly any belly. I still hold most of the same opinions, do the same things and act in much the same way. Which means I can wander back till I am in the two times at the same time.

In fact, I believe adolescence is a permanent state. All that happens is we learn to live with it. The sweating palms, the awkwardness, the blushing embarrassment, the whirlies in the gut, the rampant paranoia and the

> *milk*
> *bread*
> *cheese*
> *durex*
> *sausages*
> *yoghurt*

It's half an hour since I wrote that. I was going to say something else, but I've forgotten what it was. Helen came in to tell me she's going to bed and to ask if I'd give her a lift in the morning. I could hardly say no. It was nice of her to ask.

The ham sandwich is beside me and the milk untouched. It's cooling and already I can see a slight film skinning over the surface, steam rising from the edges and breaking in the air.

As another thing occurs to me. If I wander back, the people I meet are as they were then. I can't help feeling it's a big mistake, but can't imagine how they'd age.

Ham sandwich finished, milk consumed. Skin hanging over the rim of the glass like something I forgot to say.

No reading. There has been too much Diary. Tomorrow we're back to things as they were.

It rained today. The forecast says tomorrow will be cloudy with sunny intervals. I hope so. And I hope the sunny intervals are around lunchtime, for I fancy a walk.

But I'm much more likely to sit at my desk, dreaming of a lion crossing the veldt. And as I'm watching, the band in my head plays that bit from the Eleventh Symphony of Shostakovich, the bit after the canon of trumpet calls, the violent *Fugato* depicting the Massacre of the Tsar's Servants on *The Ninth of*

January, 1905, the bit that ends with a wallop of percussion and a near-silence of trilling strings.

Three

And now to my name, *Angus MacPhail*; christened on my twelfth birthday and called after the man I called Dad who became my father.

We were a family of five – Mother and Father, Euphemia, Cameron and me. 'You will keep my name alive,' said Dad after my christening. I had been at 14 Cuchullain Avenue for just over a year.

'Cameron was given two surnames. This, as you'll know, is something of a tradition amongst the Scottish middle classes, and even the aspiring middle class, so Cameron got his mother's surname to wear beside mine. Euphemia was called after your mother's mother. But your name is my name,' he said. And we smiled.

The most immediate change in my circumstances was that my presence now appeared to have some importance. How can I reveal the wonder and delight, the joy that surprised me when I found myself living with a family. It matters little what the family were like; they were a family, my family, and they wanted me; indeed, they had chosen me. They appeared normal, sensible, articulate and loving, and though I have no memory of being party to or part of an overt display of affection – other than when I was occasionally kissed or even cuddled by my newish parents, which more or less amounts to the same thing – how happier this place was than Greenbank House. Here I was in a warm and loving atmosphere where every member of my family appeared to me as an individual and I loved them individually, content to be amongst ordinary folk and to adjust myself to their normality.

We can hardly believe our families are human; an odd fact, which seems to confuse most folk: but to me this family were all too ethereal; their bodies were flesh and their minds were friable, thought at first it seemed all human goodness was stored therein.

Cuchullain Avenue is on the edge of town and Number Fourteen is midway down the avenue, a house which looks bigger from the outside than from within, so like other houses on the estate that, as visitors have often remarked, even the gardens have a similarity. People get lost on our estate and the police, not to mention the other local services, frequently ask, 'Where is that again?' before requesting a resumé of directions.

Knowe Lane Estate was built at the end of the war, on what was then the outskirts of town; about thirty detached and semi-detached houses, erected by an incomer who disappeared when his business was completed, having spent only the necessary time and money in the place, never to be contactable again, leaving the taste of aloes in residents' mouths.

Of these matters I record what first-hand knowledge I have gleaned and these parings came solely from my father, who, whenever anything was wrong with the house, even when part of it merely required service or replacement, be this a slate for the roof, an electric light bulb, a choked drain, or the time we were digging the garden, struck metal and three days later unearthed a bath, during these times and every time a rates demand arrived, he uttered a single word: 'Shyster.' I always took this to be a reference to the man from Glasgow who sold him the house.

My parents were married at the outbreak of the Second World War. Mother seems to have lived in Glasgow while Father's flat feet rendered him ineligible for active service, so he became a storesman at Aldershot. Mother's family came from Clydebank and were bombed in the Blitz. My father's family emigrated to Canada, where I believe there are surviving relatives. I have tried to trace his sister, who married a Canadian serviceman, but my letters elicited no response.

I can never remember my father talking about his background, except in the most casual way and usually in response

15

to my mother's prodding. 'Didn't your John live there for a while?' she asked when we learned my brother Cameron was being sent to Perth. 'There aren't many places where our John hasn't lived, at least for a while,' he said. Uncle John was a plausible-sounding man I never met. He seems to have developed a passion for horse-racing as a young man, a passion he maintained with undiminished fervour throughout his life. His sister, my Aunt Agnes, was a dancer. Father referred to her as The Floo'er o' Dunblane, which I don't think was very nice. And Auntie Annie married a Canadian. 'Shotgun,' said Dad.

Mother used to offer details of her life and family, usually of an evening in front of the fire. 'Your Uncle Edward was a wonderful man who made a smell in front of the king. His Majesty was inspecting a guard of honour and, as he passed, your Uncle Eddie dropped rather a lot of wind, which His Majesty ignored. Now, your Uncle Eddie's wife, she'd be your Auntie Annie, that's your other Auntie Annie, my sister, not your father's sister; your Auntie Annie danced with a black man. During the war. He was an American, of course, not a Matabele warrior or anything like that. Civilised. He just walked over and asked her to dance, a foxtrot it was. He had lovely white teeth, she said and she also told us he was a good dancer, very light on his feet, though she could have been saying that to annoy your Uncle Eddie who danced like a sergeant-major, though, as I told her at the time, you can tell that just by looking at them. They've got very good rhythm, haven't they.

'Then there was the time we went to Wilson's Zoo, that was in Oswald Street in Glasgow. They had an old lion there and they used to feed him mince. He just lay in his cage and slept all day. He had no teeth, so the man used to give him mince for his dinner. But what a smell. A terrible place for smells, and they used to have to clean up around the lion; he never moved.

'But your Auntie Bunty took some of her birthday cake to feed the monkey. The monkey wasn't very nice. He used to do things to himself when people were looking. Not nice to see

16

that happening. Auntie Bunty threw the cake into the cage, the monkey smelled it, took one sniff and threw it back at her. Then it did things.

'And that was the day we never paid. We went into a shop for tea and cakes and just walked out after we'd eaten it. We didn't mean to, of course. It was afterwards when Bunty mentioned it: "Did you pay?" she asked. "No," says I. "Well, neither did I," says she. Laugh; what a scream. But we never went back, though; no, we never went near the place again.

'Your granny, my mother, now, she once sat beside Harry Lauder on a bus. She knew it was him because he had his wee stick with him. When the conductor came round for the fares, Sir Harry looked out the window. "Have you got a ticket?" he asked. "Oh, dearie me, no," said Sir Harry. "I must have forgotten." Then he asked for a penny one, even though he'd been on the bus since before your granny got on. It must have been at least three ha'pence-worth.

'Now, before I forget, I had my fortune told at the Kelvin Hall Circus. Madame Zandor her name was and she was a real gypsy. She told me I would marry your daddy and that I'd live in a big house like this one, a house with a garden. She told me I would have three children and isn't that strange for I only had two till you came along. She said my lucky colour was blue and my lucky number was twenty or twenty-one, either would do she said. I got married on the twenty-first, so that was lucky, wasn't it. She told me one of my children would be a great blessing, but that I wouldn't remember my grand-children, which can't be right: how could anyone forget their grandchildren. She said I would have a peaceful old age. Mind you, she told your Uncle Tommy he'd marry a titled lady, but he got himself killed at Arnhem before he could marry anybody.'

Sitting by the fire in the big front room, my mother in pink slippers with fluffy edges, sometimes staring at me, sometimes staring across the room. The conversations ended when she thought I was my father: 'Let's have a wee cup of tea,' she'd say.

17

We lived in a tidy house. There was a small, square hall with a table for the telephone, a staircase and a Baluchistan rug which Mum said had been bought with one of Father's Christmas bonuses. 'Jesus Christ, woman,' he said. 'How much of a bonus do you think they give me?' And above the table was a Van Gogh print, *The Starry Night*, whose colours matched the rug. 'I like that picture,' Mum told me. 'The stars look real. The way they should be.'

The stars hung opposite the living room, which was comfortable, dominated by chintz, three-piece suite and curtains, a walnut coffee table and a standard lamp with a chintz shade prowling behind the television in the corner. The centrepiece was a red-brick fireplace with bookshelves in the chimney corners. Dickens, Stevenson, Scott and Hardy variegated the orange Penguins, Ernest Hemingway and Scott Fitzgerald, some hardbacks of Graham Greene and something of Compton Mackenzie, Neil Gunn and Eric Linklater. Above the fireplace hung *The Hay Wain*, and along the mantelpiece, on top of the bookshelves, were photographs of people I scarcely recognised; Mother and Father on their wedding day, Cammy and Phamie as babies or young children, silver-framed and poised between the glass and plaster ornaments.

Books were scattered around the house. Mother had cookery books on the kitchen shelves and we had books in all our rooms, books which changed as our opinions changed; on the same shelves it was possible to find Anna Sewell, Catherine Cookson, Ken Kesey and Carlos Castaneda, or Richmal Compton, Arthur Ransome, John Steinbeck and V. I. Lenin.

Father's room was between the sitting room and the kitchen. It used to be the dining room and he worked on an oblong table. It was a disordered room with notebooks piled on the work-space in front of the chair, beside a jar with pencils and pens, a dish of paper-clips, a reading lamp and bookshelves which overflowed from the living room. I always imagined he was sorting papers and assumed they had nothing to do with me. The others talked of Father's room and the time he spent there as something abstract, like an opinion he had, something which could alter in the light of fresh evidence. I can never recall the room being cleaned: we went to the kitchen through the hall.

The bathroom was on the half-landing and four bedrooms faced each other at the top of the stairs. Cameron and I were on the left; Mother, Father and Phamie slept on the right.

A patchwork garden of grass and flowers to the front of the house, with an assembly of vegetables, fruit bushes and a drying green round the back. Plumpish icteroid roses humped around the door; they stayed about six weeks and spent the rest of the year dying. One side of the house faced north; and the other side faced the Simpsons, who lived in a house identical to ours.

Every house was identical to ours; and so we were on our small estate, preserving our own in our own small way. I often wished I was a bird, to see what else was in the world, to soar above geometric order, frightened to believe there was ever more than this. I imagined everyone lived as we did. Television programmes can come as a shock to a xenophobic voyeur.

There was anxiety and secrecy in the way we lived. We had to be careful. Everyone lived beyond their means and tried not to show it; so we kept ourselves to ourselves. We did not discuss the cost of living, far less each other's salary, presuming our houses meant we, more or less, were paid the same. We exchanged cards at Christmas and fed the cat when they went away; we took their deliveries when we stayed at home; we went to the library, the shops or to coffee mornings; we went to work.

We became used to adapting what we had to what was needed. The fabric of our houses and the houses themselves became a source of misery; every home had things which needed doing, which never would be done.

When you think about it, gardening's a curious waste of time. We planted flowers and watched them die. We grew too many vegetables no one would eat, so we threw them on the compost which improved the soil so we could grow more vegetables. Everyone grew the same things, but arranged them differently. We shared our tools, our implements and our experience, complained about the soil, the unyielding weather, and we pruned our plants, hoping for new growth.

'I suppose it's time for the garden,' Father would say as though it was a medicine he had to take. I always thought he did what was needed to keep it looking respectable, but in later life he became enthusiastic in a particularly Scottish way. In this country the word *fairin* means a gift or a punishment; and it often is the case that something we enjoy can become a chore, or that we find pleasure in drudgery, a point Cameron always understood better than me.

My father spent hours getting ready for the onslaught, and, always as he tugged up his Wellingtons, he'd say, 'I'd better get out there before it overtakes us.' When he died, his love of gardening and all his loves became obvious, though the way he showed love was never obvious.

Cameron bought seeds and catalogues and helped to plan the lay-out. I think he felt not to show enthusiasm for something his father liked would border on disloyalty. And for all her later devotion to flowers, nature and vegetarianism, Phamie couldn't have cared less and didn't even use the garden for sunbathing.

On the day I arrived Mum and Dad gave me a guided tour of the house which ended in my room. 'We'll be downstairs when you're ready,' Mother said. 'I expect you'd like to freshen up.' I didn't know what she meant.

I stood in the centre of the room and looked around me. How they found such things, I do not know. There were four shelves of books, a desk and chair, an easy chair, a table with a lamp and a posy of flowers, a comfortable bed with clean sheets and new covers, a wardrobe and a chest of drawers filled with clothes which fitted me perfectly, a new pair of slippers and a blue woollen dressing gown. There was an alarm clock and a transistor radio on the table by the bed. Two days later the photograph Bickerstaffe had given me was beside them in a silver frame. I have it still.

I sat on the bed and stood up; then I sat on the easy chair and lit the gas fire, staring at the Bob Dylan poster above the bed, wondering if he was a relation. I stripped, put on the dressing gown, ran a bath and scrubbed myself red. I brushed my teeth with my new toothbrush, dressed in my new clothes and, quite rosy, went down to tea; macaroni and cheese. That night the Greenbank clothes were gone and I never saw them again.

My parents became the world to me. From an initial feeling of gratitude, I learned to love them and know they loved me in return. My father taught me an alternative to Bickerstaffe, Nettles and the like, while Mother concerned herself with our welfare and managed as best she could by washing, mending, ironing and cooking, tidying, sweeping or busying herself around the place. 'My evenings are my own,' she'd say. 'Of an evening I can do what I like.'

I was aware that my mother took small white pills. The effect of these pills is far more powerful than any novelist. They can change your personality and destroy your mind. That's what they did to my mother. They kept reality at bay and provided delusion. We thought they made Mother happy; in fact she was demented. Of course, she liked the pills, took them as prescribed or needed, and justified every one. There were pills to make her sleep, pills to wake her up and pills to keep her happy when she was awake.

It seems strange to have progressed this far and barely mentioned my brother Cameron and my sister, who was named Euphemia, known as Phamie but who called herself Debbie. 'Who needs a name like Phamie MacPhail,' she said. 'It's as if you'd been given a bag of cement to wear round your neck as you surge forward in the race through life.'

That first night we sat and talked. 'Bedtime all,' said Mother when the clock on the sideboard chimed eleven. 'Now, I want you all up bright and early tomorrow morning. Remember,

21

it's Angus's first day at school and I want you both to take him.'

I lay in bed and stared at the ceiling, afraid to sleep for what I might dream, saying my new name over again, like a phrase I had to learn, or a prayer.

'What's your name?'

In the playground at ten to nine, a cold wind blowing and my clothes felt stiff, a schoolbag with two cheese sandwiches and a bottle of milk around my neck.

'His name's Angus MacPhail,' said Cammy who was standing beside me. In the girls' playground I could see Phamie and about half a dozen other girls staring and giggling, statuesque when they saw me looking.

'And who is he?'

'My brother.'

By now there was a crowd around us, boys of different sizes, who reproved as though I was some sort of baggage, no better than I should be.

'If he's your brother, how come we've never heard of him before?'

'Easy,' said Cameron, weighing up his audience. 'Due to a tragedy I cannot mention and which is none of your fucken business anyway, our family were separated. Angus was raised by an elderly aunt who recently died, and now he has come to live with us.'

One by one they shuffled away. This was when I knew I loved him. My brother was the nicest man I have ever met. There was an easy charm about him, an affability that could only come from innocence.

Cameron smoothed the family feathers; he mediated in disputes, could interrupt my father's work and avoid the shouting, could talk to Mum when she felt alone, could deal with Phamie and guide me through school.

'I don't think you ought to deal with Angus that way,' he told one of my teachers. The man thought I was an idiot because I couldn't understand algebra.

'Right then,' he'd said, writing on the board: $X=1$, $Y=2$, ... $X+Y=3$. He stared round the room threatening an answer. 'Does anybody not understand that?' he asked.

There must have been something in the way I shuffled, something in the way I stared at the desk. 'And what do you not understand?' he asked, pointing at me.

'Why did you call them X and Y in the first place?'

'Idiot,' he screamed.

On the way home, Cameron asked why I was blowing my hands. I showed him the marks, four of the best from a good Lochgelly.

Next day we went to see the teacher. 'You can do to me what you did to Angus,' said Cammy, 'but that won't solve the problem either. The problem is that Angus does not understand and you did not explain, which seems rather remiss for how else does one teach other than by explanation. If anyone is to blame it seems to be you for not explaining rather than Angus for not understanding.'

'Right,' said the man weighing his sarcasm. 'What do you propose we do?'

'I think you should accept that Angus doesn't understand algebra and never will. Things will be much easier for both of you.'

I never did understand algebra, but Mr Delacourt never belted me again and taught me how to pass exams. 'I like your brother,' he told me when Cameron had left the school. 'I like him a lot and don't know why. He's a bit too forward, a bit too sure of himself, but he certainly is likeable.'

Everyone thought so, and it is because of Cameron that I never felt awkward or out of place at home, for the others more or less forgot about me after a while. They seemed to accept I was there and expected more of me than Cameron did. I always felt he was on my side.

'Who was last in the bath and didn't clean it, as if we need to ask,' said Phamie with sufficient pertness on a Saturday morning.

'Me.'

'How many times do we have to tell you. It isn't as if it hasn't happened before. You don't have to clean the bath after anyone else, so why should we have to clean up after you,' she said. 'It's filthy. And I'm not your skivvy.'

'I think we have to make allowances,' said Cammy.

'You make enough for us all,' she said. And before she could swirl out of the room, Cammy stopped her.

'Angus doesn't know about these things,' he said. 'It's all very well for you and I to expect him to behave as we do, but you forget where he came from. Put yourself in his position and see how you'd be. If you had never cleaned a bath in all your life, if you'd been raised in a place where it was all done for you, where baths were shared and always cold with no more than four inches of water between you and someone else, don't you think you'd forget if you came to a home where you could bathe on your own with as much hot water and scented soap as you want. Why do you think he has a bath every night? It isn't because he's any dirtier than you or I, Phamie. It's because he doesn't know. This is his luxury.'

'Suppose so,' she said.

Cammy turned to me and smiled: 'Sorry,' he said, apologising for his sister.

Phamie is three years older than me. For as long as I've known her, she has either been a woman or was well on the way to becoming a woman. Apart from mealtimes there was little contact between Phamie and myself. She went to school, came home and went to her room; then, either she went out again or groups of girls descended on us in twos or threes. I would open the door to pert, shy, often pretty girls who would look at the floor as they spoke, only to ask if Debbie was in. When two or three were gathered together, the noise from Phamie's bedroom bore no relationship to the demure, doe-eyed creatures who had come to the door.

One evening when I had been at Cuchullain Avenue a couple of months my mother said, 'Euphemia, I mean Phamie, no I don't, I mean Debbie, you know who I mean, your sister has some friends in. I think it would be nice to give them tea and biscuits. My mother always gave my friends tea.' So we busied ourselves setting up the tray, trying to remember how many were there. 'You go in,' said Mum. 'I will open the door and announce that tea is ready, then you will carry in the tray.'

There was silence, the stillness you get when no one knows what's going on. Seven or eight girls sat on the floor with cigarettes poised between two fingers, all trying to look interesting. There was a bottle of gin and a bottle of sherry, a glass on the floor by every girl. 'That's the tea,' I said. 'Mum sent it.' And as I left, someone giggled. When the door closed, the shrieks and laughter were worse than before. 'There you are, dear,' said Mother. 'I think they liked that.'

Two nights later there was a tap on my door. Phamie came in and sat on the bed. 'You're not bad, you know,' she said. 'It was good of you not to shop us. That was a near thing the other night. Everybody, but everybody, was out of their tree. And now, are you ready for this, do you think you can cope: I am going to do you a favour. A friend of mine, well she's my best friend really, Judith MacDonald, we all call her Judy, really fancies you. In fact, she's in love with you, but she doesn't know it. She's told me she feels deeply attracted to you and that every time she sees you she feels a fatal, uncontrollable urge rise inside her and she knows that if you touched her she'd be putty in your hands. I've told her you're unsure of your love for her, but that you'd be prepared to meet her to discuss certain aspects of a possible liaison.'

I knew I was staring at my sister with a certain slackness in the area of my lower jaw. 'Don't be so surprised.' She squeezed my hand. 'I have also told her that, as far as I know,' she was pacing herself, giving me time to interrupt, 'that as far as I know you are relatively inexperienced in these matters. She has told me she understands completely and it will make no difference, neither will the seemingly enormous gap in your ages. Though I am sure you don't know very much, I am equally sure you know something, even though it's only the basic and obvious truth that love can conquer any obstacle, even one as big as a three-year age gap.'

Two nights later I found myself at the corner of Cuchullain Avenue. Judith MacDonald came down the road. 'Hello,' she said.

'What would you like to do?'

'Don't know.'

'Would you like to go for a walk?'

'If you like.'

We strolled together, admiring the gardens. We wandered through the woods on the edge of the estate and round by the side of the golf course, where we sat in silence on the dampish grass, staring across the links.

'You can kiss me if you like,' said Judy. I kissed her cheek and she sighed.

'You're wonderful,' she said. 'Debbie told me how gallant you were and I found it hard to believe. Boys don't respect you. They only want to take advantage. But now you've proved yourself, I'm putty in your hands.'

'I know,' I said, remembering what my sister had told me, though I had forgotten to ask what she meant.

'Take me,' said Judy. 'I'm yours.'

'Where would you like to go?'

She muttered something I could not understand. I told her I was happy where I was, meaning Cuchullain Avenue, but I fear Judith MacDonald did not know that: she spoke of true love and how wonderful it was to have your feelings reciprocated by the man you had given your heart to. She held my hand as I walked her home.

'Look at the moon and think of me,' she said by her hedgerow. She kissed her forefinger and pressed it to my brow. 'And when you dream, dream only of me. I'll miss you and will be thinking of you always.'

I had never met anyone quite like her and told her so. I also said I found her a puzzle, did not understand what was happening, but that I would certainly be thinking of her. She skipped up the path and blew kisses from the door.

26

We went on like this for a week or two, my puzzlement deepening as her demands became stronger. 'Make me a woman,' she said. I told her that in my eyes she already was a woman.

Her parents encouraged me to visit; I was younger than Judy and the brother of her best friend, so they obviously thought no harm would come of it. But every time we went to her room we went through the same routine about where she would like to be taken as we lay on the floor, our bodies packed with steam.

'That's what I like about you,' she said. 'You really respect me, don't you.'

Phamie told me things were desperate. 'You've won her heart completely, but your inexperience means you can't take advantage of the situation.'

'I don't want to take advantage of Judy. I respect her.'

'Sure.' My sixteen-year-old sister sat on the bed and looked straight into my eyes.

And from the kitchen Mother called, 'Your soup's out, dears.'

Phamie crossed her legs and I saw a brilliant white flash.

'It's getting cold. Hurry along now,' shouted Mum from the foot of the stairs.

'What are you looking at?' asked Phamie. 'Are you trying to see up my skirt, you dirty old thing you?'

'We'd better go and get our soup.'

'Mum,' she shouted, her back against the wall, legs slightly apart. 'Angus and I have some homework to finish.'

'That's nice, dear,' Mother called. 'Your soup's back in the pot. You can heat it when you're ready.'

'The pot's quite warm,' she said, lifting her skirt. 'Maybe you'd like to stir it up a little.'

I closed my eyes.

'It's all right,' she said as she undressed us both. 'We're not really brother and sister.'

Later Phamie concerned herself with age differences. 'She isn't as old as I thought,' she said. 'In fact she's only fourteen,

27

but you're only thirteen, aren't you. It's a pity you weren't at least the same age. A woman usually likes a man to be older than her.'

After a night or two with my sister, Judy and I were fine and in spite of the age gap managed to stay together for longer than anyone expected, especially ourselves. Let's leave her for now, resting if not sleeping, young and fresh, formed and firm as she was then, breathing softly, eyes closed, her hair lapping across her face and beads of sweat on her upper lip. Judy.

We all know people who wander in and out of our lives like a phone bill. Cammy's later actions and the stushie they generated are important because of the belief which fired him, but they tell us nothing. Newspapers printed articles with headlines such as THE CAMERON MACPHAIL I KNEW, which gave as much information about Cammy as about an ornament.

All this was after my adoptive brother stood in the dock before Lord MacTavish in the Court of Session, Edinburgh, charged with a dozen or more bank robberies, committed with a person and persons unknown, except for Harry Campbell, an illiterate mental defective who turned state's evidence on hopes of a reduced sentence. He admitted the charges, but Cameron MacPhail had laid the plans and egged him on with a promise of socialist wealth. He got three years and Cameron got thirty.

It was to be said that Cameron did not help himself. He sacked his lawyer and conducted his own defence, which mainly consisted of lengthy political lectures with finely pointed analyses and a well rounded argument. He asked various witnesses if they supported the death penalty, how they felt about the Vietnam War, on their position on Northern Ireland. In one instance he asked a bank clerk what he thought of the Middle East. He also gave the court a reasonable account of his background, packed information I would never have known had it not been for the trial.

His first passion was Scottish Nationalism. He saw England winning the World Cup as a metaphor and figured we should

28

follow their lead by doing to them what Nobby Styles did to Pele and Eusebio.

He became disillusioned with the Wilson government. He was sixteen years old, I was fourteen and Phamie had gone to London. 15 October 1964, was the first time I saw him drunk. He was celebrating the end of thirteen years of Tory misrule and seemed disappointed when it rained on 16 October. And of course there was Vietnam.

A word or two about time. I have been accused of having no sense of time and am aware that it often takes longer than I think to travel from one place to another, no matter how often I make the journey and that I am frequently late for appointments simply because I have misjudged an aspect of time in relation to distance and therefore, I suppose, to space. Einstein shattered the illusion of uniform, absolute time and in my own small way so do I. Since Einstein has shown us that in the physical world time and space are part of an interlocked system, I will only relate my narrative to time when it is relevant. Irrelevancies such as years, months and chronology will be ignored.

And of course there was Vietnam. It affected us all, even those who claimed to be unaffected, especially them, for they were affected in the eyes of others. Few things diminish a person like their attitude to war. America's subsequent guilt was equalled only by my brother's impotent disillusionment at the way the Vietnamese fell behind the most expedient line. It was a crushing blow. He had barely recovered from the death of Che Guevara, the collapse and subsequent discreditation of the Cultural Revolution and the rampant revisionism that swept China following the death of its great leader Chairman Mao Tse Tung, whose thought was supposed to live for a thousand years and didn't even last as many days after he'd gone to join the big party congress in the sky.

America's guilt was easily assuaged. They ignored their memories of the war and anyone who had participated in it. As

29

homosexuals, pederasts and Fascists came out of the closet to be courted by politicians, veterans of the Vietnam War replaced them in the dark recesses of public consciousness. They were ignored and cosmeticised, even when they dragged their prosthetic appliances around Washington demanding recognition: 'Look at me,' they screamed. 'Look. Over here.' Then Hollywood found a new market.

My brother's remorse was not so simple; it must have involved some sort of resentment since he felt betrayed. Scotland did not want the kind of nationalism he was offering, they wanted a national kind of nationalism. Because they'd always voted Labour, Cammy assumed they'd want a social kind of nationalism.

He based his authority on Marx's assertion that capitalism was in its death-throes, that it was doomed to stagger from crisis to crisis until it was inevitably sent whirling into oblivion by a righteously indignant proletariat. Guevara had preached, 'Dos, tres muchos Vietnams est la contigua!' Cammy felt the time had come and was propelled in this belief when Guevara's mutilated body was thrown before the world's press on the floor of a Bolivian jungle.

That death was a watershed. Since it seemed that Guevara's dream of more than one Vietnam to weaken the US imperialists and their running dogs was unlikely to materialise, partly because revolution, as Lenin taught us, must be lit by a spark from within and cannot be grafted on to any other political situation, however ripe, and partly because the Americans wouldn't like it and would therefore try to prevent it, Cameron threw his energies into opposing the Vietnam that already existed.

I knew none of this till we met in a pub. Judy and I had gone for what Mother called a refreshment while we waited for her parents' house to free. They were not expected back and I had said I was staying with a friend. 'That's nice,' said Cammy. 'It'll be good for you to get away for a night.'

He used to leave the house every night around seven. I had no idea where he went to or what he did, nor as far as I could gather did anyone else.

'Isn't that Cammy?' Judy asked. We hadn't spoken for a while. I was staring at the gantry. Cammy was distributing leaflets for the Vietnam Solidarity Campaign.

He seemed embarrassed. 'Makes a change from *War Cry*,' said Judy and he smiled. He talked to us as though we were strangers. Judy and I hardly spoke. I think he guessed we weren't interested, his passion embarrassed him, or it could have been the return of the embarrassment I noticed when he saw us but, whatever it was, he simply stopped talking, raised his empty glass and replaced it on the beer mat. 'That was good,' he said.

I got us another. Cammy sipped his beer and placed the glass in the centre of the mat. Judith fumbled with my jacket pocket. After a judicious pause while Cameron and I discussed the relative merits of heavy beer and lager I found the key to her house tied with a pink ribbon bow.

Every detail of that evening is etched on a metal plate at the back of my memory. Cameron said he had some more leaflets to deliver, then he had some reading to do, and he finished his beer with a flourish. Judy and I ran down the street in the rain, sat upstairs on an empty bus, breathed on the window and wrote our names.

Her room and the posters; the books on the shelves, Richard Brautigan, George Orwell, Sylvia Plath, *Catch-22*, Miller and Steinbeck; the Casa Pupo bedspread; her hair; the tawny bedside lamp; the smell of lavender water she'd scattered on the sheets; the sharpness as we undressed in the dark; her Marks and Spencer knickers and all the wonderful newness of her.

I have a strange mind which has forgotten much of what would now appear to be important yet has retained a great deal of trivia I cannot remove. If I could ask Judy what she remembers of that night, it could well be nothing. It could be the roughness of my beard, the taste of my prick or the look on Cameron's face as we left the pub. Which makes me wonder about the relevance of memory. How do we know that what we remember is important? Or is it only important because we

31

remember it? Later I was to watch the woman I called Mother struggle to remember her children's names, looking for her withered memories. So if what we remember is important, what about the things we forget? Aren't they important? Time and memory would appear to be relative. Things get wiped automatically. Planned obsolescence.

Later we lay, Judith and I, drinking chocolate and eating digestive biscuits. We stripped the bed, swept away the crumbs and shivered again as we searched for the warm hollow. She lit a cigarette and put it in my mouth: 'I got a letter from Debbie,' she said when she'd lit her own.

'What did she say?'

'She's worried about being able to pay her rent.'

'I didn't know she paid rent.'

'She doesn't, well, not officially. There's a commune fund and she has to put money into that. It's the same as paying rent, but the word has such bad connotations that the commune doesn't use it.'

Sergeant Pepper was released in June 1967, and Brian Epstein took an overdose of sleeping tables in the August. His departure was the first crack in the structure. This was before the final disintegration of all but memory. Even though *The Magical Mystery Tour, The White Album, Yellow Submarine* and most of Yoko Ono were still to come, it seemed as though the centre had fallen apart, as if there was nothing to do but drift along with the aimless, ambiguous circus that was leaving in the morning for nowhere. It seemed so pointless and for many that was the attraction.

It attracted Phamie. She went away and came home to argue with Cammy. 'Jesus, man,' she shouted. 'All across the world there are millions of kids, young people like you and me, who are really pissed off with the isms society has dumped on them. We want to change, to start again, to wipe it all away, to build anew. Millions of us are turning on to love and peace and all you can think of is Mao.'

'If you think that what's taking place is anything other than the worst possible excesses of juvenile naïvety, then I am sorry to say you've very much mistaken. People have had orgasms before now.'

'You haven't.'

'I'll ignore that long enough to say as a general rule it isn't enough to build a political theory on.'

'As usual, you're really really hostile. Who's talking about orgasms? They're important. Sure, they're very important. Everybody knows they're important.'

'Drugs are not enough for a new society either.'

'Who's talking about drugs?'

'Have you been smoking dope?'

'What's wrong with that, just a couple of joints, nothing much, honest Cammy. Jesus, what's wrong with you is that all the societies you imagine are war-orientated. They are all based on really heavy theories which involve killing people and eating meat.'

'I don't believe this.' He was laughing. 'You have the social and political awareness of a retarded amoeba.'

'It's true, Cammy. It really is really really true,' said Phamie, wide eyes, legs crossed, sitting on the bed in her long skirt, long hair, Donovan T-shirt, smoking a badly rolled joint. 'We're turning away from the old world and its values. What we want is something better. A new base. That's why we're turning on to peace and love instead of war and hate. Turn on and switch off, man. Leave it alone. Let them get on with it. Millions of kids are really really rejecting the old way. All you're interested in is old Mousey Tongue and millions of kids are being turned on by something really really new.'

It was a circular discussion which always ended with Cammy laughing or Phamie rocking herself back and forward, singing softly.

She said she wanted to find herself and needed a fulfilment she could not find at home. 'It means she's randy,' said my father. But Mother ignored him. 'We all ought to be a little more self-aware,' she told us one night after cocoa.

Phamie went to yoga, then meditation classes, she planted seeds in the back-garden, changed her diet, forswore all meat,

33

coffee and tea and would not wear leather. She went to a consciousness-raising seminar somewhere in the Welsh mountains and a month later came back with Jeff, an American refugee who had deserted from the army. Phamie said she wanted to marry him. The immediate problems were a wife in Akron, Ohio, and another in Saigon. 'A one-man United Nations,' said Father. Jeff went to London and Phamie went too. We heard little else about Jeff, though Mother sent him pullovers she had knitted. 'That's what they did for us during the war,' she said.

Letters home were infrequent. They arrived in decorated envelopes with flowers drawn round the border in that strange intensity dope-smokers achieve. I stayed with Phamie in London once and came back to find someone asleep with the earphones on, someone laughing hysterically over a page in a comic and someone eating handfuls of jam. Phamie was in bed with Pete, who told me he was a musician.

'Pete's been busted,' said Judy.

'Is she coming home?'

'She's going to a pop concert in Amsterdam. Then she's going to spend the summer in Greece sleeping on the beach.'

'That'll be nice.'

'Yeah,' said Judith turning the light off. 'Fancy it myself.'

Four

There's a freedom, a feeling of release which hangs around the air on Friday afternoon. But the weekend's merriment was dispelled when one of the tellers was £25.00 short in her cash tally. I said the usual things about pulling your tights up, mind on the job, shoulder to the wheel, no slacking, but I feel a recurrence is inevitable.

The girl's name is Miranda Morrison. As she was leaving the office, I said, 'By the way, Miranda; did you know your name didn't exist until Shakespeare invented it?'

'Yes,' she said. 'I knew that.'

She said it sweetly, as if it was a secret. And because I'd broken the ice she said, 'Do you like being a bank manager?'

I stammered around while Miranda looked interested. Eventually I said, 'It's my job.'

'Good-night, sir,' she said. 'Have a nice weekend.'

When I came home Helen said, 'You look puzzled, dear.' And I was puzzled. Worse still, I did not know what was puzzling me.

Helen looked particularly well tonight. She is a handsome woman who is attentive and tidy, who is undemanding and knows when to leave me, who is attractive, intelligent and absolutely devoted. Her clothes always enhance her figure and heads turn involuntarily when we walk down the street. At parties, bank functions and the like, men always talk to her, and she handles it well, always smiling and self-assured. She is an asset.

But something about her suggests a ritual, as if she knows of a life outside me, a sanctuary she keeps inside her head. It seems sufficient to know it exists but, if I then accept its

35

presence, she issues a series of polite reminders. When her brows are knitted and beneficence curls the corners of her eyes, I want to ask what she's been thinking. And if I ask, she loosely smiles. I could take it if her head was empty, I've been with empty heads before, but a head's not empty when eyes are bright.

I've given up asking. Sometimes, during summer holidays, when puddles of light leaked through the windows, I'd watch the dust motes rise and caper and used to phone from work to tell her. The ringing tone, like a two-note cuckoo, was always full of anticipation. If she wasn't in I'd get back to business. But when she answered, she sounded as if she'd been interrupted. 'Hello,' I'd say. 'Helen, how are you?'

'Fine.'

'Isn't it a lovely day?'

'Lovely.'

Then she'd ask why I called, but usually hold the phone in silence, eventually saying, 'See you later.'

I wrote that last night, before braving The People of my Mind. I had become excited by an idea which arrived uninvited and decided to commit this conception to posterity. *Mais, j'ai trouvé cette idée dans un fumier.* For what by moonlight seemed clear invention, in the cold light of dawn was a common noumenon, but, and this is where the trouble started, your honour, in the haste of my discovery, I left my Journal open.

Perhaps a quantitative analysis of diary sales in this country would reveal why psychological analysis is so unpopular. But I doubt it. I believe we are happy with our neuroses, that we nurture and feed them in order to disguise them as national character or, in extreme cases, personality. I believe that to effect such a cure would obliterate us completely.

I have committed things to my Diary which I have seldom even committed to myself, as if I have to write to believe it, or to understand the belief.

Which forces me to ask: *Who the hell are you and what do you want? Go away. Get off my land and don't come back.*

Let not your heart be troubled, Angy. The alternative to this Diary is no Diary at all. And that is no alternative.

A word about my name. Angus can be abbreviated to Angy or Gus. I detest both, but prefer the former, except that I don't know how to spell it. It isn't Angey or Angie. Rather, it is the first three letters of my Christian name with a hard G and a Y on the end; Angry without the R. So much for pronunciation. It still doesn't look right.

2 pkts. soup
cheese
shampoo
conditioner

When I see that photograph of Marilyn Monroe, the one from *The Seven Year Itch* where she's standing on a grating, her hand cupped to the side of her mouth, whispering a secret as her skirt swirls around her waist, the one Joe di Maggio didn't like; when I see that photograph of Marilyn Monroe, I think of Helen.

We met at a dance. I went with one crowd, she went with another and we all teamed up. It was one of those Paul Jones things, some sort of dance where everybody's supposed to participate. I wasn't participating because I can't dance. I know how to walk and can walk in time to the music, but I'd hardly call it dancing.

Helen's a good dancer and, like anyone who does something effortlessly, she cannot understand why I can't do it, or feel embarrassed. 'I suppose that's why you've never bothered to learn,' she said. And it's true. I feel silly.

So there I was sitting it out when she turned and shouted, 'Angus.' When I raised my head, her upper half was exactly like that picture, though her skirt gave no cause for concern. And that's how she is locked, a fly in my mind's amber; Marilyn Monroe with her skirt down.

She waved to me to come and dance. I shook my head. 'Why not?' she asked later. 'Don't be silly. You can dance with me. I'll teach you.'

37

And for the only time in my life, I didn't feel as if I was dancing; it felt as if I was walking around.

I walked her home. Standing by the gate she told me she was in love with an artist called Gerry who lived on beans and lemonade. 'But I could see you sometimes,' she said.

We went to the pictures and held hands. We went to the theatre and walked home holding hands. We saw another film and sat in the back row with a packet of nuts and a strawberry ice-cream. I tried to kiss her. 'Please,' she said. 'Don't.' I apologised.

A week later we went to the circus. Walking home, I took her hand. It was cold and late October, the season of smells with a sun in a corner, when air shifts to a sharpness you can sense in the city, and maybe feel for a day or two after the clocks go back.

We shivered and talked about the dwarf clowns' whitewash routine and an elephant's dignity when it stands on one leg. I asked if she wanted to go straight home. She shook her head. 'I like the cold,' she said. We passed signs of warmth, pubs and cafés with steamed up windows, houses with their curtains drawn, an occasional glimpse of someone reading by the fire. We climbed a cobbled hill that broadened into a cemetery which seemed to be lit from beneath like snow.

It was a big graveyard. Clusters of weeds were knotted along the spine of the paths and some tombstones had been broken or vandalised, as though the people they commemorated were finally dead. I wondered if we die when our memory dies or do we die when people no longer remember us. I asked Helen and she shivered, peering through reflected light to read the inscriptions which indicated precisely what occupants expected on the other side.

She leaned forward. And when she turned I tried to kiss her. She did not stir. I removed my head. 'I've asked you not to do that, Angus,' she said.

Tiny points of light jumped in front of my eyes. I was almost surprised to hear myself speak. 'What do you reckon gives you the right to treat me like this? You must have some very confused notions about adult behaviour, so let me put you right on at least one thing: I don't care if I never see you again, so you can get to hell out of here and leave me alone.'

She didn't move. Her bottom lip quivered till she poised on the edge of speech, when from over the wall a woman shouted: 'You aaright, hen?'

'I'm fine. Thank you.'

'Did he take you in there?'

'I'm all right.'

'I know what he'd be after. Dirty bastard. You keep your haun' on your ha'penny, hen. Gie him nuthin'. Hey, you. Ratbag. Come oot o' there and lea' that lassie alane.'

'I'll be okay.'

'Please yoursel'. But don't say I didnae warn ye.'

And for long enough the only noise was the whine of the traffic. Helen said, 'I'm sorry.' And the sound of her voice restored my anger.

'What do you have to be sorry about?'

'I don't know. I just am.'

She followed me down the cobbles. We went into the first pub and sat in a corner drinking whisky as a woman with a one-stringed voice encouraged others to join in by waving her arms. 'I find this very depressing,' I said.

'It's just the mood you're in.'

'Of course it's the bloody mood I'm in. What the hell else would it be.'

'Will you do something for me?' she asked at the bus stop. 'Will you come and see Gerry?'

So I sat in a café reading *Catch-22*. She was late and breathless.

'I've been up to see him,' she said. 'I thought it was best if I prepared the ground, so to speak.'

'And?'

'He's looking forward to meeting you; very much. I've explained the position. I suppose he wants to meet his rival.'

'Perhaps you'd like to explain the position to me.'

'I can't go on like this, loving one man and seeing another. It isn't fair, especially to me, so I've decided to choose.'

39

'If you think I'm entering some sort of beauty contest, you've got another thing coming. He can have you; run along and live in his garret. I'm off.'

'You might as well come up since you're here,' she said.

Gerry's flat was on the top floor of a stairway that smelled of cats and cooking. Long hair was fashionable; Gerry's was short. He wore a collarless shirt and a thick black beard, a couple of teeth were missing, he had paint on his arms, hands and face. His house had a lot of canvases, bits of hardboard really, finished or unfinished, it was difficult to tell. A hundred years ago Gerry would have painted whiskery portraits, allegoric knights in armour or wistful ladies. Seventy years ago his colours would be brighter, he'd have painted landscapes with cows and milkmaids. Forty years ago bodiless heads, fungi, seashells, roses and barley sugar would have floated in a violet sea. Twenty years ago he'd have thrown paint around the room and ten years ago there would have been a still–life series with a plate of mince, potatoes and peas against a flowery patterned tablecloth with a chipped cup and a plate.

Helen dabbed her eyes at the foot of the stairs. A baby was crying in a nearby house and someone was cooking cabbage. 'What are you trying to tell me?' I asked.

'It's very difficult.'

'What is?'

'Please try to understand.'

'Understand what?'

'I can't talk when you're like this; you're so hostile.'

'Suppose I'm pissed off?'

'Do I bore you?'

'Of course not. You're wonderful.'

'You don't act as if I'm wonderful.'

'I was being sarcastic. Anyway, that makes two of us.'

'I wasn't being sarcastic.'

'I didn't say you were.'

'Yes you did; you said, "That makes two of us." '

'Oh Jesus. I meant that you don't act as if I was wonderful.'

'Don't I? And what do you think I've just done?'

'I've no idea. I thought that was what you were going to tell me, what I didn't understand.'

'For God's sake,' she said standing in a doorway. 'Kiss me and get it over with.'

And later in the rain when we walked around the city I asked if she had slept with him, though I didn't want to know.

'Not exactly.'

But she'd never met anyone like him.

They'd met in a pub. Everybody went back to Gerry's to listen to Charlie Parker records till three in the morning. And as she was leaving he asked her to call again. Next time he asked why she hadn't been back and she didn't have an answer; so they went to his place. He told her about the loneliness of the artist, the search for identity when you face a bare canvas, the struggle to get it right, how it never comes out the way it's supposed to, the way you think it will when you begin, how shape and colour can alter as new ideas occur to you; though essentially that doesn't matter, it isn't so important because you are trying to be true to the inner vision that always maintains itself. It was no hardship giving everything up: 'The hardship would have been to stay, to do something to buy the time. I don't think I was cut out for a shipping office, so there's no regrets on that score, none whatsoever. It isn't everyone who understands, but I can see you do. There isn't really time for you and I to talk just now, I've got all these other people to see to. It isn't always like this. It seems to happen when I meet someone interesting, not that I've met anybody interesting for a while. So, when are you free? Well then, come back tomorrow. Please. Promise you'll come back tomorrow. Come for lunch. We could spend the afternoon together, if you like.'

She arrived at one for a stroll around the market. 'I never knew this place existed,' she said. 'I thought everyone bought new clothes.' He laughed. 'New clothes,' said Gerry. 'Christ Almighty.'

41

The stench of human carelessness was everywhere: with the fat albino boy who played the mouth organ or the man with the accordion who sang 'O Solo Mio' with a screech like brakes at the end. This is where women squat round puddled bundles of rags piled outside the market doors raking for a bargain, where a man with a twitch wears a hand-coloured picture round his neck, a young boxer with a Benny Lynch stance and a centre parting, where fat men argue and thin men share a bottle of Eldorado White, standing by the stove or watching the stalls while the wife has a cup of tea with a cake and a smoke in Betty's Restaurant, where Jocky The Greek and One-Eyed Mary had a marriage that lasted three days and nights, beginning with the cake being pushed down the lavatory and ending when the party got a four-day remand with the happy couple shouting 'I love you' through the bars, and where Freddy The Fly sold a telegraph boy's bike to four Pakistanis and drank a bottle of wine as he watched them try to describe him to the police.

They had a pie and a pint in the Ship Bank Inn. 'Life,' said Gerry with a sigh. 'This is the life.'

'And tell me, tell me what do you say we take a taxi back, listen to some Dizzy, a little Bird or maybe even John Coltrane. So, a shared bag of chips in the back of a taxi. Has anyone told you who you looked like? Don't laugh. I'm being serious. Honest to God. I'm not kidding. Scout's honour; I'd love to paint you. What do you say? Would you like to sit for me? That would be wonderful. I don't believe it. Don't be silly; of course you wouldn't be embarrassed. It doesn't matter. Whether you've done it before or not is hardly important. It's your shape that interests me, nothing else. It's just a body and we've all got one. You're hardly going to show me something I haven't seen before. Jesus Christ. Your skin is wonderful. Don't ever let the sun get to it. Do you tan? No, I didn't think so. It's so pale, almost luminous. Like alabaster. That's a compliment. Really. It looks terrific. Firm.'

It ended when he met someone else.

'And this is what you've been trying to tell me?'

'Will you come to lunch on Sunday?'

The Mother didn't like me. She'd gone to a lot of trouble, tidied the house, prepared the lunch and set the table. The Father was chatty.

When lunch was over, Helen and I went for a walk. 'I don't care what she thinks,' she said with her lip trembling. 'I'm going to marry you and that's all there is to it.'

The blow-out came later. When we got back, Mother was in the kitchen, Father in the sitting room was reading about Rasputin. 'Interesting man; not at all as I imagined he would be,' he said as if he'd met him.

'Will you come into the dining room?' The Mother asked. 'I think we should have a little chat.' She was heavily made up and her lips didn't move when she spoke. Father sighed and raised his hand: 'Be seeing you,' he said.

Helen was crying by the kitchen table.

'Sit down,' said The Mother. 'I don't want you to think we've got anything against you personally.'

'Who's we?'

'Just hear me out, please. It's simply that Helen's had a very difficult time and she is rather young. She doesn't know what she wants. One minute it's one thing and the next minute it's something else.'

'What are you trying to tell me?'

'We don't think it would be a good idea for you and Helen to see each other.' I didn't hear the rest. I looked at The Mother. There was a look I had seen only in the eyes of the deeply religious, the suffering insane or young children, an open look through which it all flowed so clearly you could almost see her mind working.

'Who's we?' I asked.

'Please don't interrupt. I was saying –'

'I don't care much for what you're saying. It seems to me that you are intruding into a matter which essentially concerns Helen and I. And if you think I'm bad, you ought to meet Gerry.'

43

'I don't think we've ever met anyone called Gerry.'

'You haven't missed much.'

'I hoped you would understand. It's not that we've anything against you personally.'

'Who's we?'

'But you must understand, a parent has certain responsibilities towards her children.'

'Helen?'

She looked at me.

'How can you stand it? Being with this woman is like living with the weight of all the Russias.'

'I don't think there's any call for rudeness,' said The Mother.

'I wasn't being rude,' I said as I left and Helen renewed her wail behind me.

If only it had happened like that. It nearly did, except for me. The Mother certainly didn't like me, not that she gave any reasons. I wasn't good enough, not what she expected, background a bit common, origins uncertain. But I'd been raised to know my place, to touch my cap and to speak when I was spoken to, so I took what The Mother gave me and didn't answer back. I was anxious to please and tried to accommodate her. Looking back, I sense I was probably right, except that she now thinks I'm an imbecile, which doesn't bother me. She is an excellent specimen of middle-class female education brought to it's logical conclusion. We have little in common, except for a sense of humour, low and basically vulgar. Her head is stuffed with the most pretentious nonsense and there are times when she appears literally incapable of thought. And every penny's a prisoner. The accent is right and will relate unprompted tales of the many great sacrifices they were forced to make and continue to make.

Which tells nothing of how Helen became my wife. Amongst the many failures which middle-class life is heir to, recalcitrant children is foremost, which never seems to tell them anything except that children are hopelessly ungrateful nowadays and not at all what they used to be like.

44

'Go then,' said The Mother. 'But don't say we didn't warn you.'

'Who's we?'

That was six years ago. We've been happy, Helen and I. One of the benefits of the Sixties is that multiplication of the species is no longer a necessity. We are childless. She works part-time, buys a lot of clothes and overpriced cups of coffee in smart tea-rooms. She works at what she's always worked at; she's a schoolteacher.

'How's school?' I ask.

And she says, 'Fine.'

Of an evening we watch television. Sometimes we rent a video of a film we've missed. We sometimes go out for dinner, occasionally to a concert or maybe the theatre. Time passes.

We don't see much of her parents. They seldom come here and when they do The Mother brings presents which indicate she thinks we are starving, with something extra for Helen, something I could never want, make-up, underwear, handkerchiefs or a scarf, which is slipped to her when I'm not looking, but which I later find on top of the bedroom chest-of-drawers, still in the Marks and Spencers bag, unopened.

Usually on a Thursday evening, after tea, The Mother phones. If I answer, she asks to speak to Helen.

After saying, 'Hello, Mum,' Helen always says, 'Fine.' Then there's a pause: 'He's fine too,' she says.

And once every two or three weeks we go for Sunday lunch. Helen and I arrive around one o'clock and I talk to The Father while Helen helps in the kitchen or sets the table. The Father reads the *Sunday Post*, selecting items for my interest.

'What do you think of this, Angus?' he asks, reading headlines and all so that it doesn't make sense. 'Mrs McFarlane Was Black Affronted,' he said last Sunday. 'A Glasgow woman,' there was a pause while he read to himself. 'To buy a pair of tights,' he said after a while. 'Dearie me, the man in the shop didn't know what to do or where to look.' And at the end of the piece, 'A lesson for the future.' He laughed, 'That was good, eh?' he said. 'Lunch will be ready soon.'

45

Lunch is always a three-course affair, soup, meat and two veg, pudding, eaten in the small dining room, with coffee and After Eight mints served in the sitting room. Conversation is like mixing cement.

'How is that nice man you work with?' The Mother asks.

'Mr Strachan,' reminds Helen. 'The headmaster.'

'That's him; such a nice man, isn't he? Well, I think he always sounds nice; very helpful and a capable headmaster.'

'He's fine.'

'Now, tell me again, he isn't married, is he? No, I've got it wrong. He's a widower?'

'His wife died a few years ago.'

'Must be a lonely life for him. Doesn't he ever think of remarrying?'

'I don't know, Mother. I've never asked him.'

'No, dear, I didn't think you would ask him outright. But you can usually tell, can't you?'

'How's the garden, Daddy?'

'Daddy's garden's fine. You should ask Mr Strachan round for lunch some Sunday. I expect he'd like to get out of the house. And I'm sure he'd come if you asked him, since you get on so well, at school I mean.'

'I know what,' says The Father, as though he'd never had such an idea before in his life. 'We can do The Quiz. The *Sunday Post* Quiz is always good, isn't it?'

'I like Pete,' says The Mother. 'Pete asks, it's always a teaser.'

So it goes. Driving home, there's never much to say. We go to bed, read hardback novels, put out the light and eventually sleep.

A word of advice: *Never sleep with a woman whose troubles are worse than your own.*

Of course, we still make love. Once or twice a week there is a kind of coupling. We both know what the other likes and can't be bothered trying anything new. Occasionally we surprise ourselves, if we're drunk, if we've had a good meal, if it's a special occasion, if one or the other isn't feeling too well, if we're about to be parted for a day or two. But such events are rare.

It happened last night. We put our lights out at the same time, which is usually a good sign. She lay on the crook of my arm and kissed me. She still feels good. We were facing each other, her legs around my waist, shagging gently, when Miranda Morrison walked into my mind.

'You enjoyed that,' said Helen.

Mmmm. And I lay awake with Miranda Morrison, who moves well and looks good, who doesn't lower her eyes when she smiles, who always speaks to me, even if it's only 'Hello', but, if encouraged, will talk about anything. Beside her the other women seem sullen and lumpish with nothing to say.

I am spending more time in the outer office. It has become very difficult. I would like to see her privately, but if I invite her into the office for a cup of tea and a long chat, I would alienate the others and you've no idea how they gossip, washing their cups when the morning tea-break's over.

Today I looked at her personal file. She lives with her parents in the West End of the city; I imagine a red sandstone tenement with a tiled close. She has a brother and two sisters. The brother is older and has been through university. The sisters are younger. One is a nurse and the other's still at school. She's twenty-one. Her hobbies are reading, cooking, cinema and hill-walking. She's been with the bank for four years and moved to my branch eighteen months ago with excellent references.

This little entry has taken three nights. I'll have to give it a miss for a while. Helen could become suspicious. She might even read it. Helen, if you are reading this, I have one thing to say: It serves you right.

I'm going to bed, though I doubt if I'll sleep. I'll probably lie awake and wonder. There's a lot I wonder about. I sometimes wonder about my name. Would I be different with a different name? Would I be different if I knew my real name? Who was my mother? And how did she meet my father? Who was he?

47

Would I be different if I'd been adopted by someone else, if I'd stayed at Greenbank House, if I hadn't met the people I've met.

I write the answers on the bedclothes with my toes so no one can see. And I think of Mozart: Second Movement (headed Adagio in the autographed score and Adante in the others) Piano Concerto No. 23 in A, K488, written, with two others while he was working on *The Marriage of Figaro*; in much the same way as I have written bank reports while working on this.

Listen.

Sunday, March 16:

'You'd better get up,' said Helen this morning. Nothing unusual about that, except it was five-past ten and I do enjoy my Sunday lie-in. The *Observer* crossword is still unfinished.

She had answered the phone, then came into the bedroom, shouting at me as she flicked her dresses along the rail, looking for something to wear.

'What's going on?'

'This is,' she said, showing me a dress. 'Or do you think it's too showy?'

'What's happening?'

'Mr Strachan's coming round.'

'For Christsake, Helen.'

'I couldn't say no.'

'Why not?'

'I just couldn't. Are you getting up?'

'Only to tell Strachan he can come round later. What's his number?'

'Don't you dare. He'll think we don't know what each other's doing, or that we've had a row about him coming.'

'He can think what he likes.'

'You don't have to work with him. He'll mention it tomorrow: "Sorry if I caused some friction, Mrs MacPhail." Anyway, he won't be in. He'll be at church. He's coming round afterwards. I said he could have lunch.'

'In that case, we don't know what each other's doing. Why

48

did he call in the first place? Did he just invite himself round here?'

'Not exactly. I can't go into it just now.'

'Why not?'

'Please, Angus. Please get up.'

'Why did he phone?'

'Jesus, I don't remember. All I said was that some Sunday, when he wasn't doing anything, he could come round to the house and meet my husband.'

'Supposing your husband doesn't want to meet him? Sweet Suffering Christ in the Firmament, you could have said. You might have asked.'

'I forgot.'

'Fuck sake.'

'Language. Please, Angus. Darling. Please. Just this once. I'm sorry. It won't happen again.'

So after we'd tidied the place, with lunch in the pressure cooker, we waited for Strachan.

The man is a Charles Lamb model of English restraint. I imagine his wife died of boredom. Poor woman; she must have willed herself away.

He was well dressed, fat and tried to be cheery. The kind of man who likes to look at prostitutes; he enjoys the window-shopping. There is something oleaginous about him. He oozes perfection. His eyes are like milk and he glances around the edge of things, never straight at them, watching Helen as she moved round the room while he sipped his sherry. I had the feeling he'd like to have gulped it down and demand another.

'Well, well, well, Mrs MacPhail,' he said after lunch, his sausage fingers linked across his stomach, still at the table. 'So, cooking is another of your many accomplishments.'

She smiled. 'Why don't you call me Helen.'

'Good idea. We're not at school now, are we.'

He has the ways of the Calvinist, a horny old bastard with the passion submerged. I made a point of giving him drink and calling him Douglas, though he never addressed me by my

Christian name. He left after tea and thanked us for a lovely day . Most pleasant, he said.

Washing the dishes, Helen smiled. 'Poor old Mr Strachan,' she said. I wondered if she'd told her mother, but didn't ask. That isn't always an easy subject to broach. Helen is sometimes very protective and acts as if I don't know. Having told me once there's no need to be reminded.

I'm tired and now there's the crossword to finish. No more work tonight. Work in the morning.

And a new thought strikes me; I'll work on that chapter for later on, the one about Helen.

In the full and certain knowledge that diaries are written to be read, it might as well be that as anything else.

I'll see if it fits.

Five

Reader, I married her.

On a wet January Wednesday. We sat in the registry office foyer, where our wedding clothes, flowers and gaiety seemed underrated, out of place. My bride wore a floppy hat. We looked at each other often, smiling for reassurance as we waited for a breathless touch of the eternal.

The reception party was slow, everyone sober, stiff and awkward, suffering from the speeches. And just when all seemed lost, my father made an announcement.

'Never has it been my misfortune to find myself stranded amongst such a stiff-arsed bunch of pretentious drouths. One's as bad as the next. You're frightened to ruin the reputations you think you have for moderate conduct; and here you are, on the verge of seeing your big secrets come alive. There may, however, be one or two amongst you who do not care for such niceties and who have actually come here to celebrate my son's wedding. For them, and them alone, I have a small announcement, after which I will say no more, but will use my mouth for the God-given function of consuming alcohol. After an adequate sufficiency I will pass amongst you, distributing insults and wisdom. The bar, ladies and gentlemen, is open and, for the next hour, drinks are free. If you make use of this facility, I will consider extending it, but only if you're good and behave like Scotsmen and women who know a gift horse when they see one, rather than the church-going, pious bunch of Karl Popper devotees I presume you to be from your previous and current behaviour. So, let the wild rumpus begin. And he who does not join us is a coward and a knave, for ever enshrined in popular memory as the idiot who refused free drink.'

51

Helen's mother offered us a clean white cheek and we kissed it. Her father shook my hand. 'My wife isn't feeling too well,' he said. Helen sighed.

Half an hour later, my father made a second announcement. 'Ladies and gentlemen, I feel I may be pissed, so before understanding leaves my speech or my person, let me say, you have so far behaved splendidly. To ensure this adequate state will continue, I have instructed the bar staff to be liberal in their measure and to obey this instruction to the letter: anyone standing at the end of the night will have the feet cawed away fae them. I have personally found that a good going sweat and a warm atmosphere is conducive to an assault on the frontal lobes by any quantity of drink heretofore consumed. With this dictum in view, I hereby instruct Willie Thomson and Harry McCallum to produce their squeezebox and fiddle so's my daughter and I can lead the company in a Strip The Willow. And when this is done we will have another the same, as it used to say in the Church of Scotland Hymnary. As an interval entertainment, I myself will lead the company in a rendering of "The Bonnie Wells O' Wearie" and anyone who does not know the words, or makes no gesture towards pretending to know the words, will be immediately papped oot, with no appeals considered. Again, I bless you. Get steamed in. And good luck to the lot of yous.'

We stayed beyond our time, and left to a battery of foot-stamping and whistles, five minutes after a married couple I'd never met: 'Babysitters and all that,' the man said, his wife smiling drunk by the door.

The taxi arrived, black and shiny. The air was chilly and someone said it looked like snow. 'I hope my Daddy remembered the cake,' said Helen.

She stared out the window, lit when a splash of city light crossed us. The cab smelled warm of cigarettes and cheap perfume. I pulled down a window and the driver slid the adjoining panel: 'Do us a favour, pal,' he said. 'Let us know if you're gonnae spew. I'll stop the motor and you can bring up as much as you like outside. If you do it in here I've got to clean it up and it takes days for that smell to go.'

'I'm okay,' I said, leaning on her shoulder. She raised the window slightly.

'I know. That's what they all say. Then they open the window and the fresh air makes them sick. Just let us know if you think you'll start honkin'. Yous can coorie in as much as yous like in there; in fact, you can do anything you want, so long as yous don't mind me watching.'

The city was a different place, a smaller part of another illusion. Our home was in a building we shared with seven other families, each with their own front door. We had a small hall, a living room, bedroom, bathroom and kitchen. We had seen the house advertised in the paper and never met the man who'd owned it, but dealt with his solicitor who asked if we'd like him to deal for us to make it cheaper and push things along that little bit quicker. Then he asked if we'd arranged a mortgage. The bills were paid by standing order, except when I was overdrawn. I paid the rates on the third reminder or by instalment, the electricity and gas were metered, and I now had a wife.

For weeks, after work, we ate Chinese or Indian carry-outs, fish suppers and pizzas while we scraped the walls, painted the woodwork, then repapered our home, covering the cracks as best we could. My wife made curtains, bought a rug for the hearth and a bathroom shade. We rented a television, bought furniture from salerooms, a new bed, a gas cooker and a washing machine on hire purchase.

I had a stag night with people I no longer know and remember nothing after nine o'clock. Cameron was allowed out of jail for the ceremony. He was my best man and the wedding was attended by two prison officers who returned him to Perth when Helen and I were man and wife. During the speeches, my father insisted on making an additional toast, to absent friends.

While the driver kept talking: 'I mind one night I picks up this old thing, in the toon it was. Jesus Christ, you want to have seen her, done up like a fucken' Christmas tree. Her hair was up on her heid. She looked like a cake. I takes her to where

53

she was going; Govan. "We won't bother with the fare for now," she says. "Just come up to the flat and we'll have a refreshment." The flat was a room and kitchen with an ootside lavvy; and the refreshment was half a bottle of Eldorado, that fucken' red stuff. I has a keek at her; she was about ninety. "Oh no," I tellt her, "listen, missus; I'd rather have the cash."

'That's okay if you're bevvied. If you're drunk, you'll jump the kip wi' anything, so you will but. I'm tellin' you, I've gone tae bed wi' Marilyn Monroe and wakened up wi' Bela Lugosi.'

Outside, it's snowing.

'Sorry, hen. I don't mean tae be vulgar. It's just my way. I can see you're broadminded. I like a woman who can take a good joke. I must have this thing about hair; don't know what it is. I minds one night I gets off wi' a cracker. She had lovely blonde hair. When I wakes up in the morning I thought I had a big bahooky on the pillow aside us. She'd an Irish jig on and it must've come aff when she was sleepin'. Jesus Christ, you want to've seen the state o' her trying to find her fucken wig, then get it on withoot me seeing. Bald as a billiard ball, so she was but.'

Thick snow, heavy as cream.

'Where are we going? Is this it? No, it's the next one. Tell you what I'll do wi' yous; I'll drop yous off at the corner to save me turning. Okay? You've only a wee bit tae walk. It'll calm yous doon. Mind you don't fall in the snow, hen. That's right, son; you haud her up. Right, sir. Thanks for no spewing in my motor. And three quid makes five. Very good of you, sir. Thanks very much. Tell you something for nothing, pal, I wish I was you the night.'

She stood on the pavement in a thin blue light. Her head was bent. She put her arms round her waist and swayed from one leg to the other.

'Come on,' she said.

The weak snow had set along cast-iron railings and bulbs of water hung from the spars, single beds for the melting snow that ran down their length or detached with a plop. I kicked the slush and we walked to the close. The streets would be flooded by morning.

The noise of our feet echoed up the stair and at the back of my head my mother said, 'Neighbours.' Key in the lock and now we're home. No one had seen us.

There were flowers by the window, but the house didn't smell right, it was unfamiliar. Helen draped her coat across a chair, lit the fire and a lamp in the corner. We had a cup of tea and sat on the sofa with the empty mugs.

I left them to dry and opened the window, stretching my stomach across the sink, with my head in the night to cool me down. I'd suddenly felt hot and my scalp was tingling which I took to be a sign I'd have a headache in the morning, if not sooner. I wasn't drunk but had had too much to drink and felt full up, so I stayed like that, looking out the window and trying to feel better, poking the snow on the sill with my finger till it was numb.

'What's wrong? There's a terrible draught,' she said. My chest was sore and I now felt sick though I knew I wouldn't bring anything up even though it would have helped the headache. I closed the window and brushed my teeth. She was in her nightdress, between new sheets, staring at the ceiling.

The light above the street lamps was a misty blue and orange. It was snowing again and big flakes drifted past the window. Outside this room we're part of a memory; and even although it's supposed to be new, the lamps and the snow and the shouts in the night and the noise of the traffic remind us we've been here before. The room reminds us we thought we were happy and were sure we were right and being here forces us to remember promises we made when we thought this time would be different to the way it was.

4 a.m. and she is sobbing.

'I want to,' she said. 'I want to. I can't, but I want to. Honest to God, I really want to do it.'

The sun came up without remark. Mists had gathered in the closes and ran along the empty streets, where freezing snow lay in marzipan lumps by the side of the road. And as the sun scattered a 40-watt light across the city, I made up a bed on the sofa, with my heart as hard as an unripe pear when I finally slept.

She laid the tea cup on the carpet and kissed my brow. 'I've made your breakfast,' she said. We ate slowly.

'Is it all right?'

'What?'

'Your breakfast; is it all right?'

'Yeah, it's fine. Thanks. The breakfast's great. It's just that I don't feel too hungry.'

'You ought to eat it. Everyone should have a good breakfast; sets you up for the day.'

By the sink, in her housecoat, she was singing to the radio as I dried. I leaned across and touched her breast. The song on the radio clung to the air as I took my hand away and sighed.

'I'm sorry,' she said.

'You're not half as sorry as I am.' Something I hadn't meant to say.

She leaned on the draining board, against the sink in a gesture of defeat. 'I can't,' she said. 'I'm scared and I don't know what I'm scared of. It isn't you. But it isn't really me either. It's not my fault, or I don't think it is. Though I don't expect you to believe me.'

'Tell me this.' I was probably shouting. 'You came over pretty bloody strong. Do you know what I mean, or would you like me to explain. No, I didn't think you would. How is it then, that while we didn't actually have a performance, we had a couple of pretty reasonable rehearsals and now I can't even get into the same bed as you and we're supposed to be married.'

'We are married,' she said, but not to me. 'Before; well, it was okay, because I knew that if you wanted to, I could put you off till we were married. I hated it. A couple of times I was nearly sick.'

'Thanks a lot. Very reassuring.'

'For God's sake, Angus, it was because of me, not because of you. Because of me; because of what I felt like, because I knew I wouldn't be able to let you do it. And if I couldn't let you do it, what chance did I have with anyone else.'

'I must say, this explains a lot.'

56

'Gerry had nothing to do with it either.'

'He never crossed my mind. But no wonder he was smiling.'

'I didn't want you to know. It might have put you off. I hated it and I still hate it. I hate the very idea of it.'

'Why?'

'It's dirty.'

'Helen, I don't believe this. I can't believe it. Tell me it isn't happening. Reassure me. Tell me I'll waken up and find it isn't real.'

'I'm sorry.'

'Stop saying that. Please. What the hell are we going to do? Learn to play dominoes?'

'Don't tell anyone. Please. Please, Angus, promise me you won't say. If anyone found out I wasn't a real wife to you, I'd kill myself. I couldn't face them. I'd want to die.'

'Do you think I want to tell people?'

'I mean doctors or anyone like that. I'll try. I will. I'll try. I'll make it up to you. Let me get used to it. Let me get used to the idea. I want to be a good wife to you. I want to; you're my man. There's things I haven't told anyone and I want to tell you, because I love you. I'll manage. You'll see. I'll manage.' She smiled: 'Make up your bed in case anyone comes,' she said.

Her father came round with the cake. He sat on the sofa with his tea cup balanced on one knee and said, 'My, this is cosy.' He stayed for half an hour and left without seeing us, always polite as he took in the walls and furniture. He spoke to them and answered us, trying to cover the embarrassing silences too quickly. 'Well,' he said at the door. 'That was lovely. Have a nice time and, yes, well I'll see you soon.'

We'd bought the house three months previously, having saved for almost a year. Both parents helped us out. My mother used to slip me a fiver when no one was looking. 'Get something for the house,' she'd say. 'You're the only one of my children who will ever get married and I want it to be all right.'

'Don't be silly, Mum.'

'It's true. Phamie's ruined herself and Cameron, well, everyone knows what's happened to him and his politics. So you take it. But don't tell your father.'

When Helen's parents came round, The Mother looked at the place as though she was lost in an art gallery. 'You can't have this wallpaper,' she said.

'Especially since we've started to scrape it,' said I. Helen looked at me and pursed her lips.

'Well then, tell me what you are going to do?' she asked. As I spoke she looked around the room and sighed when I'd finished. Then Helen told her in a different way. 'That'll be nice, dear,' she said.

Her father nodded. 'Good, Angus,' he said. 'It's a nice wee place. It's good for you to get a start like this.'

'Poor Daddy,' she said. Evening, television over, ready for bed sitting by the fire with our mugs of chocolate. She is wearing a neck-to-ankle nightdress, pink candy-striped housecoat and fluffy slippers. 'Poor Daddy. I always loved my daddy.'

She sighed. 'You'll never believe this,' she said. 'I know you won't. I just know it.'

'Tell me.'

And she did what her father had done; she looked round the room. The battery-driven clock shifted rather than ticked. Its sound was audible when she spoke, slowly at first, to herself, her hands clenched together till the skin was white, resting on her knees with her arms straight.

'Before you begin, tell me this. How I'm supposed to believe you. I mean, you have given me accounts of your past which weren't quite accurate.'

'Let me know if you don't believe this one. I told you I would try and this is me trying, Angus.'

'Sorry. I mean it, love. I am sorry.'

She stared at her knees and nodded as if to accept the apology. Then she was silent. Her eyes were closed and she sighed, and after another pause, she nodded again.

58

'When I was wee, he used to work away a lot. I thought he was away for months at a time, but it was probably only a couple of weeks. That was when she did her gallivanting. And she always took me with her; that way the neighbours thought she was taking me out and never suspected anything; that way they had no gossip, nothing to tell my daddy.

'It was always houses we went to. I've no idea who the other people were or how she arranged it, but they never came to see us and the only time I saw them was when we went to their houses. And they were always expecting us. "Hello," they'd say. "Come away in." I'd get a juice and she would drink whatever was going.

'After an hour or two, I'd have to go to bed. They always laughed. There were men there and I'd get embarrassed about taking my dress off in front of them, of letting them see me in my knickers or anything like that. And do you know this; I've just remembered, she always stuck up for them. She made me feel silly for behaving like that. "Come on, Helen," she'd say. "Don't be daft. Nobody wants to see your drawers." And then she'd laugh, along with everyone else. I mean, I always cared about how I looked. I was always neat and tidy. I always had a clean frock and my hair in plaits or bunches with nice ribbons. That was what I hated about going to these houses; it was the strangeness. Nothing was the same as in our house.

'There was always an awful smell of dirt. I hated going to bed in these places. The sheets were all scruffy and there was a dry, sour smell off the bedclothes; sometimes they were damp. "There you are," she'd say. "That's nice, isn't it." And she'd tuck me in and give me a kiss on the cheek. I hated that, her kissing me. It was nice at home. She smelled clean there. But in these places her breath smelled of tobacco and drink and she always had make-up on. She'd put it on when she got there; her and another woman, running around, sometimes in their underwear, with a drink and a cigarette in their hands, putting on make-up or trying on each other's clothes, giggling.

'That's what I don't understand. At home she was always

neat. The house was immaculate, scrubbed and spotless. While my daddy was there she was a good wife. She was like she is now, well, not as bad as she is now, but she never wore make-up, she didn't smoke; in fact, I can't remember her taking a drink in our house. Then my daddy would go away for a day or two. "We've been asked out for the evening," she'd say. "Some friends who want to meet us. Daddy doesn't know them," she'd say. "They're friends of mine, really." And away we'd go. I can see it all now, but when you're eight years old, you don't see that much.

'One night in a house, I don't know where, I used to know the woman's name, but I've forgotten it, I wakened up in the middle of the night and the bed was moving. Take my hand, Angus. No. I'm all right. Just take my hand. Hold me.

'She was at the other end of the bed and her leg was near my face. I opened my eyes and saw another pair of feet and, well, you can guess what was happening. She was moaning and gasping for breath. I got scared, but didn't move. I couldn't. Christ, I was terrified. Then they were still. And she started whispering. "Come on then. I thought you said you could ride me. What's the matter with you? Worn out?" There was a lot of fumbling and he went over, his dirty smelly feet were next to my face. But she kept on talking. She was saying terrible things, cursing and swearing. I don't remember anything else, except what she said and I want to block that out. I put my fists to my ears and I must have gone back to sleep. I was only wee.

'Next morning she wakened me. It was always the same. She'd get up and scrub herself clean, then she'd get me up and wash me all over. I had to strip right down. Then she'd say, "We shan't breakfast here, dear. I've got a wee treat lined up for you." And we'd leave the house around seven in the morning with everyone still sleeping, tiptoeing downstairs and running along the street; sitting on the buses with the men going to their work looking at you.

'We'd go into town, to a hotel and I'd have bacon and eggs, tea and toast. She usually had a couple of tomato juices and some coffee; nothing to eat. We'd usually get back by eleven o'clock and if there was school, I'd have the day off. "We won't go there again, dear," she'd say. Every night, after a bath, in my own clean bed with a nice clean nightdress on, she'd tuck me in and say, "We won't go back again, dear. I promise. We won't go back. Best not to mention to Daddy we were there at all. He doesn't know the people and I don't think he'd want us to go. So we shan't go back. And you'll tell me if any of the neighbours ask where you were, won't you; or anyone at school. Just say you didn't feel well and tell the neighbours you were at an auntie's, and then tell me who asked. That was the last time, Helen. The very last time." And I always believed her. I thought we'd never go back. But we always went back.'

'How long did this go on for?'

'Till I was ten,' she said, standing up to kiss my cheek. 'Night–night,' she said and went to bed, closing the door tight behind her.

The snow melted. All day it rained so we stayed indoors, watching television, playing patience, playing Scrabble. 'There's no such word as oogamy,' she said, and we didn't have a dictionary. I slept for most of the afternoon and when I wakened she was cooking. 'I thought we might go out tonight,' she said.

We didn't plan a honeymoon. Helen had said, 'We might go away for a day or two, if the weather's nice.' We had three days off; this was Friday, work on Monday and Friday night's the same as usual.

While I washed up, Helen had a bath. She started to get ready just after six o'clock. 'It's easy for men,' she said. 'All they do is fling something on and that's all there is to it. A woman has to prepare herself.'

Watching her dress, I learn her secrets. Never use soap and just a touch of mascara; use a hair toner, a good one, once a week and wash your hair every second day; a woman has to have a bath every day, twice a day, at least, during certain

61

times and always carry a spare youknowwhat, just in case, you can never be too careful; buy a good bra; brush your hair when there's nothing else to do; never have more than one scent about you; cheap perfume's a waste of money; always see yourself from the back; plain is nicest; brush your teeth whenever you can; rub your gums with your finger; a drink of hot water and lemon juice every morning is good for your skin; a raw egg white is a good face-mask once a week; vinegar in the rinsing water's good for your hair; a woman ages quicker than a man and has to keep up with the style; a man can wear anything, but a woman must be careful.

'A woman wants men to want her,' she said as we crowded round the back-room table. The Marland Bar: mahogany counter, bar and dado, dark green walls, tattered light and the same old mirrors, shelves and gantry, optics, tumblers, glass and bottles, a pewter measure and a tray for the slops, places where light was caught and sparkled on the rim, cases for sandwiches, rolls and pies, a brass footrail and a raw smell of beer, tobacco and disinfectant. The bar was always busy with whisky glasses, blinking like fireflauchts through the smoke, around the fire and by the tables the hum of chatter was lost when you passed. They'd kept the old ways because anything else would have cost too much and the old ways now were back in style.

The back-room had benches and tables round the walls, fancy glasses and mirrors, nice lights, a bell that worked and a barman who was on to a good thing with the best job in the shop, Friday or Saturday nights.

Someone said, 'You're looking tired.'

'Have you had a nice time?'

'God, girl, you're blooming.'

'Has he been treating you right?'

And nobody spoke to one alone, but red faces came to the table for a few words: 'How's it going?'

And Helen smiled as she took my arm; looking into my face, she brushed imaginary fluff from my shoulders; bent her head towards the table, suddenly straightening as she spread her hand through her hair; she blushed when William told a joke and clasped her hand around her mouth: 'I want you,' she whispered into my ear.

'Jesus Christ,' said Cash McColl. 'Have yous two no had enough?'

Helen looked straight at him. 'No,' she said.

It wasn't the place. It could have been the Zeffirelli light, the cosiness, the mixture of nostalgia and desire, the warmth and the smoke, but it's more likely to be memory, which seldom is what we want it to be, or seldom tells us what we want to know, which soothes or comforts by comparing and is likely to remind us of what we need or what we're missing rather than delight us with what we've got. The third and fourth movements of the String Quartet, Number 15 in A minor, Opus 132. Judy and I. 'Nice that,' she said. 'It's very strange, a bit creepy. Every time I hear it, I'll think of you.' How many times has she remembered, and what did it remind her of; did it remind her of something she couldn't place, could she remember having heard it before, or, more likely, has she never heard it since that time? The hardest part is not knowing.

'Sorry?'

'What were you thinking?'

'Nothing.'

'I know what you were thinking,' she said, laughing. 'Anyway, what I wanted to know was why do you call him Cash?'

'Oh, that. He's always trying to borrow money. He'll start with a quid and work his way down. He once asked me for the loan of three-ha'pence to buy some fags. I'll say this for LSD McColl, though, you always get your money back. William says there's a common float, that when you give Cash money no one ever knows from then on who it belongs to.'

She laughed. 'Doesn't he mind?'

'Not now. Nobody ever gives him money. They think he's kidding, but he isn't. He needs it. He's got a wife and six kids no one's ever seen.'

'Christ Almighty,' Cash said later taking a piss, his other hand leaning on the wet concrete above the urinal. 'That's some woman you've got there, son. Sorry, Gus. No offence, it's just that I've never seen anyone looking so bloody raw, know what I mean?'

'Sure.'

'Hey, Angy. You couldn't give us the loan of a quid, could you?'

'Sorry, Cash.'

'Fair enough. You'll be needing it. Jesus Christ, man. You must be knackered.'

'I missed you,' said Helen, rubbing my shins with her feet.

'Shut your horrible mouth,' said Lindy. 'I'm not speaking to you.' And William blew her a kiss.

Lindy worked in a bookshop; no one knew what William did. They were a pair rather than a couple, strangely matched; William in his suits and ties, his suede shoes and a folded copy of the *Guardian*, Lindy in her cheesecloth skirts, loose blouses and shoulder-length hair. She liked to sing. The bookshop played records as a suggestion of music rather than an interruption and Lindy's voice trailed like a scent behind her as she moved around the place.

'Pound says somewhere that the rich have butlers and no friends. Then he says, the poem's called "The Garret", then he says, we have friends and no butlers, meaning the poor. Right?'

'He was a Fascist,' said Sugar Daly.

'Good-night,' said Cash. 'See you.'

'Night, Cash.'

'Hey, Cash, will you be in tomorrow?'

'Don't know. Yeah. Think so.'

'Then bring your fucken wallet.'

'Anyway,' said Lindy, 'my point is that the middle class have neither.'

'That is rubbish.'

'They only have themselves.'

'And what's the matter with that?'

64

'Wasn't Pound a Fascist?'

'Not really.'

'I thought he was.'

'That poem,' said William. 'That poem has the line about dawn entering with little feet like a gilded Pavlova.'

'It also,' said Lindy, looking at me, 'says pity the married and the unmarried.'

' "Nor has life in it aught better/ Than this hour of clear coolness,/ the hour of waking together." '

'I like that,' said Helen. 'Tell me it again.'

'A good time to get a round,' said I. And Helen smiled at me, pushing her glass across the table.

Joe the barman saw me and came over: 'Did you ring?' he asked. I gave him the order. 'You should always ring, sir. I'll come, sir, if you ring. Please. Thank you.'

He brought in the drinks and took an order from Lindy. 'Nothing for me,' said Helen and Lindy smiled. Helen's hand was resting along the inside of my leg. 'I don't want to go anywhere afterwards,' she said. 'I want to go straight home. Okay?'

'Same again?' asked Joe, bringing in another round as the bell rang.

'Give us a song,' said Sugar and Lindy shook her head, wondering what to sing.

'Thank you, madam. Shall I arrange your carry-out.'

'Come on, Lindy.'

'You might as well, Joe. I'll pick it up on the way out.'

'Lindy?'

'What?'

'Are you going to sing us a song?'

She spun the whisky around the glass. Her voice was dark, husky and a little sad:

> For you took what's before me and what's behind me,
> You took east and west when you wouldn't mind me;
> Sun, moon and stars from my sky have been taken
> And God as well, or I'm much mistaken.

Black as the sloe is the heart that's in me,
Black as the coal is the grief that binds me,
Black as a bootprint in shining hallway,
'Twas you that blackened it, forever and alway.

'Right then, drink up, that's the time. Please.'

'Who's for an omelette and a few cans, *chez moi*?' said William.

'The carry-out is waiting.'

'Good. Who's coming?'

'Don't mind,' said Sugar.

'I expect the newly-weds will be having an early night,' said Lindy.

Helen smiled and put her arm around me. William and Lindy went off arm-in-arm, Sugar carried the carry-out.

Walking home with my hand beneath her coat she scratched a wee bit of my side that itches when I think of it. Her head lay beneath my shoulder and I played with her left ear-lobe as we tottered home, slightly bevvied, adjusting to her and the cold.

She is a slender woman, finely boned with pale and deceptive, thin hands. Because her face is tightly skinned, pale flesh taut over high cheek-bones with clear, straight joints and small temples, she will grow old always looking young. Her eyes are large, her nose short, straight and flared. She has a look of fragile, reluctant youth.

Buses passed on their way to the garages and taxis ran to the housing schemes around the city. The night was sharp, fresh, dark and nearly February with the air again poised for snow. The house was cold. She lit the gas fire and I boiled a kettle.

'I've put the blanket on,' she said. 'Please, Angus, bring in the tea. I want to talk.'

Teapot, cups and a tray in the living room. She stared at the fire: red, blue, yellow, red and blue.

'I was ten,' she said. 'The first time I saw him, saw him properly was when I was ten years old and he came to the house. He wasn't like my daddy. His features were sharper

66

and his eyes were brown. He dressed different and had wavy hair.

'Obviously, my daddy was away. It was wet and I'd stayed in. She'd been ironing. I remember the smell, that nice ironing smell was around the house, a warm smell. She'd folded the clothes and put them away. She asked what I wanted for tea. I must have said sausages; we were getting ready to go out when the bell went and she said, "That'll be the butcher with the sausages." Funny, me remembering that.

'I went to the door. He must have been expecting her; he was smiling. His smile died a wee bit when he saw me. But he recovered quick enough. "Hello, Helen," he said. "You don't know me, but I'm your Uncle Bob. Is your mummy in? Good. Go and tell her, tell your mummy Uncle Bob's here."

'I went into the bedroom. She was putting her coat on. I stood there looking at her and when she turned I said, "Uncle Bob's here." It's funny, you don't remember what happened, but you remember the feeling. I remember feeling scared. I'd never been so frightened. When she looked at me, I thought she was going to hit me. She rushed out the room, but when she saw him, she ran out of steam, as if she'd been punctured. The fight just went out of her.

'He said, "Hello." And she just stood there.

'I didn't know who he was or anything about him. But I knew it must be something dirty and I hated him.

'I'll say this for her, she didn't give in easily. She soon got her wind back. "Don't you dare come here," she said. He said, "I'm sorry. I'll go. I thought you'd be pleased to see me. I'll go." But he didn't go.

'Bit by bit he got in, you know, "It's cold here, any chance of a cup of tea?" that sort of thing. After an hour they were talking away as if nothing had happened, as if he lived there. He was all about wanting to bring flowers and chocolates, presents for me and if he'd thought about it he'd have done that, but it was a spur-of-the-moment thing, he was in the area, just passing actually, on his way to see an old mate, Jock, "Did you ever meet Jock?" and all that crap, just for the sake of talking. She must have mentioned that the butcher's was shut or something. "Don't tell me," he said. "I've come at a bad time. Of course, your tea."

'You can guess the rest. "Get ready," he said. I'll be back in half an hour. She changed, ran around singing, all excited. I hoped he wouldn't come back. But he did. Taxi at the door, into town, Miss Rombach's Restaurant opposite Central Station, it's away now. A treat for the young lady, he said. Strawberry ice-cream. He wanted to give me more, but she said I'd be sick. Then we went to the pictures. I tried to sit between them. I knew, even at that age, I bloody well knew. She moved me up and that was it. I don't know what the film was, can't remember. I remember wondering what they were doing, what they could do and I kept my eyes opened. Nothing happened. We got a taxi home and that was all. He went away. "I'll call again," he said at the close and she nodded. He smiled. It was as if she was all shiny, her eyes and everything. I didn't understand that look then, but I understand it now.'

She turned down the fire and watched the firebrick fade. Without thinking, I went into the kitchen, leaned across the sink and stared out of the window. Again the city is cold and gaudy with silly lights sparkling.

'I'll tell you.' She is behind me. The kitchen is narrow, almost a corridor, with the window and sink at one end, the door at the other and everything else in between. She is white and trembling. 'You bastard. You fucken cold bastard. I'll tell you. I'll tell you now and no more. I'll tell you now and there's an end to it. Uncle Bob may not be important to you. What you went through at your Greenbank House must make him seem like a nice, reasonable chap because he bought me ice-cream. Bet you never got ice-cream. No one took you to the pictures, did they? So Uncle Bob is not important. But he bloody well should be. He's important as far as this marriage is concerned and I'll tell you why. He came back. That's why. He bloody well came back. And look at you, standing there with your lip trembling, looking out the window because you

68

can't look at me. You don't need to look at anyone when you stare out the window, do you, Angus. Jesus Christ. You're so bloody cold, frozen stiff because you can't get your nookie.'

Milk hissed in the pan. And this is the way my mind works. I thought of Mr Simpson, the Greenbank janitor, an old man who wheezed and spluttered; he'd hold his chest and shake his head while his spit burned and sizzled on the fireside hob.

'Do you want some chocolate?' I asked and she battered the door shut. I mingled milk and chocolate, enough for two half-cups.

She was crouched by the fire. She cupped the mug in her hands and drank the chocolate quickly, slurping, as though she was thirsty. 'Do you think I like this?' she asked. 'Do you think I am enjoying telling you this? I haven't told a living soul. Needless to say, it isn't exactly the sort of thing I could discuss with my mother. But I'll tell you. I'm telling you because I'm married to you and I want this to work, Angus. I want this marriage to work and I'm telling you what happened because if you understand then you can help it to work too. You have to know, you have to understand and that's why I'm telling you, so's you'll understand. Jesus. Look at you. Look at your face. I shouldn't have to say this to you. Have you no sense of anything outside yourself? I'm going on with it. I am going to get it out, because it's necessary, not only for you and I, but also for me. But one thing more and then we'll continue. One thing more. Do you believe me?'

I stared at her too long, was too aware of my timing to get it right. 'Sure. Of course I believe you.'

'Liar. You don't know whether to believe me or not. You look at my mother prim and proper and you look at my dad and you wonder about them only from what you can see. But there are things we can't see, Angus, wounds that can't heal and these wounds are important.'

'Well, now that you've insulted me, you can carry on.'

'Is that all you got, an insult? I'll tell you what, let me finish; let me finish talking and then we'll see what happens. You can think about it. Okay?'

'Sure.'

'Hold on. I've got to go a place. I'll carry on when I get back.'

Sitting, looking round the room, I took an inventory. There is an anima of things, a Gospel of Objects. They can be loved, though they serve no useful purpose. They are uncluttered by their past.

By the window stands a table made from the cast-iron base of a Singer sewing machine. The guts have been removed and all that remains is the useless treadle with a slab of varnished pine screwed on top to make the table. There is a lamp on the table. The lamp has a pink shade which purls a soft reflection across the varnished pine. It has been made from the base of an oil lamp, formed like an Ionic column with fluted curlicues around its neck where the bevelled glass container held the oil and its mellowed portable light. On the other side of the table is a dark green ewer with dried reeds and grasses in a winter arrangement. Sorrel, hogweed and Solomon's-seal. And the picture of my mother in its silver frame stands between them. All were now what we chose to make them.

There is a small mirror in the bathroom. A photograph of Marilyn Monroe has been printed on to the glass. When you look into the mirror, your face is superimposed over Marilyn Monroe's face. Helen is staring into the mirror. 'Just coming,' she said.

'Are you all right?'

'Terrific.'

'Do you want some tea?'

'No. No thanks. I've just had some chocolate.' And she followed me through.

'There isn't much more,' she said.

I am looking at the table and the winter arrangement. 'Are you listening?'

'Sure.'

Silence.

And when she talks, she talks to herself: 'There isn't much more.

'I came in from school one day about a week or two later and there he was. I felt as if I shouldn't be there, as if I'd interrupted them. "Go out and play," she said. But it was raining, so she let me stay in. But I was the stranger. He was sitting in the big chair by the fire, my daddy's chair, and she carried on working, doing things about the house as if everything was as it should be, normal.

'She was hanging up a pair of curtains. I'll never forget this. She was on the ladder and she asked him to hold it for her. He got up from the chair and looked at her. I was doing my homework at the table, so I saw the lot. I turned round and he had his hand up her skirt. She's fixing the curtains and he's got his hand, running it up and down her leg.

'They couldn't get me to bed quick enough. I cooried in so's I wouldn't hear them. But I heard them. It was awful. I kept thinking I'd tell my daddy. But I didn't. I thought it would hurt him, so I kept it to myself. But it didn't, it didn't hurt him. He was almost pleased, as if a big weight had been lifted, as if he'd known and was glad it was out in the open. The way she did it too. I came home from school and there was nobody in. I only had to wait about an hour for him to come home, sitting on the stairs I was when he got there. He smiled too. He smiled at me with his wee apologetic smile. "Sorry I kept you," he said. "I couldn't get away sooner." As if we were strangers, as if I had an appointment with him. But that's just my dad, it's his way. He made the tea and then he told me. She'd sent him a letter, posted it to his work. She took none of her clothes, nothing. She never even kissed me goodbye. I went to school, same as usual, and she said, "Cheerio."

'All that time, I've hated her. At first I hated her for what she did to my daddy. It changed him. I used to hear him crying at night. He changed. He just got more into himself and he was the same when she came back.'

'When did she come back?'

'Ages. She was away about a year, maybe more, a year and a half. I don't know how it happened. She came back. I came home and there she was. "Hello," she said. And do you know, we've never talked about it. This last year or two, she's got to be the way she is now. "Men are dirty buggers," she said. That's what she said. It's as near as we've got to talking about it. And my daddy is the way he is because he doesn't want her to go away again, as if he's scared she'll leave him. That's why he took early retirement, I'm sure of it.

'Now I look at her and think I must be imagining it, think it can't be the same person. But it is. I know it is. She's got older, that's all. She's settled into something. God knows what happened to Uncle Bob. I'll never know.

'They got that place when my daddy retired, so we're away from it all, as if it never happened. But I've only got to look at my daddy to know it happened. Then there's my part in it. I still feel guilty. But I couldn't have told him. Couldn't. I think he knows that. I hope he does.

'When I grew older, there was nobody to show me anything, how to dress, nothing. Once she said to me, "You should never wear green and blue together. They clash." Christ. I nearly went for her. "How am I supposed to know that?" I said. "You were never here to teach me these things." And when I turned round, she wasn't there. She must have walked away and I didn't hear her. Honest. I don't know if she heard me or not. I hope she did. Not that it would bother her. She can't have a conscience. Not a real conscience.

'I mean, what does she think when she thinks about it? What does she know about me? What did she do to tell me the things a mother tells her daughter. Where was she? I had my first period when I was twelve. The woman next door told me what to do. I didn't know about these things. I had pains in my stomach and when I started bleeding, God, what a fright I got. "It's all right, hen," she said. "It's only your illness." Then she took me to the doctor. What way is that for a girl to learn anything. The doctor's explaining about ovaries and my mother's not there. And now she tries to tell me who I can marry. See that time, when you came over and she talked to you, that's why I was crying, really crying. I was crying from rage, from my own stupid rage. I wanted to say, "What right

72

do you have to tell me what I can do and what I can't do? What right do you have to tell me anything. The things I needed to know were told by a doctor.''

'And when I saw the way men chase you, I hated them. I hated the way they looked at you, hated the way they tried to touch you. I hated the way they chased me. And I knew why. I knew why they chased me. I was her daughter. They could see her in me. Men know these things. They can tell. Gerry knew it. He told me. Gerry said it. "Jesus," he said. "You'd be a passionate woman." That bit of her was still in me. So I got rid of it.

'I got rid of it by ignoring it, by not letting myself believe it was there. It was a kind of revenge, if you like. Play them along, take them for what you could get, but no deal. Mugs do deals. You can get what you want without giving them anything, without marrying them, for God's sake. Play them along and give them nothing, then Ta-ta at the end because they'd hurted me. Some guys I felt sorry for, but some guys like Gerry had nothing to give and the rest I took to the cleaners. I played them along till they were going daft, then I gave them the push.

'So, that's how it is, Angus. That's how it is. I want to. Honest. I do. You're different. You're my husband. And I want to. But I can't. Funny, I never thought I'd want to. I always believed, somebody told me if you did it too much you'd turn into a hag. I never thought I'd want to, but I do with you.'

'Why me?'

'Because you don't know who you are either.'

'Tis not the frost that freezes fell
Nor blawing snaw's inclemancie;
'Tis not sic cauld that maks my cry
But my luve's hart's grawn cauld tae me.
When we cam in by Glesca toon,
We were a comely sicht tae see;
My luve was cald in the black velvet,
And I masel in cramasie.

Christ. Lying awake, listening to lorries. Gears crunched and brakes hissed as they approached the corner. A chilly and harsh ascending note as they accelerated if the road was clear, another crunch as the note dropped and faded. Coming the other way there was a splash as they hit the puddle by the Drive Carefully sign on the corner.

Next day was Saturday. We went shopping in the morning and to the pictures in the afternoon. The film was about people like us, a young couple. In the end they got married. The last frame showed them holding hands and smiling over the wedding cake, all dressed up.

It was raining when we came out. 'I want to go home,' she said. 'You can go to the pub if you like.'

'What's wrong?'

'Nothing. I don't feel too well.'

'Then we'll both go home.'

'I'm all right, Angus.'

'Do you want to be on your own?'

She nodded.

'Is it your period?'

'I don't want to talk about it.'

'Jesus Christ, Helen, women have periods.'

'It isn't here yet. You go to the pub. I'll go home and go to bed.'

'I'll walk you to the bus stop.'

'No. I'm going to walk for a bit. It'll clear my head. You be sure to get something to eat. Don't drink on an empty stomach.'

'How's the wife?' asked Sugar.

'She's fine.'

'I'll bet she is.'

'Is she having a wee night in?' asked Lindy. 'Washing her hair.'

'Where's William?'

'Seeing his kids.'

74

I remember arguing with Sugar. I remember standing up to order a round, then having to sit down again. I remember being told to be quiet by Joe the barman and I remember buying a carry-out. We had a lamb Madras, pilau rice, onions, one chapati, a popadum and a bottle of beer. I remember saying goodnight to Sugar, but have no idea where the others went. I remember Lindy saying, 'You can't go home in that state.' And I remember we went for a walk.

I don't know how we got there, but I remember her room. The creaky floorboard on the stairs, a poster of the Manolete bullfighter; and I remember pouring whisky from a half-bottle into two mugs of coffee. I remember a wee Vivaldi concerto and Lindy lighting a joss stick. I remember the bottom bar of the electric fire sparked when I used it to light a cigarette and I remember the look when I handed her the cigarette. I remember talking. 'Sooner murder an infant in its cradle than nurse unacted desires,' she said.

I remember rising to go. I remember she placed her bare arms on my shoulders, against my neck. I remember inhaling the odour of her armpits, repugnant and marvellous, reminding me of the dampness of scrambled sheets in the morning, and I nearly fainted.

'Where were you?' Helen in her dressing gown was sitting by the fire.

'Guess.'

'I don't need to guess. Cow. Did she sing you a wee song before she did it.'

And she thrust her left wrist towards me. She had a razor blade in her right hand. She drew the blade across her wrist in a single, deep movement. The blood gathered slowly in a black lump, then, without any significant change, the clot spilled on to her hand, across her wrist and the rush began. Her eyes never left my face.

It was six in the morning when the taxi brought us home in the rain. 'I'm not staying here,' she told the doctor. 'If you don't let me go, I'll sign myself out.' He looked at me and shrugged his shoulders.

'You're in there,' she said, pointing to the bedroom door. 'It's Christmas.'

She undressed in the dark.

'We don't have to, Helen. It's all right.'

'What are you suddenly? Have you had a vision that's changed your life? Are you going to become a priest?'

'This is not the way I wanted it to happen.'

'Me with my wrist slashed and a period nearly due. It isn't here yet, Angus. It might be here in the morning. So it might be a little messy. Not very messy, just a little messy, Angus.'

'It's all right. Really. It's all right.'

'No candlelight, is that it? No music. No romance. No seduction. Sorry, son, but you're getting what you wanted. No cow's taking my man. Don't you fancy me any more?'

'Of course I do.'

'Then kiss me and get it over with.'

I leaned across and she opened her mouth. She sobbed a little, her left arm round my neck, biting the back of her right hand, her body rigid.

'Are you finished?' she asked.

'Uh-hu.'

'Do it more. Do it again. Go on.'

'What?'

'Take more. Men want more. You can take as much as you want. It's all right. It doesn't hurt now.'

'I've had enough.'

'Get some paper. I think I'm bleeding.'

The sheets were stained. She soaked the sheets in salt and changed the bedclothes. She put a wad of toilet paper inside her pants. 'I've no towels,' she said.

Two years later she showed me the paper. 'Remember this?' she said. She had found it in a drawer, stained to a salmon colour. She smiled and put the paper back in the drawer.

I didn't go to work on Monday. I left the house on time, but

76

knew I wouldn't go. The weather complemented my mood, so I prowled around the city, looking for areas I did not know.

I passed a primary school and for no reason stopped at the railings. And while I was standing there, the bell rang. For a moment the playground was deserted. The dull Victorian elaborations centred on a heavy Gothic doorway with Glasgow School Board chiselled into the grey sandstone in letters two feet high. Six worn steps staggered up to swing doors which had long ago been painted green. There were six square windows on either top-panelling and unpainted plywood on the bottom panels. From the pavement I could see the wood grain on the window spars where the paint had been worn away by chamois leathers. Two dirty fingerplates on either door were surrounded by a Brasso grey border which merged with the paint.

Then the doors swung open. They bounced off the walls. The hinges tried to stagger back into their sockets, but the doors rebounded off the walls till every child in the school had emptied down the steps and into the playgound. The doors slowly finished swinging, the glass intact.

There wasn't a quiet face in the playground, nor a stiff body. The kids ran nowhere, round and round and back and forward then round and round and round again, neither chasing nor being chased, simply running round the playground in all directions, shivering and shouting.

Soon, on the edges, the girls pulled out skipping ropes, others drew beds for a shoe-polish tin of peever and a couple of boys centred around a football, waiting for the others to finish their morning shout.

I turned up my collar and walked away.

Six

Saturday, April 5:

There are things in my attic I know nothing about. I don't know how they got there and am always surprised with what I find.

I go up occasionally, usually when Helen's out. I like to rummage around and have often sat there, shivering in the dark. I could lose myself in my attic.

It is a wide and convenient space with a warm, cosy smell, running the full length of the house, floored, insulated and filled with nothing but what I have put there. I keep meaning to do something to improve the place, especially the lighting, and of course am filled with good intentions I never get round to beginning.

If I think I've lost or misplaced something, I have a look in the attic and there it is. It has also happened that I've thought something's there, only to find it's been thrown out. Like everyone else, I relish the joy of discovering something I thought I'd lost or something I didn't know was there, as if someone had put it there, as though it had never belonged to me, even though it may be very familiar and full of memory when I find it.

There are also times when the attic is the last place on earth I want to visit, when I'd do anything rather than go there, even though I'm half-way up the stairs. But mostly my attic represents none or few of these things. It's a good place to hide, where I wander freely, rest and be undisturbed. And the attic is full of wee surprises.

When Father died, handling his clothes, especially his shoes, seemed bad enough; but the thought of going through the papers left in his room seemed like an intrusion. I always imagined he would walk in and find me.

About nine months after his death, after Helen and I had a row, I went round to Cuchullain Avenue. Phamie was on her knees with a cardboard box in front of her, tearing sheets of A4 paper. There was no doubting what it was.

'Terrible,' she said. 'What a waste. Imagine a grown man ruining his life doing something like this. Rubbish. All of it. Waste paper.'

'Couldn't the kids use it for drawing?'

She shook her head. She'd been at it since morning and had filled five cardboard boxes. 'No,' she said. 'He asked me to do this, though God knows why he wrote the stuff if he wanted it destroyed.'

'Perhaps he didn't know he'd want it destroyed. Maybe he was full of hope. He always seemed hopeful. It seemed important to him.'

'Nothing was important after Cammy got nicked and Mother died.'

'Have you read it?'

'What? Here; take this box will you?'

'Where to?'

'Outside. Anywhere, Angus. Just take it into the back-garden. No, I've never read it. I couldn't do that. It would be like spying.

And as the smell of autumn filled the air, I watched the paper scraps of my father's life burn amongst the garden refuse. We carried the ashes to the compost heap.

We had divided the estate when Phamie gave me a clutch of folders, box files and so on. 'I've burned most of it,' she said. 'You deal with the rest. I don't expect you'll find much, maybe a Premium Bond or two.'

Last night I went to the attic. Melancholy hit me in waves, the way seasickness does, so I scratched around and found the folders beneath a discarded Open University Foundation Course in Humanities. The elastic band had lost its bounce, but I found what I was looking for: my father's handwriting. A small script, cramped, with each letter formed in blue Quink, written with his orange Waterman pen with the black top, gold nib and filling lever. Cammy has it.

Each piece of correspondence was filed. Replies were clipped to the originals, the bills marked Paid and dated, gathered in years, with five folders and a box file. And just as I was tiring, I found the following, a fragment, about one-third of an A4 page:

decided to let you see my book because your list seemed eccentric enough to accommodate it, but also to test whether anyone, other than myself, would be interested in reading it. How I could have been so ingenuous, I do not know. I now realise your list is varied because its compilation is random.

I am appalled at my own gullibility. This, I do assure you, has nothing to do with the fact that you have rejected my book, but is entirely in keeping with the alternative terms you offered.

As far as your proposal is concerned, again I find it

Then Helen came home.

Monday, April 7:

11.35 p.m. This will keep me beyond my bedtime, but I must tell all.

Helen and I spent the weekend in the garden of our suburban home. We planted spuds, shifted the herbaceous border and pruned the roses to allow new growth. As I left for work this morning I thought the garden was neater after looking much the same for four or five months and didn't mind the stiff back.

I decided to capitalise on my good humour. Around 11 a.m., when I knew the tellers would be busy, having made certain someone was at the ledger counter, I stuck my head around the door, pointed to Miranda Morrison and crooked my forefinger. She came over immediately, carrying the wisp of a smile.

'What can I do for you?' she asked, closing my office door.

'Are you still interested in hill-walking?'

'Haven't done much during the winter,' she said, 'but now the weather's a bit better I thought I might try again. I didn't know you were interested.'

'I wasn't until recently,' I admitted truthfully.

'I'm more interested in rock-climbing these days.'

'That's very different.' It came out wrongly and now there was silence. 'It's just that I don't fancy wandering through the Lairaig Ghru on my own,' I said.

'I'm sorry, Mr MacPhail. I really must go.'

'Of course.'

'I promised a customer I'd phone back at a quarter past eleven and it's nearly that now.'

'Mustn't keep the customers waiting.' That also came out wrongly. Why did I feel awkward and say foolish things?

'Are you ever in the city?' she asked.

'Often.'

'Then why don't we have a drink tonight?'

'I beg your pardon?'

'I know it's a bit forward, but I do enjoy talking to you and realise your position could be awkward; I mean, you couldn't ask me for a drink, could you? I also happen to know a few hill-walkers and, if you liked, I could give them a ring and see what they say, then pass the information on to you tonight at eight o'clock in, say, Sloan's pub off Argyll Street. Do you know it?'

'I'll find it.'

'Good.' And she closed the door behind her.

When I left for lunch she didn't even look at me. I spent most of the afternoon visiting a shyster who wants more money to piss against the marble slab. Every once in a while, as I pondered over a balance sheet, met a partner or surveyed a piece of equipment, my stomach tingled, my knees were ginger and I lost the place entirely as I considered my good fortune. I left early and walked around the shops, generally going daft.

Helen was a problem. I felt guilty. We had chops for tea. This was one of her teaching days, so we had chips. 'I've got to go out tonight,' I said.

81

'That's all right.'

'I'm really sorry. I don't want to go.'

'It's okay.'

'I'd much rather help you plan the vegetable garden, but I'm afraid there's no alternative.'

'I don't mind.'

'I've got to go. It's a customer. I tried to get out of it, but the arrangement was made with head office and there's nothing I can do.'

'It doesn't matter.'

'Sorry.'

Why didn't she mind?

Then the problem of what to wear. I decided something casual, the sort of clothes Miranda had never seen me wear: jeans, bomber jacket, trainer shoes, sweat-shirt, all fairly ordinary really, with Eau Sauvage dabbed lightly across my cheeks.

'You smell nice,' Helen said when I kissed her.

'I decided to shave. I don't know why. No reason really.'

'You'll be late,' she said.

'I've no idea what time it'll go on to. I expect it'll finish about eleven, but there's no telling.'

'Doesn't matter.' She switched on the telly.

'Hello,' she said. 'Let me get you a drink.'

'Not at all. I'll get this.'

'Do you find it insulting for a woman to buy you a drink?'

'Large whisky.'

The lounge was smoky and dimly lit. I watched her screw her face and blink. She turned from the bar and caught me staring; then she smiled and gave the barman her order, whisky and fresh orange juice. I wondered how women always know you're staring.

She brushed her hair with her hand in a gesture of defiance and it fell back to where it had been, around her face in a fuzzy, straggled cut, parted somewhere in the middle, flat across the head, corrugated to the tips, newly washed and blown. Her skin looked pink and fluid. I imagined her sitting by the dressing table, squirting Johnson's Baby Lotion on to cotton wool balls before she brushed her teeth, coming to bed tasting of peppermint.

She put a single whisky and a jug of water in front of me. 'I didn't know if you'd want ice,' she said.

'This is fine.'

She smiled and squeezed into the seat beside me. Her breasts were firm and tilted; she wore a blue Shetland wool jersey, an anorak and gold bracelet, jeans, long legs, bare feet and sandals. 'Cheers,' she said.

Then she smiled again, shaking the ice in her glass. 'I wondered what you'd wear,' she said.

I realised I had nothing to say, neither small-talk nor conversation. She steered us around my hill-walking extravagance, mentioned one or two people at work, a couple of television programmes, films and books. She asked the questions and I answered until the differences were obvious: she was a product of the freedoms Phamie had won; I felt chilly, grown old.

'To be a woman and be amongst women who have accepted their new roles, who took them in with their school milk and haven't had to go through an unlearning process is so uplifting. It's wonderful. What makes it even better is that they're all around my age. You look sad, as if you're intimidated. I'm sure we can find a place for you.'

'Don't be so patronising. I've always believed that freedom for women would ultimately mean freedom for men.'

'A lot of men say that. It's a fine, trendy sort of statement. But they don't mean it. The next thing they say is that it's a woman's struggle; she must find her own way to independence and men can't help her. Watch out when you start thinking that, Angus. It means your legs are crossed, both hands are protecting your genitalia and you're wearing your mental cricket box.'

'I'll bear it in mind. Fancy another drink?'

'I hope men become able not only to say what they feel, but

to show what they feel and to follow their feelings, to trust them and show some real affection. Men give themselves to passion so well, but they do it less readily than women.'

'How do you know?'

'It's common knowledge. Everyone knows that.'

'I didn't know it.'

'Well you do now; so don't say you weren't warned. You see, not all that many women can abandon themselves to passion either. If they try it and are ill done by, then they naturally feel vulnerable and don't want to try again; they don't trust it and don't trust themselves. But it's also true that women generally give themselves more superficially than men.'

'Where did you learn this stuff?'

'Listen. Women are cunning in matters of love and very manipulative, which most men aren't. That's the trouble, women are often afraid to be themselves, so they're either playing safe or else they're manipulating. It's a generalisation, I know, but there's some truth in it. Get us another drink, would you?'

'Orange juice?'

'Yeah; with a vodka in it.'

When I came back from the bar, she smiled at me. 'I wondered when you were going to ask me out,' she said.

'How could you tell?'

'The way you looked at me; other things as well.'

'Feminine intuition?'

'Don't be silly.'

And she had youth on her side. Jesus, how shameful. I felt ridiculous and wondered how I looked in my casual gear. As she told me about her family, I wondered about tomorrow and the other mornings. Would she start coming in late, five minutes in the morning, another five at lunchtime, would she begin a series of secret confidences? What was I doing here? I wanted it over as soon as possible. I had proven my point and she had proven hers; the boss fancied her and had made a fool of himself; that would be something to tell the girls, especially since she'd asked him out.

'Must be difficult for you at work,' she said.

'Not really.'

'It will be now, especially if the others find we've been out together.' This was it. Blackmail.

'I certainly don't intend to tell them.'

'You wouldn't, would you?' she said, staring at the bar.

'But you might?'

'I might, but I'm not going to. There's no reason why I should. I realise I could make things awkward for you, or rather, we could make things awkward, both for ourselves and for the people we work with. But that would be silly. It would also mean you'd never want to see me again.'

'You know I'm married, don't you?'

'Mmmmhmmmph.'

'Why do you say it like that?'

'Why even mention it? Of course I know you're married. I've thought this out long ago. You don't strike me as being happily married, though if you were you wouldn't tell me. I don't know what you want from me any more than I know what I want from you. But we both want something. In fact, we probably need whatever it is we're not getting and I'm sure we can get it from each other. These things don't happen in isolation. There are always other causes. I know that people my own age, even those who are slightly older, bore me and I'd hate to be married to someone who hadn't at least lived with a woman. It would be awful. That way you'd put all the blame on the other person and take the credit for yourself. Nothing in my background has made me ready for any kind of permanent relationship, as much as I want it, so that's probably why I find myself attracted to people who have been through the relationship trap before. At least they know the dangers, if not the actual pitfalls.'

'Is everything else in your life compartmentalised like this?'

'It's just that I've always fancied older men and I don't see why I can't have what I want; not that I always get what I want, but in matters such as these it seems important to be going in the right direction. Maybe I believe it's better to travel hopefully than to actually arrive.'

'You seem to have it all worked out.'

'I'm not sure. In some ways I suppose I know what I want, but I get so depressed about it all. No wonder there are so many divorces. Everyone I know enters hopefully and comes out hopeless. It seems such a shame, a terrible trauma and an awful waste. People don't seem to know how to stay married or even how to stay together any more. God knows why; maybe it's a hangover from the Sixties. I'd have hated to have gone through all that nonsense. I only know I don't want to get into anything till I'm sure of what's going on.'

'Are you telling me you want an affair?'

'If that's all you want, fair enough. We can have an affair and it will all be over in a week or two. I've told you, I don't know what I want, but I want something and it has to do with you. Suppose we see each other, do things, hill-walking if you like, go to the movies, but let's just take it easy. The thing is that guys your age always want to rush into bed with girls my age and that's about all they ever get. They don't get any of the benefits, such as a different approach to life or a new sense of direction, which I am sure must come from something like this.'

'Sounds wonderful.'

'Mmmm, might be nice.'

As I drove her home, she stared out the window and spoke into her hand as it fretted round the corners of her mouth.

'Don't tell me you love me, Angus. Don't ever tell me unless you're sure. And don't do anything silly at work. We'll keep things as they are; Mister MacPhail and Miss Morrison. You can phone me at home and we'll see each other as often as you like, or as often as you can. I've thought about your wife and I don't like it much, but that's how it is. I know I could be hurt and so could you. But you could also be silly and that would hurt us even more. If we do it this way, at least I won't be silly. I know what you're thinking, married man and all that. I've no reasons and no excuses, except how I feel.

Tomorrow at work will be interesting, quite exciting really. Phone me tomorrow night and let me know what you think.'

She dabbed her lips against my cheek, pulled the handle but couldn't open the door. I leaned over and opened it. 'This way I get to feel your leg,' I said. She laughed and swung away from me.

That was two hours ago. And I still can't sleep.

Friday, April 11:
    No work.
    I've kept things ticking over by being there and find it appalling how little I have to do. It is true to say I have been distracted.

Not that Miranda seems to bother. She floats around like weeds below water. Just once, on Wednesday, our eyes brushed as I came back from lunch. Her head was bent. She could have been praying. I opened the pass door, she looked up and our eyes met. Had anyone caught that look, the ball would have been up on the wash-house roof.

'You surprised me,' she said on the phone. 'I was thinking about you, I looked up and there you were.'

I've been phoning of an evening when Helen's in the garden. We don't talk for long; ten minutes at the most. 'You'd better go,' she says.

And my other little project, *der Meisterverk*, seems to have been pushed aside. I used to do little bits in my head; sometimes in the bank, driving home or when reading the paper at lunch an idea would grab me. I'd write it down and develop it later. But now I'm filled with other things. I suppose I'm stuck.

> *cheese (brie)*
> *eggs*
> *ham*
> *tights*

That was a near thing.

I don't know why I'm not writing. It could be anything or nothing.

87

I am not making excuses. It isn't good enough to write escape clauses into your fiction. If you set out to cover something, you must be judged by how well you succeed. My consolation is that not everyone remembers the same thing; but even that does not explain why I have written about the Beatles and Rolling Stones, who were unimportant to me, and have omitted Bob Dylan, who was very important. I have missed Phamie's Jesus phenomenon; there is neither Scott Mackenzie nor Paris '68. Another consolation, another excuse, is that I am not writing history. I am attempting fiction. I am making things up, telling lies.

Miranda tastes of rain and grapes and mystery. When I think of her, I think of cherries, the juice transparent through the skin. I raise a bunch and see them vivid against a clear, blue sky as I float down a slow stream to God knows where.

Wednesday, April 16:
Roll on Friday.

Before I forget, I've discovered more paper in Daddy's hand.

Tonight I needed to be alone and could not even consider sitting with Helen. No fault of hers, poor girl. *Mea culpa.*

'I think I'll go up to the attic,' I said after tea.

'It's raining anyway. Well, just a shower, but it will stop us doing anything in the garden.'

'There isn't much to do.'

'We'd better get some lettuce seeds sown. And there's the flowers for the herbaceous border.'

'Of course.'

'Well, off you go. I've got some sewing to do. Alan Whicker's on at nine o'clock, will I give you a shout?'

'No thanks. I want to see if there are any more papers up there. I really must do something with them.'

'I'll give you a call if I make some tea. It's a pity about the rain. It's been such a nice day up till now.'

I settled with my torch and cushion. And opened a new folder. These papers appear so randomly. Father's filing system has been disturbed, the papers gathered quickly and placed into separate folders.

When I opened this new folder, I found a title page:

THE HUNGRY WORMS
by
Angus MacPhail

I wet my finger, turned up the corner and the second page said:

Amang the hungry worms I sleep.
The Ballad of Clerk Saunders.

And beneath the epigraph, a dedication:

To Dr Karl Adler, who discovered the inferiority complex,
with a grateful nation's thanks.

I must have stared for half an hour, unaware of heat, cold or hunger beyond these two yellow pages. I could see my life running before me like fire before paper and I could see the big black Underwood typewriter which sat on the desk like a stuffed bird.

One Sunday afternoon I went into his room when he was typing. He typed in jerks, concentrating on the keyboard. It was a misty afternoon, but the house was aglow with the warmth of central heating. His head was bent, his right forefinger prodded the keyboard while his left hand supported his head. When he reached the end of his line, the bell went ping. He looked up and smiled at me: 'The sweetest sound in all the world is the sound of the Underwood bell,' he said. And it was then I realised he would die, that death was a certainty for all of us.

There was no more novel after the two title pages. This first letter was hidden amongst correspondence to the Gas Board and is obviously part of something longer.

the case, but the fact of the matter is that you cannot wait until posterity decides you are a wonderful genius. If you believe your work is worthwhile, you should want it to stand the test of critical scrutiny and your opinions would be unaffected, either by the process or by the outcome. For however you undermine or claim to be unaffected by the process, it is a hoop through which you will one day have to jump, either when you are around to withstand the vicissitudes or when your work is published posthumously.

I personally believe you are hiding and no matter how you claim to be unaffected by critical praise or damnation, you are, in reality, scared to let your baby go. While it is with you, it is safe. And so is your reputation. Anyone can imagine themselves an undiscovered genius.

It really is too easy to make jokes at the critics' expense. There are few who would deny that there is truth in

And that's all there is, something to, rather than from, the Old Man, typed with an electric typewriter on good quality paper.

Thursday, April 17:

Last night, before retiring to the attic, I had a word with Helen. I've been buying magazines such as *Hill Walker* and *Rambler* and have taken out a family membership for the Scottish Youth Hostels Association, which I explained as part of a self-improvement plan.

'You've been talking about doing something for years,' she said. 'I never thought that a game of golf once a month with the other managers was enough exercise for someone who sat around all day.' And I couldn't help but agree.

I've discovered a wonderful way of speaking to Miranda. I have an outside line on my desk, so I call the bank from my office and when Miss Pemberton answers, I stuff a handkerchief over the receiver and in my best bourgeois drawl ask to speak to Miss Morrison. The first time was best. 'How wonderful,' she said. 'I can see you. You've got your blue tie on.'

I have been fortunate. Several people have given me advice. I have been told that it's a great life if you don't weaken, that you're only young once, that cleanliness is next to Godliness, that mony a mickle maks a muckle. But no one has told me how to deal with this.

Life with Helen is rather difficult. But she hardly notices, having begun to discuss her appearance, asking if I like certain clothes, lipsticks, eye shadow, hair toner.

Some women talk about their looks and what they do to preserve them as a kind of housekeeping whose very difficulties become a source of pride, substitute fine lines for a burst washing machine and you'll see what I mean. Other women make it clear they do it for men, for sex, and though Helen was previously amongst the former, I feel she is moving towards the latter.

And she has been giving me my favourite food lately. And my favourite parts of the food, in much the same way as Mother used to serve Father. He would always get the top of the milk, the burned bits of pudding, the extra roast potato and so on. 'Your father needs it,' she'd say, though no one questioned her actions. 'He's working.' Now it's me who gets the top of the milk. I enjoy the attention, but wonder what it means.

It is not surprising that all the great events in a family's life, all the big pronouncements, happen at mealtimes. It is the only time they are all together. It is even so with Helen and I, as though we are tied by convention.

Last night I mentioned going hill-walking at the weekend. 'That'll be nice for you,' she said.

'Don't you want to come?'

'Don't be silly, Angus. You know I'd hate it. No, you go off and have a nice time. You need it after being stuck indoors all week. I get plenty fresh air in the garden.'

'What else will you do?'

'Don't worry about me,' she said. 'I've got quite a lot on my plate. I'm going out on Friday night, but you know that already.'

'Where is it you're going again?'

'I don't know how many times I've told you. One of the assistant teachers is getting married and she's asked us over for a show of presents. You could come if you like.'

'Will Strachan be there?'

'I don't know. He might be. He usually turns up for staff things.'

'I've never heard of men being invited to that sort of thing, far less turning up for it.'

'I said you were busy.'

'Thanks.'

'You'll be going on Saturday morning?'

'I think that would be best.'

'Do you want me to pack some sandwiches, make up a flask or something like that?'

'No no no. It's all right, love. If I need anything, I'll get it myself.'

'That programme about shepherds, "One Man And His Dog", is on tonight. I always like to see these dogs. They're so lovely. Or are you going up to the attic.'

Monday, April 21:

Her hair was tufted to the back of her neck and gathered in a red elastic band. She wore a dark blue donkey jacket. The turned-up collar made her face look clear, bright and scrubbed. She threw her gear into the back seat, on top of the anoraks we'd borrowed; smiled.

We wandered round a supermarket, threw food in a basket and ticked off the meals. Then north with the windows down, singing songs and eating chocolate, a chilly freshness in the air and frothing green nonsense all around us, listening to a radio play about a woman who was having an affair with the postman while her husband was about to stand on a land mine in Northern Ireland.

About forty miles on and we drove through a smirr; we

92

turned a bend, the smirr was gone and a rainbow grew from the hillside. Down the length of the glen with the noise of rushing water at every bridge and bend, then upwards, off the track, where the daffodils were leaving, beyond the bluebells and laurel to the cottage at the end of the forestry road with the green sticks of a rosebush sprouting along the fence and round the side of the whitewashed porch with the dark blue door, yellowed brass knob and flaking paint.

Birch logs were piled by the fireplace and the smell of winter mustiness hung around the house. We lit the fire and made up the big double bed that stood four feet above the floor. Blue and gold pagodas and willow trees covered the bedspread, dark green roses and a view of Ballachulish ferry covered the walls.

The window was slightly ajar and framed a web of red geranium on top of the pine dresser in our bedroom, with two cane tables, a bedside lamp and an ashtray, A Present From Bournemouth, beside the bed.

We sat by the fire in the sitting room and spread a map across the carpet, after tidying little flakes of birchwood into a companion set with a Spanish galleon floating across the handles.

'I don't think we should go far,' she said, turning on the radio, then switching it off at the sound of an alien voice. 'I think we ought to take the forestry path along by the woods, up through the crags and on to the top of whatever hill that is behind us.'

We picked bluebells for the jam jar by the window, with uncurled fern shoots. We gathered last year's pine cones and scraped and scuffed along the soft tread of needles as a misty light, brighter than the sun, filtered through the trees. We climbed upwards, hardly aware the land was rising except in our breathing. And the path reappeared as suddenly as it left us, running beneath the telephone wires that came from nowhere and went over the hill, wires that trembled as we ran, sideways and upwards, along the path with rough red chips and railway sleepers, across a stream of rushes and bog lily where we could see down the glen where the grey ribbon road curled over the stream broken by sunlight that came from the left; and the place has done it again: it has caught you unawares, reached out and grabbed you.

Climbing up, the air is cooler and every ridge is like the summit. The wind grew sharper, louder as we cross a scrambling of stones to the top where we bent against another wind from the other side, a wind that rushed across the world to reach us. We stumbled through it, catching our breath to see the road we'd climbed fall past the trees, across the strath to the green hills and brown, where blue and purple charge through the grey till all colours melt into sky, though hills and outlines still are visible in spite of the wind and the tears from the wind as the sun dazzles upwards from the loch where its reflection is changed in the air.

She grabbed my hand and shouted. I heard the wind and shouted back and she shouted again and pulled my hand. We ran down the hill, which was harder than the climb, for we had to be careful, to mind the steps and potholes, rabbit burrows and clumps of fern, the heathers and bogs, and we kept on running although we were breathless. In the wood she stopped by a cluster of primroses, blinking in the half-light by the edge of a tree, and that's where we gathered handfuls of air till I almost slept as I stared at the patterns of wind in the branches, and my head was spinning with the start of a headache, as she leaned across and stroked my hair, told me to rest on her lap, that she wanted to see what my face was like when I was sleeping. It seems silly to write it, but mostly I remember opening her shirt, then wakening with her blowing into my face, saying, 'Time to go home.'

Walking back, we sang the songs we'd sung in the car. I peeled the potatoes and she did the cooking. We turned on the radio so's we could switch it off again and, as the smell of woodsmoke seeped through the house, I read to her, lying by the fire drinking chocolate and whisky, malt whisky, with custard cream biscuits because that's all there was.

Lying in bed, peering beyond the window and smelling the

night as it passed the geranium, turning off the light, watching the stars from the darkened room and the sound of the latch as she opened the door in her long white nightdress as the birch logs fell in the grate. And in the nowhere between sleep, when she thought I was sleeping, she touched my face, she touched that wee bit of my left cheek just by the jawbone. 'Darling,' she said.

In the morning it was a matter of time and now we were dressed there was nothing to help us. It was over. We sawed some wood and cleared the grates, left the key beneath the stone and drove back the way we had come, stopping for a bar lunch in the middle of the afternoon, ordering from oversized, four-colour menus, wrapped in clear vinyl.

I drove to the end of the road and we sat in the car. Bunches of women were coming from church. Every now and then a head detached from the group like an ostrich getting ready to run, turning to look at us in the car, wondering what we were doing, as we stared ahead and said nothing, scared to let go. 'It's different,' she said. 'There's no going back. Not now.'

I got home at the back of ten. The News was on ITV. Helen was sitting by the fire with the Sunday papers, waiting for me. 'Graham Greene's on "The South Bank Show",' she said. 'Would you like to see that? I've kept you some dinner. There's warm water if you'd like a bath and the blanket's on because I knew you'd be tired.'

I yawned. 'That fresh air's good for you,' she said. 'You're not used to it. That's what's wrong. You're just not used to it.'

But I sat by the window while she was sleeping, looking across the strip of city lights, imagining how we could keep the pretence, when of a sudden there came to mind 27 August 1978, Usher Hall, and Alfred Brendel is playing the Waldstein as part of a Sunday afternoon Edinburgh Festival concert. I'd waited fifteen years to hear my first live Waldstein in a big room. Some Waldsteins have been with a few friends, always in a small room and so many Waldsteins in little rooms alone. This time I am taking the music for granted, as though it were

95

accompaniment to his performance rather than the result of it. His hand rises like smoke. It is difficult to believe this wonder is real and, as the final theme creeps in, a girl beside me sobs, then smiles, embarrassed.

A monk on stage, behind the piano, knees together, hands on his lap and half a smile around his face, applauded and smiled and did not stop, and two rows behind him a blonde girl in a blue dress did not move until she sighed, smiled, clapped and clapped and clapped.

Thinking of the music, the applause and Miranda, I must have slept.

Tuesday, April 22:

Helen is too attentive. I think she knows more than she pretends to know, which would not be hard since she pretends to know nothing.

Miranda's eyes are everywhere. On Monday I phoned her and she phoned me today. The message is always the same.

Last night I went to the attic and found three pages, typed on the Underwood. It's bad enough discovering your father was a closet radical without extra evidence arriving daily.

If I find more of my father's writings, I'll burn them.

SOME OBSERVATIONS ON SCOTTISH DEFINITIONS WITH A VIEW OF THE NATIVE PHILOSOPHY

The ensuing remarks are not intended to trespass upon the domain of such specialist publications as *The Scottish National Dictionary* or Dwelly's *Gaelic–English Dictionary*. I merely wish to inform our English and foreign visitors of certain usages which are common throughout the Lowlands, Borders and most tracts of the English-speaking Highlands and Islands.

A Braw Bugger(1)

One who can shite(2) with the best of them.

A Dour Bugger

One who cannot shite yet refuses to take the medicine.

A Thrawn Bugger

One who can't shite, takes the medicine yet refuses to shite.

A Canny Bugger

One who can't shite, takes the medicine, still can't shite, returns the medicine and has his money refunded.

An Uncanny Bugger

One who can't shite, takes the medicine, won't shite, returns the medicine, has his money refunded, then shites.

Note that the braw Bugger and the Uncanny Bugger, the alpha and omega of this spectrum, have one common characteristic – their bodily functions are unimpeded by normal imperatives.

THE SCOTS AND THEIR PROPERTY:

The Scots, like many deprived races, have a passionate attachment to the basic essential of food, drink and slumber, which they underline by their frequent deployment of the personal pronoun:

> *Do you want a bit of my fish?*
> *I'm going home to my bed.*
> *You'll have had your tea?*

However, the male Scot's lack of all proprietorial instinct toward the female will gladden the hearts of the most ardent

---

1: The term *bugger* when applied by one Scotsman to another has no sexual significance, even in sheep-rearing parishes. Since, to the Scot, a man is the highest form of created life, to call a man 'a man' is to overpraise him.

2: The male Scot prefers excretion to sexuality because, although both are equally inevitable, the first is less expensive.

feminists. It is shown in his preference of the indefinite article over the personal pronoun when identifying his spouse, actual or intended:

> *No thanks, I'm going home to the wife.*
> *No thanks, I'm going out with the bird.*

Contrariwise, the acquisitive and rapacious attitude of the average Scotswoman towards the male counterpart is nowhere more evident than in her heavy-handed insistence on the personal pronoun:

> *My man kicked hell out of me last night.*
> *My fiancé's done a bunk again.*
> *It's aff his da my boy gets his nae brains frae.*

SCOTTISH POSITIVISM, THE PERENNIAL PHILOSOPHY:

Scratch a Scot and you will find a philosopher. Scottish philosophical thought is so deeply ingrained in the national psyche that the works of Hume, Hamilton, Miller and Carlyle must be regarded as mere outcroppings of the native bedrock, whose quality is best revealed in the following dicta, which may be heard in any launderette, turf accountant's office or wine bar.

What's for you will no go past you – The world is all that is the case. (Isness is all. Is replaces If.)

It'll aa be the same a hunner year frae noo – In that the past is irremediable, any finite point in the future will display the same characteristics.

It'll no be this in the mornin' – Since the present is tolerable, it is highly unlikely that a finite point in the future will display the same characteristics.

This by no means comprehends the extant. Further observations may well yield fruit.

Part Two

GROUCHO: The party in the second part will be known as the party in the second part.

A Night At The Opera

Seven

Mother said, 'I got a letter.'

'That's nice,' said Dad.

'Who's it from?' asked Cammy.

'I'm not telling,' she said. 'If you know who it's from it won't be a surprise.'

Dad looked at me and shook his head. 'Do you find this behaviour strange?' he asked. I nodded. 'I'm glad,' he whispered, 'I thought it was me.'

'No whispering at the table,' said Mother. 'Only naughty boys whisper. And no reading either.' She snatched Cammy's newspaper. 'What's this you're reading?'

'*Grandma*.'

'Comics. You should read a good book rather than waste your time reading comics.'

'It isn't a comic. It's the official organ of the Communist Party of Cuba.'

'You'd think they'd be able to find a better name for their comic than that.'

'*Grandma* was the name of the boat from which Castro, Guevara and –'

Mother sighed. 'Would anyone like more lasagne?'

'Are you taking your pills?' asked Dad.

'Of course.'

'And you're sure you're taking the right amount?'

'What do you mean? Gracious, I wouldn't do a thing like that, Angus, you know I wouldn't. It says so on the bottle; every bottle you get from the chemist says it is dangerous to exceed the stated dose.'

'I wouldn't like you to become dependent on them.'

'Neither would I,' she said. 'Lasagne anyone?'

We ate in silence, Cammy reading, Father and I eating, Mother picking and fussing around. 'I got a letter today,' she said.

Father looked at me.

'Wouldn't anyone like to know who the letter was from?' she asked.

'You said you weren't going to tell us because it wouldn't be a surprise any more,' I said. Father's voice would have brought petulance. Cammy carried on reading.

'That's true,' said Mother. 'And thank you for reminding me, dear. But I've changed my mind.'

Father and I stared at her as she picked at the lasagne. Her face lit with surprise as a new idea wandered in from nowhere: 'Would anyone like more lasagne?' she asked.

'Who was the letter from?' asked Dad. 'The letter you got today.'

'Oh, I couldn't tell you that,' she said. 'It wouldn't be a surprise.'

Those were the days when pills were considered to be an aid to mental stability and emotional equilibrium, when amphetamines seemed the panacea humanity had craved since the dawn of civilisation, or at least since Freud. They were cheap to make and easy to sell because everybody wanted them. And medicine used them rather than investigate the alternatives. Research into the human condition, which had been the basis of medicine since Ancient Greece, was virtually abandoned, or was conducted on a private scale, which meant the same thing. So lunatic theories abounded and for a while we forgot what medicine was supposed to do while we worried about what it was doing. Doctors gave you pills, found out what was wrong, then prescribed other pills to help you.

'Great stuff,' said Dad, clearing his plate. Mother asked if he would like some more. 'We're going to have to do something about this,' he said, as Mother watched the News on television.

'I quite agree,' she said. 'There seems to be nothing but bank robberies these days.'

102

'I beg your pardon,' said Cammy.

'I said that lots of banks are being robbed just now,' said Mother. Cammy looked at her and shook his head. 'Are you coming with me?' he asked.

We are skipping the years like a stone over water. It is February 1969. Having left school six months ago, I am now working as a teller with the Royal Darien Bank under a scheme whereby energetic youngsters were allowed to work for nothing, providing they were well dressed, well mannered, well behaved and turned up on time. I was taken on at my fourth attempt and not allowed to touch the money, in fact I seldom see it. 'A necessary precaution,' according to my trainer. 'If you saw it, you might want it, but this way you learn to treat it as a commodity like any other, tins of soup, for example.' I am a Trainee Systems Analystic Accounts Executive, which pleased Judy.

'When you're trained and working and have a salary, perhaps we'll be able to get married,' she said coyly.

'Why not?' said I.

We sat in a pub, watching the activity dwindle. 'Cammy's right,' I said. 'We have so much money they've invented machines to take it off us.'

'What do you mean?'

'Fruit machines.'

'What about them?'

'Nothing,' I sighed.

'I hope my Dad doesn't come in here.'

'Why not?'

'It's a nice place and he'd ruin it.'

Cameron said, 'Are you coming with me?'

'Sure,' I said. 'Won't be long.'

'It's nice to see you two going out together,' said Mum. Dad was writing his novel and Mum went singing into the kitchen. 'It keeps me company,' she said when I asked what she was singing.

'Did I tell you I got a letter today?' she said, drying her hands on her apron. I was washed and shaved, changed and ready.

103

'You mentioned it,' said Cameron.

'For once and for all,' said Dad, who had come into the kitchen for some tea, 'get the letter and read it to us.'

'Very well, dear,' said Mum. 'There's no need to get angry.'

Dad filled the kettle and we waited in silence till the hum of the water preparing to boil stirred us.

'I can't find whatever it is I'm looking for,' said Mother, standing by the doorway.

'It's in your hand,' said Dad.

'You read it,' said Mother.

Dad read the letter to himself. 'Well, she isn't pregnant,' he said.

'Really, Angus,' said Mother. 'Imagine saying such a thing; of course I'm not pregnant.'

'I wasn't talking about you, dear. I was talking about your daughter. And if it wasn't for a so-called miracle of modern science, I'm as sure she'd be pregnant as I'm sure there is shite in a nanny goat.'

'How is she?' I asked.

'Okay,' said Dad. 'She says there have been some really heavy scenes and the whole trip has been something of a downer. But she's going to hang on in there and see it through because she's got this incredible belief in the forces of gravity which she realises might conflict with her belief in reincarnation but that's not too heavy since she's quite confused anyway. Not much else, except she's coming home.'

'Really,' said Mother, sitting on the sofa. 'Who's coming home?'

'Your daughter.'

'When?'

'Soon. She's trying to arrange a lift.'

'That letter sounds hopeful,' said Cammy. 'It shows the awakening of a new politicisation, entirely opposed to her previous policy of opting out and the far worse anarchosyndicalist pseudo-revolutionary tactics she was engaged in, such as squatting and the like.' He smiled at me and I smiled back.

Dad carried his tea into the study.

Mother was sleeping, so we closed the door quietly.

Cameron's meeting was at the other side of town, a location which will confuse my reader since the action hitherto has largely been confined to indoor locations.

I therefore include this small section from *Where No Queen Slept* (Being a Brief History of the Burgh of Invercullion and an Introduction to the Town, With Maps and References, Written and Compiled by Angus MacPhail), my father's only published work, alas no longer available.

Seen from the top of Conic Hill, which rises to 1,411 feet above sea level, Invercullion displays all the timelessness of a small Scots town.

The Conic Hill, which is visible from every part of the burgh, gives an illusion of countryside, even though parts of the town are heavily industrialised, producing beer, carpets, steel, and biscuits, with many secondary and service industries. At the time of writing, there is talk of a Japanese multinational corporation setting up on one of the industrial estates and an electronics giant from America has also shown interest.

But native Cullioners know the worth of such speculation. Invercullion High Street was built as wide as a boulevard because our town was to be the site of a new cathedral, whose foundations can be seen to this day.

The Reformation not only stopped the cathedral being built, but also contributed to most of the contemporaneously contiguous buildings being pulled down since they were largely adjuncts of the cathedral. This has left our town with few buildings of antiquity and fewer still of architectural merit. But the cathedral foundations are still there, between High Street and Market Street in what is now called Cathedral Park, having been brought into public ownership in the middle of the last century when proposals to open a coal mine on the site were narrowly defeated in the town council.

But let's go back to Conic Hill and see what the poor, mad Higgins saw:

> Dancing like a wraith before me,
> Ever stretching on and on;
> This road and view, the wind implores me:
> 'Go young man, to Samarkand!'

Traces of the Beaker People have been found on Conic Hill and archaeologists assure us there used to be a broch at the top. From here Picts and Brythonic Celts looked down the estuary of the River Cullion and out to sea; from here they watched the ships go by. Even the Romans passed us, which is not surprising, for today Invercullion lies inland, though there was an earlier settlement at the mouth of the river.

These were the peoples St Walter described in his *Accounts Of The Curings*. 'Journal The First' gives a detail of those he met on his journey northwards, Invercullion's earliest inhabitants:

Those are quick and fiery in spirit, fierce in their enemies, loving death itself as much as slavery; they count it slothful to die in their beds and glory and manhood to slay or be slain in the field. They are people of sparing diet, bearing hunger long and rarely eating before sunset. They make do with meat and foods of milk, which is also their drink. And though they are generally fair of face and of comely bearing, they are much disfigured by their peculiar dress.

Noble falcons there are, of towering flight and splendid spirit, and hawks of the highest courage, cresting the hill behind this place. There is some iron and lead and nearly all metals, two colours of marble with a manifold wealth of fish and beasts giving milk and wool.

'Journal The Third' tells what happened on his second trip, 'Journal The Second' being a meditation. He hoped to consolidate his earlier conversions, but found the place destroyed by plague and razed by fire:

We came by boat and thought it deserted. Only when we were amongst them did we hear their moans, which were piteous, especially the children. With Holy Jesu stretched before me I did go into their huts and give what food and drink they could take for with this plague comes also the spueing boke. I covered their nakedness, which was chief amongst the women, and, ere death's black shadow stole them, did save every soul for Jesu, clasping their hands in prayer when dead. When all were gone and with night approaching I did put their place to the torch and climbed the hill with berries singing unto Him who delivered me from sickness and pleading redemption for the souls of the dead.

Then came the Reformation. Nearly having a cathedral is worse than never having been considered: to have the foundations dug and then find everything has been brought down about you, knowing the destiny of the ages has been snatched away, no gold, no finery, no low voices singing to candlelight, no soft sigh of the monks, no altercloth, paintings, jewels, ritual or confession; to have your foundations replaced by nothing is to have salty brine soaked into the incision.

The first written reference to the River Cullion does not appear until more than 150 years have passed.

The Reverend Mr Samson breakfasted with us. Dr Johnson expatiated rather too strongly upon the benefits derived to Scotland from the Union, and the sad state of our people before it. I am entertained with his copious exaggeration upon that subject; but I am uneasy when people are by who do not know him as well as I do and may be apt to think him narrow-minded.

We saw the foundations of the Cathedral. Though it rained much, Dr Johnson examined them with a most patient attention. He could not here feel any abhorrence at the Scottish reformers. 'One cannot destroy what was never built,' said he. Later we walked by the river. Dr Johnson always said that he was come to Scotland to see wild objects, – mountains, – waterfalls, – peculiar manners; in short, things which he had not seen before. 'A man who has seen the Thames may not call this Cullion a river' – Johnson. 'If not a river, sir, pray what is it?' – Boswell. 'Water, sir, 'tis all. It has not the vigour to be called a river.'

They stayed at the Invercullion Arms Hotel, Boswell sleeping in the room where sixty years earlier Defoe had written:

. . . a town in the full perfection of decay, and is, indeed, a most lamentable object of a miserable, dying corporation; the only support which, I think, preserves the name of a town to it, is, in the lands adjoining, an excellent vein of Scots coal and there is a good salt-work in the town; close to the sea there is a small pier or wharf for ships, to come and load both the salt and the coal.

Other travellers concern themselves with what Invercullion should have been, or could have been if we'd had our cathedral. Such a considerable amount of time and energy has been dispensed upon this speculation that at least one visitor has remarked that our sense of the past is more important than the reality of our present. Everyone agrees, things would have been better had our cathedral been built, even if it was built and knocked down again, which is probably why to this day the town's children learn the Montagu d'Alton poem, 'Aspiring', in Primary Six:

> *'Cross corrugated fields I see*
> *Where Invercullion's spire should be;*
> *As man-made smoke climbs ever higher*
> *My eyes are raised to the assumptive spire –*
> *That strong, invisible dominion*
> *Draws my gaze upward, nearer Heav'n.*

D'Alton was a frequent visitor. His notes to our local worthies are displayed in the library and, of course, Mrs

108

Trilling, who comforted his last days in Rome and shared his dying misfortunes, came from Invercullion. She was working at the Invercullion Arms Hotel, a chambermaid when they met. It is interesting to consider that she may well have served William and Dorothy Wordsworth, Coleridge and de Quincey when they came. They did not, of course, mention Invercullion directly, though local scholars believe oblique references to the place can be traced in certain of their works and journals.

I am well aware of the fact that Invercullion has become internationally famous through a variant of that popular genre of which 'The Ball of Kirriemuir' is probably the best known item:

> There was a lass, a tinkler lass
> On the road to Invercullion;
> She met a lad wi curly hair
> And twa ba's like a stallion.

> Singing, blaw your pipes, my darlin Jock,
> And play upon your chanter,
> You've maybe lain wi a lass afore,
> But no wi Meg the Ranter.

I do think it a pity that a place of such antiquity, charm and variated wonder should be known for something which in no way reflects the range of its history or activity. I suppose citizens of Kirriemuir will feel the same.

High Street is our main thoroughfare, a busy trunk road for, as you are surely aware, Invercullion stands between Dovedale and Glenfield, with Hollyburn and the city beyond. To the east of the town, High Street becomes Basie Brae and the area around there is the worst we've got, a slum known as the Bottom End. Residential properties are mostly in the north-west corner of the town, by the Toatie Glen which leads, of course, to Conic Hill, and is on the road to Dovedale, with Dovedale House, home of Sir

William and Lady Basie, who own the town and surrounding 160,000 acres, standing two miles off the road, beyond the cairn of white bricks, between stone pillars with a pineapple and banana on top. The pineapple was Sir William's grandfather's favourite fruit, whereas Grandmama preferred a banana. Together they planned the estate and developed it to what it is today.

Perhaps we can pause on our brief tour to hear a story, doubtless apocryphal, as it would be told by one of our local townsman. It has been said that our present laird's grandparent was shocked to find a miner from Glenfield pit walking across a field and ordered him off with threats of dire consequences. 'Ah'm no' daein' nuthin',' said the collier. 'Ah'm jist oot fur a walk.'

'Then walk somewhere else,' roared Sir Geoffrey. 'Get off my land!'

'Yese cannae own laund,' said the pitman. 'It belangs tae aabody.'

'It certainly does not. This land belongs to me.'

'An' how did you get the laund?'

'My ancestors fought for it.'

'Then get your jaiket aff,' said the collier. 'Ah'll fight ye fur it.'

It is doubtful if Sir William's ancestors did fight for it. It seems more likely that the lands and property came to the family by the same route as anyone gets anything, they either bought it or they stole it. However they acquired the estate, having it seems to entitle Sir William to a great deal of respect from the townspeople. Sir William in turn feels this respect brings obligations, especially a continuation of the patronage his family have traditionally dispensed. He also feels the townspeople are better off than he; they live in centrally heated houses while he and his family are forced to stay in a large and draughty mansion which was intended to have fifteen servants run it. Sir William continually complains of poverty, but refuses to dispose of a single asset. The Basies live apart from us, mingling at the edges. Sir

110

William meantime prepares to pass the estate on to his eldest son at the earliest opportunity, but it appears the aristocracy are as good at controlling their children as the rest of us.

From here *Where No Queen Slept* goes into a section on popular walks and rambles, a description of the town's industries, architecture, day trips and so on. But now we know where we are, the narrative can continue.

'I'm telling you,' said Cammy. 'The time is right.'

We were walking across town. A soft rain had soaked us and my feet squelched in elastic-sided boots. Cammy's head was down, eyes aglow.

'Last year was wonderful,' he said. 'Think of what this year could bring. There is the continuing crisis of capitalism which Marx predicted and which they cannot counter any more than they can contain the great revolutionary tide which is presently sweeping the world. This time last year we had the Tet offensive with disastrous consequences for the Yankee imperialists at Khe Sahn and Hue. The full extent of the Vietnamese victory still hasn't been realised. They're not only holding their own, they are winning, beating the mightiest army the world has known.'

'Is there much further to go? My feet are soaking.'

'Ho Chi Minh's war has penetrated the very fabric of American society. Already in this year we have seen the demise of several leading American politicians. Two have died violently. They were entirely dissimilar; they came from opposite backgrounds and in many ways represented opposing ends of the political spectrum and stood for opposing values. They died. There have been continuing riots and demonstrations, culminating in what happened in Chicago last August. But, more importantly, we have seen the demise of LBJ, who was the leading exponent of the American war machine. The fact that he refused to accept the nomination for another term of office is no accident. It was a cop-out. The continuing crisis of capitalism has penetrated the fabric of the

111

White House. And now there is Nixon to contend with. He's supposed to stand for many things but, you mark my words, one of the things he will have to stand for is the removal of his troops from Vietnam.'

I could smell the sea. Its freshness gave our surroundings an air of incongruity.

'Where's this?'

'Bottom End.'

Four houses in a block, scattered along the street in an awful symmetry that appeared random because of the abandoned gardens, which were separated from the pavement by wired fences, privet hedges or a trestle of fish boxes. Some gardens had been cultivated, but most were wasted. There were gaps in a row because someone didn't use the gate, but had walked a path to their own front door, and the wiry plants or bushes were now mutations.

Cars in varying states of decay or repair were abandoned along the road. A couple were garaged where the gardens should be, with tarpaulins slung across them. Motor bikes roared and flooded past us, noisy in the rain. Most of the cars had flat tyres and a couple were on stilts of supporting bricks with newspapers taped along the windshield.

Nothing shone except the rain. Even the lamps seemed dull. A curtain flashed open as we passed. There was drunken singing, a raised voice or a scream. Dogs loped sideways and cats were huddled on the window-sills. Tin cans, trash and broken bottles lay along the pavements and an ice-cream van roared past with chimes of 'Popeye the Sailor Man'. Every home had a live television set in the corner. Women sat by their gas fires with raw, hopeless faces; children with eyes like stone stared as the TV roared with music and laughing visions of a good time.

Cammy opened a gate. The house looked like all the others and the woman who opened the door started talking immediately. 'In the name of the wee man, look who it is, the Big Bopper. And is this poor-looking soul new? God help you, son. If you've any sense you'll go back the way you came, even though it's pissing rain. Well, lads, since you're here, I've only one word to say to you. Rent. Tell that old bastard to take up a wee collection amongst the faithful and see if you can rustle up the price of a cabbage between you. We had a wee encounter last night, your mighty leader and myself. "Pay your rent or get to fuck," says I. "You're a fine-looking woman," says he. "Have you only noticed?" says I. "I've admired you from afar," says he. "You've been here for fifteen years," says I. And then do you know what he does; he pulls out this shrivelled-looking object which maidenly modesty forbids me from naming, but between you and I it hadn't seen light since VE-Night. "Hows about it?" he said. Apart from trying to keep a straight face, I was quite shocked. But I didn't like to hurt his feelings, though I was forced to enquire if this was as well as the rent or instead of. Oh, he's such a merry little prankster, isn't he. Laugh a minute when he comes to power. Well, I must be off. Can't stand here all night; there's a half-bottle to be drunk. So if you two stalwarts of the revolution could tell him it's R-E-N-T instead of R-I-D-E, I'd be much obliged.' She turned to go, then grabbed Cammy as he passed on the stairs. 'Get it up you while you're young, is one of the Thoughts of Mao Tse Tung.'

We were with an obviously Adullamite gathering, six or seven people in a bedroom at the top of the stairs. 'Who's that?' shouted a girl with straight hair.

'Get him out of here,' said someone else.

'It's okay,' said Cammy. 'He's my brother. I thought it would be okay to bring him since we were related.'

An old man stood up. He'd been sitting on the bed and, though it creaked when he rose, the indentation of his body remained on the mattress and cover.

'I'm afraid you'll have to leave,' he told me. 'I'm sorry you've been brought here under false pretences. Cameron has mentioned you to us before and we were interested in meeting you. However, we are presently discussing business of such importance that only the closest of our comrades are allowed entrance, and Cameron should have known this.' He turned to a small girl beside him. 'Add Personal Criticism to the agenda,' he said; and as she started writing he turned to me: 'If you don't mind risking yourself with my landlady, I'm afraid I must once again ask you to leave.'

I closed the door and could not make out what was being said. Someone shouted, 'Order!' There was silence and the bedroom door was opened quickly. The small girl said to me, 'Will you go. Please.' When I was half-way down the stairs, I heard the door close. I remember nothing of the room and can only place the faces of those I have described because I saw them later, in circumstances I can hardly forget.

'Don't you worry yourself, son. I've been trying to get in for ages. They're a very select crowd.' The sitting room smelled of carelessness. 'Do you want to come in?' she asked. 'Tell you what; there's a pub at the bottom of the road. You go down there and get us a couple of bottles of Eldorado white, red if you prefer, come back here and you and I will have a wee party, or a sing-song at the very least.'

Night and the street with rain all over. A car went by like tension; water sprayed in little fan-shapes away from the wheels and glinted like a mayfly.

I couldn't find the bar on the corner. Two streets away, on the road before High Street, there was a place with a neon sign jerking red, blue and white. I bought a pint and watched television.

My glass was half-empty.

'You don't live around here,' said the man next to me.

'No.'

'What brings you to this place?'

'Visiting.'

'We don't get many visitors.'

When I left, the rain had stopped. A wind whistled through the streets, carrying a salt spray from the sea. I walked along High Street, over the bridge and up towards Cuchullain Avenue with crowds of kids still hanging around the chip shops, shouting and pushing, silent when I passed, then a burst of giggles. When I got home I knew I'd caught a cold.

114

Eight

My sister was in the living room with Mum and Dad.

'You're early,' I said and kissed her cheek. She stiffened slightly and did not kiss me. 'I got a lift,' she said.

'You two were always fond of each other,' said Mum as she went to bed. She'd given us tea in the good china as if we were visitors. It was well past her bedtime, but she had stayed up to be with Phamie, eventually sitting with a look of rapt wonder on her face as she stared at her daughter, hardly talking, nodding agreement, verging on speech every now and then but afraid to talk, sitting with her hands on her lap, smiling at her strangely beautiful daughter.

Dad went to bed a little later when Phamie launched her latest theory. 'He's dead,' she said. 'He is, he's definitely dead,'

'How do you know?' I asked.

'Night all,' said Dad.

'Well, there's signs, lots of them. On the cover of the *Sergeant Pepper* album he's looking the other way. His back's to us. Now that shows he's not with us, doesn't it?'

'Not necessarily.'

'On the cover of *Abbey Road* he's barefoot. Now dead people are always barefoot, aren't they? And there's a car on the cover. The registration is 281F, or twenty-eight-if. He was twenty eighty years old, see. But what's really freaky is that if you play the last track backwards it sounds like "Paul is dead".'

'I'm not convinced.'

'That's because you're not into signs and symbols. There's a really good book about it. I've got it somewhere. Hold on.'

She raked through a bag and produced a copy of Hesse's *Glass Bead Game* and the Penguin *John Lennon*. 'You should read them,' she said. 'They're great. Really, really great.'

115

'I've read the Hesse.'

'Isn't it great?'

'I didn't understand it.'

'Try this one.' She gave me the *John Lennon*, which I read later and replaced without comment, a book derivative of Ivor Cutler, a man who refused to grow up, with a bit of Thurber thrown in for pedigree. 'It's great,' she said. 'Really, really great.'

Cammy came home and apologised for the embarrassment: 'I don't seem to have pleased anyone tonight,' he said. 'The group are upset because I brought you along without asking, and they're right. We must learn to abide by collective decisions.'

'If there had been a collective decision not to bring me, you presumably would not have brought me.'

'What is this?' Phamie had made us coffee and missed part of the discussion. 'You guys seem really strange.'

'It's okay. We were on about what happened earlier.'

'Cammy took me to a meeting where I wasn't welcome, that's all.'

'Big deal. Happens to me all the time.'

'Yeah, well; I don't suppose your friends add Personal Criticism to the agenda because of it.' Cammy was trying to joke and not succeeding.

'So what happened?' I asked.

'I made a mistake and was properly criticised. I feel I've let them down, but I'll make it up. It means developing a correct attitude, that's all. I'll regain my position.'

'For Christ's sake, Cammy. Don't tell me you've started living your life doing what other people tell you to do or think you should do. That's nowhere, Cammy, fucken nowhere. You've got to do what you know to be right.'

'The greater good outweighs personal ambition.'

'Who's talking about fucken ambition. I'm meaning everyday things.'

'Then we're not talking about the same thing, Debbie.' Cammy smiled his smile. His head tilted to the left and his

116

eyebrows raised, which caused his eyes to open wider and his brow to wrinkle.

'So, how did you get on with the landlady?' he asked me.

'She wanted me to get a carry-out.'

'Nothing revolutionary in that, I'm afraid.' He yawned. 'Time for bed. Good to see you, Debbie. I'm sorry. I'll have to get to bed. I'm tired. See you in the morning.'

'He isn't tired, is he?'

'I don't suppose he is; no.'

'There's something on his mind.'

'And how about you?' She didn't answer. 'How have you been, Debbie?'

'Me? Fine.' A cat cried in the rain, wind howled through the draught excluder and rain lashed the window.

'And how's your man, I've forgotten his name?'

'I'd rather not talk about that,' she said.

After a while, pale and pulling the loose threads at the hem of her skirt, she shivered. 'Bastard,' she said. 'He used to write poems and said they were for me. He wrote "You are someone/ Who came with the snow/ Kept me alive/ And will not go". That's nice, isn't it? It's a good poem.'

'It's a bit ambiguous.'

'He was really really jealous. What do you mean it's ambiguous?'

'Nothing, Debs. Nothing at all. Carry on.'

'He was really fucken jealous. He never had any reason to be jealous. He didn't need a reason. He just was, all the time. If I spoke to someone, he'd ask, "Who's he? What does he want? Have you slept with him?" Stuff like that. All the fucken time. You know,' she said. 'You know that the best way of finding out if you're stoned is to touch noses, right. If you're not sure, go up to someone and try touching their nose. Right? If you miss, you're out of your tree.

'There was this guy at a party really really stoned and so was I. I stood up and he came over and said, "Touch my nose." So I did. I went like that and I touched his nose. Jesus.

'George did his nut. "You fucken whore," he's shouting.

117

That was the first time. He dragged me out of the place and gave me a doing. Called me all the whores of the day. That was just the start. It went on and on. He'd get pissed and start throwing his weight around. If I left, he'd come and get me. God, this happened four or five times before I started to suss what was going on; I mean, what a fucken hassle, your old man kicking fuck out of you once a week.

'I've got a friend. A spade. Sam. Great guy. A good laugh. He's a poet, a West Indian poet. I told him what was going on, so he goes round and gives George a doing. I didn't know and when I got in George went for me with a broken bottle. Look.'

There was a pale luminescence on Debbie's skin, just below the shoulder, a soft ivory glow in the light and a white scar across her shoulder shaped like the letter U. The whiteness made it uglier, somehow purer.

'I had to have a transfusion at hospital. Four pints of blood. The doctor knew what had happened. "Charge him," they said. "Jail him." I couldn't, couldn't do it. You can't jail your man.

'But it kept happening. I don't mean that I kept having transfusions. I can't tell you all of it. You wouldn't believe me anyway.'

I gave her whisky, stolen from the drinks' cupboard. 'I never take this stuff,' she said, sipping slowly and pausing because she expected to cough. 'I left him a couple of months ago. I didn't escape, run away or anything like that. It was all settled nice and peacefully; no third parties, the stuff was split down the middle and that was that. Finito. I could hardly believe it was over. I couldn't believe it was as simple as that. It was easier to split up than it was to stay together.

'Then, after about a week I started bleeding. I thought it was strange. It wasn't my period, but I'd been under a lot of stress, which sometimes affects things. My periods usually last about three days, four at the most, but this bleeding kept on and on. Then I started to get pains whenever I sat down; I got a stitch. A friend suggested I go to a clinic. It took me ages to go. You've no idea what they're like, the shit you've got to put up with if you want the pill. And this, this was something else.

'I went and left then went back again without being seen. The receptionist got really pissed off with me. I stayed away for about two weeks, but the pain got worse and the bleeding got really really heavy, so I had to go back. I went on a Tuesday because there was a woman doctor on then. She was a bit strange, asked all sorts of daft questions, what sort of a pain, stuff like that. She examined me; you know, with my legs up on these stretcher things. Listen, get us another drink, will you?'

I remember feeling bewildered. I moaned and tried to change it into a cough, but she knew. When I turned with the glass, she said, 'I've got to tell someone.'

'I'm sorry,' I said truthfully. 'I didn't mean it.'

We sat shivering, me with the cold. When I sneezed, she turned up the gas fire, dabbed her eyes and gave me the tissue.

'Thanks. Women always have tissues.'

'We need them.'

There was a silence so long that I wondered if she was going to speak.

'That kind of examination is horrible,' she said. 'An invasion. I remember trying to imagine it was happening to someone else, wishing I was stoned, trying to sing songs, "Yellow Submarine", "Lucy In The Sky With Diamonds", going tra-la-la when I forgot the words. I was singing, I don't know what, "Ob-la-di, Ob-la-da", something like that, when the doctor screamed. She looked at me and said, "OhmyGod," like that, as if it was one word. Then she tried to smile, but her face was still and her mouth twitched. "It's okay," she said. "Don't panic. It's all right. Carry on singing."

'I asked what was wrong. She wouldn't tell me. These people tell you nothing anyway. She went and got another doctor, a man. He looked inside me and they whispered together. "Don't worry," he said. He said, "It's okay. We're going to give you a little injection." I was crying. Fuck you, I thought. Fuck you. You fucken bastard. Fuck you, you

119

bastard. He gave me the injection. "Good," he said; and I was on my own for about half an hour. I couldn't feel anything. It was as if my body was ice. Then he got clamps. They got a fucken clamp and stuck it up me, to hold me open. I stared at the ceiling. There was a nurse. They still wouldn't tell me what was happening. She had ginger hair, a badge and an engagement ring. She was crying. I didn't look at her, but I could hear her. She ran out of the room and sniffed a lot when she came back. I just stared at the ceiling. I couldn't look at anyone. I was just there. I was ice, that was all. I was ice because they'd given me the injection.

' "Let us know if you feel anything," he said. I couldn't feel a fucken thing. You know what it's like when you get a tooth out; you don't feel anything except the pressing. You feel the pressing, then you feel the tooth being ripped. Right? It was like that. I felt a little pressure. I told him. "It's all right," he said. "I've got it." Then I felt something slide inside me, as if the pain was sliding away.

'He had a pair of forceps up me. I felt this strange sliding sensation. I looked down and just caught a glimpse of the end of them when they came out. It was almost black, covered in blood. But when it caught the light the colour was a very deep crimson. And it reflected the light, which made me scared.

' "Dish," he said. And the nurse got one of those metal, kidney-shaped basins. He opened the forceps and the crimson thing dropped inside. There was a clang, a little ring that stayed in the air. He put the forceps down and pulled the rubber gloves off his hands with that awful noise, like suction.

' "Show her," he said to the nurse. The nurse looked at the woman doctor and she nodded. Then he, the man doctor, looked at me for the first time. "That's what you've been carrying around inside you," he said. I tried to sit up, but could only lean on my elbow, and I looked in the dish. It was a razor blade. Wilkinson's Sword.'

A long string of saliva ran from her mouth and nose. Her eyes were red and puffy. Her cheeks were wet, but she did not sob.

When I wakened I realised I must have slept, though my mind was numbed, racing through sleep without rest.

I phoned work to say I had the cold.

Phamie and I walked along High Street. 'Nothing's changed,' she said.

February in Scotland, rain from a lustring sky and the weather matched our mood. We spoke around things rather than about them, but soon settled.

'I don't understand how you didn't know.'

'Christ, not you as well. The folk at the hospital seemed to think I put it there myself. "It must have been uncomfortable," they said. "Didn't you notice?" Of course I bloody well noticed; that's why I went there. Look, I don't know when he did it. I couldn't stand having him around at the end, so I stayed stoned and I took pills. That combination plus a little whisky tends to zonk you out. Flat. So he must have done it when I was stoned and pilled and drunk and sleeping. Satisfied?'

'I can't get it out of my head. Even when I was asleep I kept thinking about it. I mean, imagine if you'd slept with someone.'

'It's over,' she said.

The rain stopped. We sat on a bench by the river. There was a smell of wet earth, a straggle of snowdrops, celandine and the three notes of a pigeon.

'I've got a guru,' she said.

'Tell me about him.'

'Phan Huan Quat. He's Vietnamese. Lives in Paris. He's taught me everything, everything I know I've learned from him. He's amazing. He taught me how to forgive. I'm not into relationships at present. I need to find myself, I need to know who I am before I can enter into a meaningful relationship. And I'm getting there. Phan Huan Quat has taught me that no matter what happens, I mustn't be afraid of sex, I have no need to fear it; that no matter how it's been abused, or how it's been distorted, it's still God-given and beautiful, it's still the source

121

of life and the only true way of feeling a sense of oneness with another human being. It's impossible to abuse. It's like a flower. You destroy a flower as soon as you want to possess it; when you pick it the flower begins to die. He teaches us that sex and love are like that. He says that no matter how you abuse a flower, pick its petals, tear off its head, no matter what you do there will still be other flowers to bloom and grow and they are part of a cycle that man enters only when he plunders.

'There are seeds,' she said. 'They are carried by the wind to bloom where they're planted. They grow in the sunlight, up towards heaven, and when they bloom the bees come along and take the pollen back to their hives to make honey and honey is the best food in the world. Nothing is better for you than honey. Phan Huan Quat teaches that no matter what we suffer, our real feelings cannot be destroyed because they are like flowers and we are also like flowers as we proceed along the path God has ordained for us which we learn through prayer, towards the place in our lives where we can blossom like flowers and bloom where we are planted.'

'Sounds fine.'

'Don't say it like that. I know it's simple. Phan Huan Quat says things have to be simple. We must live our lives one day at a time and keep things as simple as possible.'

'Have you told him about George?'

'Not yet.'

'Too complicated?'

'No. It's because I'm too ashamed. I want to meditate, Angus. There's a nice tree I'd like to talk to.'

'I'd be as well to go to work.'

'Why don't you meditate with me?'

'I couldn't.'

'Then wait for me. Please. I won't be long.'

I left my sister on a bed of leaf-mould beneath a tree. An hour later she ran down the path towards me, smiling. 'Wow,' she said.

'Good?'

'The best.'

122

'Are you cold?'

'Freezing.'

'Then let's get warm.'

And we walked back the way we came.

'How's Judy?' she asked.

'Fine.'

'What's she doing?'

'Working. In Pittsburgh's.'

'What's that?'

'A shop.'

'The shops are shut. Is this their half-day?'

'Uh-hu.'

'I knew it. I got this really strong feeling about her when I was meditating. Let's go.'

I phoned Judy and said a surprise was on its way. 'Good. I like surprises,' she said.

Phamie hid behind the door and when Judy opened it there were squeals and hugs. They tried to include me in their conversation, but after a while they gave me up, so I read a little, then went to Judy's room. If they noticed me go, they didn't say.

It was strange being in the room without her, as though I wasn't there either, as though I was imagining the room rather than experiencing it. I lay on the bed and stared at the ceiling.

If not then, it was around this time I began to imagine life without her. Our conversations had become little more than a series of information exchanges; there were long silences, which made me feel uncomfortable, though she seemed happy.

I'd give her books and find them unopened, sometimes in the bag or wrapping paper, on top of the dresser at the end of the bed. She'd smile, then look away. 'I've been busy,' she said.

She often seemed worried. If I asked what she was thinking, she'd smile and say, 'Nothing,' staring ahead. She liked the Beatles, the Rolling Stones and the Dennis Brain recording of the Mozart Horn Concertos, but rarely expressed an opinion.

123

She said she didn't like foreign films because she couldn't understand what they were saying. She told me this running from the cinema in the rain. I thought it was a joke. She laughed later than me, on top of the bus going home when she took my hand and stared out the window.

Listening to the laughter rise through the floorboards, I considered none of this. But the time is significant for we had a series of arguments that year, 1968.

She liked Esther and Abi Ofarim singing 'Cinderella-Rockerfella'. It was Number One in the hit parade for three weeks and while her parents were on holiday she lay on top of me cooing and purring the words, which I found embarrassing.

She complained when Marmalade reached Number One with 'Ob-la-di, Ob-la-da', relenting when she learned they were a Scots group whom we had seen performing in Invercullion Town Hall as Dean Ford and the Gaylords, reverting when she heard *The White Album*: 'The Beatles sing it better,' she said. 'I don't know why they didn't release their own version as a single.'

'Jumping Jack Flash' pleased her; Engelbert Humperdinck's 'Man Without Love' and Tom Jones's 'Delilah' annoyed her. 'That song really annoys me,' she said.

Louis Armstrong sold more records than anyone that year with a song called 'Wonderful World'. Judy was singing the bit about seeing babies cry and watching them grow; I was reading *Portnoy's Complaint*. 'That's nice,' she said.

'What is?'

'Watching babies grow.'

'It's a terrible song. Louis Armstrong is partly responsible for one of the most important musical developments the world has known and is one of this century's greatest musicians. That he should end up mouthing this dross is unforgivable. It's tantamount to prostitution.'

'You sound like Cammy.'

I knew she was right. We'd been through a bad row earlier in the year. It had hurt her and I was still smarting from my insensitivity.

'No one's supposed to disagree with you,' she said. 'If they do, they're stupid. Okay then, I'm stupid; and I have all sorts of other problems as well, like how I feel and where I live and the people I live with and what they do to each other, never mind what they're doing to me. But it's not very nice, Angus; nothing you could put your finger on, just the fact that my father isn't too sociable on account of the fact that he's pissed all the time, but that's a cross we have to bear, nothing compared to Grunting Hall and being adopted which are two of the worst things that could happen to anybody. So we're agreed, I'm stupid; but I don't care any more, I don't care what you think; in fact, I've come to depend on it; if I like something, you will hate it and sound superior, which makes me wonder what you're here for anyway, apart from the obvious.'

'You are never in any way even remotely apart from the obvious,' I shouted.

The trouble was caused by a television series called 'The Prisoner', which starred Patrick McGoohan, who wrote and directed some of the programmes. Judy told me about it. They appeared to concern a prisoner, though even that was a bit ambiguous, and in every episode The Prisoner was pursued by an unseen character called Number One. In February, 1968, they ran the last episode and promised to clear all previous mysteries, including the identity of Number One. So we stayed in to watch Part Seventeen on ITV.

She sat on the sofa, legs drawn up and her chin on her kness. She didn't move till the final credits, even though her mother told her to, 'Sit properly.'

'I still don't understand it,' she said in her room. 'Who was Number One?'

'He was.'

'Who?'

'Him. The Prisoner.'

'How do you know? You've never seen it.'

'I don't know. I'm only guessing.'

'You've been watching it, haven't you? You've seen it and didn't tell me.'

'Don't be silly.'

'It isn't silly. People go to a lot of trouble to make television programmes. They wouldn't make something that didn't matter.'

'Come here,' said I.

'What for?'

'Guess.'

We didn't see each other for weeks and I thought it was over. I sat at home and played Dylan records, wondering what she was doing and who she was with.

But the biggest row started when Apple Corps released their first record, 'Hey Jude'. We'd patched up our differences, largely because I was casually passing the shop at closing time.

'Hello,' I said. 'I'd forgotten you worked here. How's things?'

She smiled and said, 'It's nice to see you.'

Judy changed her name to Jude, then Apple released their second single, Mary Hopkin singing 'Those were the Days'. It was Number One for six weeks.

'Twiggy saw Mary on "Opportunity Knocks",' Jude told me. 'Mary won it and Twiggy told Paul. He signed her up and they made that record. He produced it and everything.'

'If those were the days for anyone, it was the Czechoslovakians.'

'The tune's Russian.'

'It may have escaped your attention, though I can't imagine how, but earlier this year the Russians invaded Prague.'

'I know that,' she said. 'You don't understand, Paul was saying something with that song. He knew about the Russians and Czechoslovakia. That's why he made the record. Paul's cleverer than you give him credit for.'

'What was he saying?'

'It's irony.'

'What is?'

'What he's saying, it's irony.'

I wakened and stared at the ceiling. Judy and Phamie were whispering. 'We didn't like to waken you,' Jude said. 'Sorry.'

'Her dad came in,' said Phamie.

'And you know what he's like.'

He was thumping about downstairs. 'I'm surprised he found his way home,' said I. And Judy looked out the window.

'Debbie gave me a book,' she said. '*The Hobbit.*'

'You'll enjoy it.'

'That's what Debbie said, didn't you.'

'It's great, really really great.'

'It's for children.'

'Don't listen to him,' said Phamie. 'He's only interested in Hank Jansen.'

'Well, now we're all awake,' said I, 'what are we going to do?'

'George used to read these books,' said Phamie, giggling. 'Then he'd get me to read them. Honestly; I used to make up bits about the Good Fairy coming in when things weren't going too well. She'd wave her magic wand and give the guy a stiffener. "Never mind the fucken fairies," he'd shout. "Get back to the action." '

'You haven't tried that yet,' said Judy.

Phamie took a pamphlet from her bag, one of a series issued by the Vietnam Solidarity Campaign. The picture on the cover was repeated throughout the pamphlet: a car with the bonnet up, Buddist monks surround the car while to the right foreground a monk sits impassively, his body on fire, flames leaping from and around him; the ground is blackened with petrol, there's a discarded white canister behind him and the air above is black with smoke which wafts to the right and off the picture.

Phamie sighed. She tapped the pamphlet against her left knee. 'It's the signs,' she said. 'You feel these things, you just know them. You don't even need to believe it, you don't need to be in tune with it or even to fucken well like it, you just have to feel it and you can't deny what you feel or if you do then you're so screwed up that you might as well not bother with anything but go on pretending you're part of the human

127

race, but you're not, you're not, you're not; the only people who are human beings are the ones who feel, Phan Huan Quat says that: the ability to feel distinguishes the human, and if you deny that you are in deep trouble, the worst trouble because you tell yourself you're all right, you tell yourself you're not in any kind of trouble, you're okay, you're coping with it, but you're not. You might be coping inside your head, but that's a good indication that you're not coping at all because you have to feel it first and if you deny what you feel or pretend it's something else or, worst still, pretend you don't feel anything then you're a psychopath, psychopaths don't feel anything; and if you're anything like that you're only storing up trouble because it has to come out somehow and it will come out in your discontent, your resentments and all these dull negative things instead of saying yes, everything is so yes and I can feel it because I allow myself to feel it, I have opened myself up to the yes.' She closed her eyes and rocked herself back and forward, making a little sound at the back of her throat, humming a song without words, a joyful little exercise, back and forward and back and forward singing the little refrain till Judy looked at me and smiled and Phamie opened her eyes.

'I want to start a group,' she said. 'I want to start a women's group in Invercullion, a small discussion group where women can discuss the things that affect us, talk about women's issues and get something done about women's rights in the community.'

I sighed.

'You and I can be first members, Jude. We'll form the group together. What do you say?'

Judy looked at me. 'Would you mind?' she asked.

Nine

Saturday, May 3:

Just as Pepys recorded the topics of his day together with the ordinary, the mundane and trivial, then considered their separate and collective implications, my little journal does the same.

If Helen's magazine article is to be believed there has been an ultra-increase in sexually transmitted diseases here and in America. First there was herpes, which seems to sum up the twentieth century – it's smaller, brighter, brasher, more functional, easier to spell and worse, with none of the style, tradition or even the syllables contained in either gonorrhoea or syphilis. This new thunderclap would appear to be incurable, recurring and achieving what centuries of moral teaching have failed to achieve: people are shagging considerably less for fear of contraction.

I showed the article to Cammy. 'They're waiting till a cure becomes profitable,' he said. 'If they cure it now they won't make any money, but if they hold off for ten years till everybody's got it, then they'll obviously make a lot of money. Capitalism, dear boy. Capitalism. Supply and demand. By the way, did you bring my fags?' Jail has turned him into a smoker. The fact that tobacco is rationed and has to be earned has made it desirable.

The Protestant work-ethic, which for centuries has allowed us to glory in our degradation, has seldom known such success. Perhaps Mr Calvin's dicta suffers from over-familiarity, or maybe this herpes is just a flash in the pan.

The virus is a variant of the herpes-simplex family, which minimises its threat by making it sound as familiar as an obscure Roman consul whose historical significance we have temporarily forgotten. Herpes Simplex the First is the common cold sore and Herpes Simplex the Second is pretty much the same except it's worse. How it developed and spread is anyone's guess, but it's apparently dormant in more than half of us. I don't know about you, but I've had a good look.

It seems an equivocal piece of handiwork – incurable but dormant, highly contagious but latent. No matter the equivocation, this serpiginous ailment is taking over the world, as I suspect a similar catastrophe must have afflicted the Greek and Roman empires, since this country, for all its little quirks, is no worse than these.

So this is the end. The Beautiful People of the Sixties celebrated the birth of a social and sexual revolution and a cold in the cock threatens us with a counter-coup. People like me are getting scared. I mention this because, as an adulterer, I am obviously eligible. And because Helen gave me the article to read.

'What do you think of that?' she asked.

'There isn't much I can think about it, apart from the fact that it doesn't seem very nice.'

'Is that what's wrong with you?'

'I beg your pardon.'

'Do you have herpes?'

'Not as far as I can tell.'

'Then what's wrong with you?'

'Nothing.'

'You haven't been near me for weeks.'

And here we'll pause for meditation. Gentle reader, assuming there is a reader, and I assume someone will read my Diaries because all diaries are a form of fiction, written to be read. They are our fictions about ourselves and, if not written for another to read, they form a testament to self-indulgence that makes masturbation seem like communion. Apart from anything else, not to have your diaries read renders the exercise pointless. Therefore, accounts are falsified and we show ourselves in the best possible light, or, and this is much more devious, we present a portrait of someone we dislike, someone who has hurt or even injured us, someone we resent,

130

as though the world perceives them as we do, as though our opinion is common. To tell the truth, assuming you can, is to bore or render your reader speechless with disbelief. Fiction is elaboration and elaboration involves choice; as soon as you choose you are fictionalising, for choice is the very fundament of fiction. Therefore, yet again, I bid you welcome to my little world. Passports please. Who the hell are you and what do you want? My paranoia is simple: having stated my case I fear it may react against me.

Now for the meditation. I am the first to admit that one in the bush is worth two in the hand, if you take my meaning. Yet I am stuck with primary narcissism, cathecting on object choices, occasionally using women as a substitute for the real thing. Onan's delight, the poor man's Valium, has previously relieved the boredom and occasionally fulfils a similar function, though nowadays we've seen it all before. Women are as well as, rather than instead of, which extends the range and increases the options, for what was a sin in the nineteenth century has become a cure in the twentieth. So much for fiction. I suspect this knowledge formed the unspoken force behind Helen's euphemism. (When Helen resorts to euphemism, I run for cover; breeding will out.) I had, of course, been near her, but not in the way she meant.

I considered telling her I was going through an identity crisis, that I thought I was homosexual and had become deeply attracted to a young man who worked at the bank. I thought of asking her to bear with me through my present difficulties, but decided against that line.

So I went on the attack. 'What's wrong?' I asked. 'Aren't you getting enough attention?'

'Do you think you're giving me enough attention?'

'What I think would appear to be secondary. You've obviously decided for yourself.'

'You'll be telling me I've imagined all this?'

'No, I shouldn't think you've imagined anything, except that there's a reason for my behaviour.'

'Are you seeing someone else?'

'I beg your pardon?'

'You heard.'

'How dare you.'

'All I want is some honesty.'

'What makes you think I'm being dishonest?'

'I can feel it. And I hate that feeling, Angus; I hate it. All my life, because of my mother and the way I was brought up, all my life I've tried to put a face on it. I've always felt it was easier to be immune from that sort of thing and I've tried not to care, I've said to myself many times, okay that's how it is, let him get on with it. You're okay. I'm a married woman. I thought I'd never let you go, that I'd never need anyone else. Don't forget how we met, Angus. I was on the rebound. I've been hurt before and I'm not going to be hurt again, not that way. It's too dangerous. So if you've got a wee bit on the side, then I hope you're having fun. But tell me, Angus. Tell me. Don't hurt me like that because that's the deepest, worst hurt you can do. There's nothing worse than thinking your man's having an affair and not knowing for certain. Anything would be better than that.'

'I'm not having an affair.'

'What's her name?'

'I said I'm not having an affair.'

'My God, Angus. Why are you so angry? What are you defending?'

'You've made your mind up, haven't you? All this talk about the way you were when we met; how about the way you were when we married, do you think I'm liable to forget that?'

'Or me. You still think of yourself as the injured party, don't you? Not that it matters. You've made my mind up for me and now I'll need to look at my own life and see what I want.'

'What's that supposed to mean?'

'It isn't supposed to mean anything. I've got a decision to make and it isn't going to be easy. I know you're lying and I've got to decide what I'm going to do about it. There's no need to look so scared. I don't suppose I'll do anything now. I haven't done much in the past.'

'What past are you talking about?'

'I'll say this for you, you're magnificent when you're angry; most men are, but it's so unexpected in you. I suppose that's how men have domineered women, by being better at being angry. It comes naturally to men, but women look ridiculous or pathetic. Goes against the grain.' This was said in her cool, flat voice usually used for ordering groceries.

Upstairs, later, after the row: 'Baby,' she said. 'You're a child, Angus. You need your mother.'

She pulled her nightdress down, wrapped it round her, snuggled in and went to sleep. She was snoring when I went up to the attic. No reason, except the need to look at the moon and wonder who made us all, the need for familiarity. Change and decay.

These days there is no privacy. The public arena is in your home. You can, of course, refuse to own a radio or a television set, freedom of choice, but that would deprive you of their benefits.

So we have a problem. The only private place is inside your head, which is fine, except that many of us have forgotten how to live anywhere else, and a few others never learned.

'I believe your brother's in jail,' said The Mother.

'It was an interesting case, that,' said The Father.

'Really,' said The Mother. 'And what may I ask did you find interesting about it?'

This is when Helen's story becomes believable, when The Mother acknowledges her husband's existence. He's always there, maybe as a prop or maybe he has nowhere else to go; and his role is passive, though he is cited to underline The Mother's opinions.

'Your daddy and I were wondering if you wouldn't be better off in a house that's a bit bigger, dear, maybe with a wee garden, not too much of course for a garden can be an awful bother.'

Or: 'Your daddy will tell you, babies can be a nuisance.

133

They ruin your social life. And it isn't just a matter of looking after them when they're wee; no, that's just the start of it. And the expense. You take my advice, dear, and stay as you are. I wish I did; more money in your pocket, you can go where you like, when you like, your time's your own. It's different for a man, of course, so Angus may have other ideas.'

I watch her face and try to catch her unawares, but such an obvious innuendo seems unlikely. There's no doubting her influence: we moved to the suburbs and do not have children. There is nothing, neither statement nor action, to confirm or dent Helen's story, though why should she lie? The Mother is certainly insensitive and selfishness is the basis of insensitivity, but her remarks could also be seen as evidence of a crystaline conscience.

Not that it matters. Time has done for us what we could not do for ourselves and little or nothing suggests our early difficulties, except menstrual secrecy. We do not discuss the subject and she smuggles her requisites around like a humiliation.

Sunday lunch and all is well.

'I believe your brother's in jail.'

'It was an interesting case, that.'

'Really. And what, may I ask, did you find interesting about it?'

'Cameron's in jail,' said I. 'He is doing time for participating in a series of politically motivated bank robberies.'

'And your sister's a hippie.'

'Was.'

'Still is, from what I can make out.'

'Even so, it's not unusual.'

'It may not be unusual, but it could be dangerous.'

'What do you mean?'

'I mean this new plague, what's it called, dear?'

'Aids.'

'That's right, now surely someone like your sister is going to be affected.'

'Why?'

134

'I think you know why.'

'You seem to know more about that sort of thing than me, so perhaps you'd like to explain.'

'Well, it isn't only men, is it?'

'Sorry, what isn't only men?'

'It isn't only men who get the plague, is it? It's women too, women who sleep with men.'

'Then why should Phamie be eligible and someone like yourself, or even Helen, be ineligible, since it seems obvious that you have slept with a man more often than my sister, purely on account of the fact that you're older and you have been married for a number of years. Yourself, Helen and thousands of women like you sleep with a man every night and don't catch Aids, now why should my sister catch it?'

'I didn't say man. I said men.'

'While I am prepared to bow to your obviously superior knowledge of promiscuity, I would have thought –'

'Funny name for it,' said The Father.

'I beg your pardon.'

'I don't know why they gave it that name. I mean, they say Lucozade aids recovery, don't they, and now they're calling this thing Aids, it's confusing.'

'Especially if you can't distinguish between advertising and reality.'

Saturday afternoon. Helen's in the garden and I am collecting my scattered wits. She thinks I am reading the *Scotsman*, otherwise known as the *Two Minutes Silence* because of the time it takes to read.

No more to record. Tonight's the night.

Monday, May 5:

Mid-afternoon. Half-past two and last year's blackbird is singing in the rowan tree, two songs in one, with a drone almost echoing beyond itself. God knows why it came back here.

Dovedale X
Past pub on rt.
Down hill
Under bridge
Up hill
On
Left at r/about
On
Another r/about
Keep going
Bells whisky sign
Maybe White Horse
Johnnie Walker?
2.30 p.m.

Don Calder's instructions are rococo. As far as I can make out, to get to the golf course I drive to Dovedale Cross, turn left at the roundabout and carry on till I find it. Monthly match on Thursday. It will be worth going, if only to watch the cheeks of Calder's arse tighten as he takes a swing at the ball.

'Hope I didn't disturb you,' he said. 'They told me you were working from home. All well is it?' Not much to say. He has recently joined our little circle of sportsmen and has chosen the course, since the rates have gone up at our more regular venues.

Saw Miranda on Saturday. We ate spaghetti and drank a cheap red wine which tasted of mud.

'What's wrong?'

'Why do you think there's something wrong? Because the waiter smiled at me.'

'I think you've got a period?'

'Wrong time of the month, dear. The bad week. Sorry, wrong again. It isn't here yet.'

I had considered myself lucky with Miranda and Helen. Their periods came at different times and during a lighter moment I thought things had worked out rather well.

'I never see you.'

'That's nonsense.'

'It's time you saw more of me.'

'I can't.'

'Then we'll have to separate.'

'Why the ultimatum?'

The waiter brought the spaghetti, placed the plates and moved the cruet. He refilled our glasses and smiled at Miranda: 'Thank you, madam.'

'Does your wife know about me?'

'No.'

'Then I'll tell her.'

'Why?'

'Because we can't go on like this.'

'Why not?'

'For Christ's sake, Angus, it's obvious. There's no future in it, that's why.'

'Then what do you want me to do?'

'Tell her.'

'Can't.'

'Why not?'

'It would hurt her.'

'What do you think is happening now? Do you think she isn't hurt?'

'I know she is.'

'She must know about me, she must. A woman always knows. So why not get it over with? Why not tell her what she already knows? She must know.'

'I will tell her.'

'When?'

'I don't know. Not yet.'

'Do you love her?'

'No. I don't think so.'

'Do you love me?'

'Yes. Of course.'

'How did I know you would say that? Doesn't it seem odd to you that you love me but live with her?'

'Is that all that's wrong?'

'No, it isn't all. I can't love your properly, that's what's wrong. And I'll never be able to love you properly as long as you live with her, or anyone else for that matter, because she's got you and I haven't. I want your children, Angus. I want to look after you, I want to care for you but most of all I want to be with you.'

'Don't shout.'

'I'm not shouting.'

'Yes you are. People are staring.'

'I don't care.'

'Everything all right, madam?'

Miranda smiled.

'Enjoying the meal?'

'Lovely.'

The waiter smiled and left.

Miranda sighed. 'I'm not prepared to accept the fact that you sleep with someone else. I'm not sharing you, Angus. You're mine. Reverse it. Let's pretend I'm married and you're single. How do you think that would work out? You'd screw me a couple of times a week in the back of the car if I was lucky, then you'd come in and have a drink with my husband. You'd tell me how much you missed me, say how much you loved me, but would have no more thought of marrying me or being with me than you'd have an understanding of thermo-nuclear fission. I'd be your bit on the side; but what lasts a week or two for a man is a lifetime's love for a woman.'

'Do you want me to divorce Helen?'

'No, not like that. I want you to want to divorce Helen. I want you to want me more than you want Helen. I want you to stop telling me how wonderful I am and start showing me. I don't want you to say you need me, I want you to show me. Show me how much you want me, how much you adore me, don't just say it. All these bloody words you've been saying. All those God-forsaken phrases.'

'I don't believe that kind of devotion is exclusively female.'

'Oh, for Christ's sake.'

138

'What I mean is . . . oh Miranda, don't cry.'

'Do tears embarrass you?'

'No.'

'In that case I won't cry.'

'Have a drink.'

'That wine is awful.' She sniffed and looked around her. 'I don't suppose you have a tissue?'

'Sorry.'

'Give me your napkin.'

She stared at the tablecloth, playing with crumbs from the breadsticks. 'I went into a shop today,' she said. 'Pittsburg's. I walked up to one of these floor-walker types and asked him, "Can you please tell me where I can get felt?" I said it very sweetly and looked straight at him. He sent me to the second floor: dress materials. He was neither shocked nor surprised. Bet it happens every day.'

'Why did you do it?'

'I was bored. And my period was due. You know, no reason. Take me home. I don't know why I told you; now you'll think I'm unstable. Take me home. Christ, that meal was lousy and the wine was unspeakable.'

The waiter helped her on with her coat, held the door open and smiled as we left.

Helen was reading by the fire. 'All set for tomorrow?' she asked. And went to bed.

'Don't, Angus. Please,' she said later. 'I don't feel like it.'

So I lay awake, staring into the darkness with our toes touching, thinking of sleep, of how tired I'll be in the morning and how the Third Movement of Haydn's 67th Symphony is a swaggering minuet with sturdy legs and black mustachios, separated by a delicate wee trio that's over and done with, vanished as the minuet comes blustering back.

Miranda was waiting.

'Sorry,' she said. I didn't answer.

'How do you feel?'

'I'll let you know when we get there.'

From where the city left us and the road wound away we could see the hills shimmer through the heated light.

Miranda went over what she had said about knots and pitons, footholds, handholds, ropes and traversing. Then, within a mile of the car park, on the slow walk uphill she put a square of chocolate in my mouth.

'Did you mean what you said last night?'

'Every word. And now I'm scared you'll leave me.' She waited for me to speak. 'Will you?'

'I don't know.'

'I love you.'

'I know.'

'I'm not apologising.'

'There's nothing to apologise for.'

'Do you know what that sounds like? By the way, my period came this morning.'

'Really.'

'Yeah; exciting, isn't it.'

'And do you feel any better?'

'I feel washed out; but whether that means better or not, I've no idea. Better than what, Angus?'

'Better than you were last night.'

'I've already told you, I'm not apologising for last night, nor for what I said, I said it because I love you. If I made a mistake it was in speaking so directly, but I felt it so I said it. Things don't always work that way, but that's what happened last night. Anyway, I told the truth and I'm sure you'd prefer me to be honest rather than say what I thought you'd want to hear. I don't suppose you thought things could have gone on the way they were.'

Last night I wakened sweating with fear, trembling and clutching the bed to bring myself back to the reality of nightmare since the humiliation was too great.

'We'll give you a scramble to begin with,' she said.

I watched her move upwards, silhouetted against the sky with the grey rock glistening. She hammered in the last piton, then abseiled down to rope me up. 'You'll be okay,' she said. 'It's only about twenty-five or thirty feet.'

Then she climbed again, faster this time and sat at the top with her legs dangling over the side.

From the ground I could see her hair against the sun, squinted, not quite centre; the sun keeked behind her every time she moved. If I shaded my eyes, the brightest thing was her red laces.

I started out all right and did what I'd been told. I didn't stretch and always kept within easy reach of another hand-hold. About six feet from the top, with Miranda giving instructions, I realised where I was and what I was doing. My body refused to move.

'Come on,' she said. 'This one. Grab this one here.'

I couldn't speak and couldn't move, but stayed there clinging, feeling the space around my back, feeling the wind though there was no wind moving. My insides looping and sweat trickling down my body. I wanted to scratch. I moved in close and then I swayed. That was when I felt it, felt myself turn as my stomach tightened into a feeling that was vaguely sexual until my legs and arms began to quiver, then to shake, and I was crying. Miranda stretched her hand towards me: 'Take it,' she shouted. 'Here. Take it.' I cannot remember her pulling me up or even how I got off the rock.

I lay with my knees drawn up to my stomach and my hands round my head, sobbing. Miranda cradled me. She took me down from the rock, away from the hills, down through the bracken and back to the car. We drove to a pub. She bought me brandy and we all sang songs.

> We've never climbed a great big hill
> And I hope to Christ we never will,
> For the highest we've climbed is the windae sill,
> We're the bar room mountaineers.

I was sick outside the pub. She held my head as I struggled and retched. A line of spittle straggled to the ground. She wiped my mouth and kissed it. 'Come on,' she said. 'I'll take you home.'

141

To her house. She went in first and told the family Angus wasn't well, taken ill on the mountain. Her mother made tea and Miranda phoned Helen.

'Hello. Sorry to bother you. Mrs MacPhail? How do you do. My name is Sally Munro; my husband, Jack, was climbing with Angus today. Yes, that's right. No, he's fine. They're both fine. In fact, if you ask me, they're too fine, pissed as rats the pair of them. Bobby Scott brought them here and I'm afraid Angus is a bit worse for wear. I really don't think it would be a good idea if he even tried to drive home, so I've made a ramshackle bed up for him in the spare room and we'll see what kind of breakfast he wants in the morning. Oh, really. Yes. No, I don't think it happened often. He hasn't said anything about work, but he certainly can't go into the bank dressed as he is. I'll remind him in the morning. Good. Well, I'm sorry we've had to meet like this. Yes, I hope so. I don't know what it is, must be the euphoria of the hills or something; they've been going over the same bit for an hour and a half now. Isn't it, very boring. Good. It's been nice taking to you. Night-night.'

I slept in her room. Early this morning while I shivered with remembered fright she opened the door and crept beside me in her long white nightie.

At half-past eight she brought me tea and drove me home. She phoned the bank and asked for me, told my secretary she wouldn't be in and giggled. 'My period's really heavy,' she said. 'But don't tell him that.'

I phoned to say I was seeing clients, then working from home, and would call back by three. If anyone called, take their number and I'll call them back. I was told Miss Morrison wouldn't be in today; stomach cramp. I called back four times. The place ran well enough without me.

Helen's come in and made the tea. I told her about my imaginary piss-up with someone who didn't exist. 'His wife sounds nice,' she said. 'I'd like to meet her.'

She's going to see her headmaster tonight. Working late; doing French with Mr Strachan.

And I've worked out what a Munro is; a Scottish mountain over 3,000 feet as listed by Dr Munro in his Tables. To say nothing of a sally.

Thursday, May 8:
And this is the sentence the inveterate Diarist craves:
I think I am going mad.
Ignored Calder's instructions and made my own way to the golf course. Four of us play on the second Thursday of the month, all bank managers with the same bank except Calder who works in computers. It's supposed to be socialising.

Anyway, I played golf and had a few drinks, told a few jokes and slapped a few backs.

All too soon the party was over and everyone had to be home for tea. I thought about asking Calder the way back just to confuse him but decided against it since he looked lost. I wasn't exactly lost, but I didn't know where I was and proceeded with hopes of finding a recognisable landmark rather than actually anticipating one. And just when I thought I knew where I was, I saw Judy.

She was wearing jeans and a sweatshirt, her long hair lifting slightly to bounce around her shoulders. It was her and no mistake. Judy.

I abandoned rather than parked the car and watched her approach from twenty-five or thirty yards. She walked in the same old way, landing on the ball of her foot and slightly bouncing up again, making her skirt swing and her breasts tremble. The sweatshirt said University of California. She was pushing a pram with small wheels and striped canvas, collapsable with the handles turned away, coated in red plastic, carrying a child, perhaps a year old. A shopping bag hung round the left handle. *Robertson's Jam*, it said. *Look For The Golly*. Her jeans were tucked into brown, knee-high boots, she wore no make-up, a little eye-shadow and the trace of a tan.

I stared as she approached, all the way down the street. There was no hint of recognition. As she came closer I smiled.

143

She must have thought I was trying to pick her up. I said, 'Hello, Judy,' but she kept going, eyes like stones. She walked down the High Street and as she turned into Strawberrybank she glanced back. I was sure I'd lose her, so I ran up to Market Street and round Cathedral Square looking in shops, but she was gone; as if I'd never seen her.

And all that long ago when I left her I figured part of me would stay with her, that I would spend my life looking as ghosts are supposed to do. This evening at tea-time, somewhere on the High Street, just before you turn into Strawberrybank, not too far from where I lost it, I found it again.

I suppose I have loved what women offered, rather than who or what she is. In my mind I am compiling a saga where I am hero and she is a character.

Judy, away from her time and place, her mum and dad, would cease to be the Judy I had loved. Or so I figured until today. For sitting here remembering, compiling and attempting truth, it is as though the encounter has become less real, as though it happened on a mythological level, as if it was a riddle.

And though it may be an illusion, I cannot rid myself of the need to decipher my existence.

Ten

Television brought carnage into our homes, as though the Vietnam War had been staged for the news teams.

'It's a disgrace,' said Mother.

'How often do you ask yourselves what this conflict is about?' said Cammy. 'How often is the word money mentioned? The only thing we hear about is the Domino Theory, as if it was a game.'

'You can switch the damned thing off as far as I'm concerned,' said Father. 'I don't care if I never see anything about Vietnam or anywhere else for that matter.'

'No sense of anything beyond your own front door,' said Cammy.

Father smiled at him. It seemed he would say something, but he went to his room. These past few weeks he had looked tired, grey and yawning, listless.

'I ought to stop doing that,' said Cammy.

'Doing what?'

'Goading him.'

'It's disgraceful,' said Mother.

'Sorry,' said Cammy.

'You ought to sue whoever cut your hair. It's a damned disgrace.'

'I cut my own hair.'

'In that case you're even dafter than I thought.' She ran her hand around his hair. 'It was nice when you were a baby,' she said.

His appearance had changed, as though he had lost interest.

'It's the same with dentists and opticians,' he said. 'A dentist will fill teeth that don't need filling and an optician will give you glasses whether you need them or not. It's capitalism,

Mother. All part of the system. Private enterprise. Making you buy things you don't need.'

'That's terrific, son, and so's your solution; walk about blind and bald and gumsy. You've got them on the run, it's a matter of time, they won't be able to recover from a body blow like that.'

'Who does this remind you of?' Cammy asked me.

'Mother.'

'Me too. Great, isn't it.'

'I feel like myself again,' she said. 'But it never lasts.' She switched on the television. 'I was thinking just the other night, all those bank robberies seem to have died down, or maybe they're not reporting them so much, maybe they think folk are fed up hearing the same old stuff week after week, so they give us a different News.'

Cammy went into the kitchen. Mother looked at me. 'How's Whatshername?' she asked.

'Judy.'

'How's Judy?'

'She's fine. I haven't seen her for a day or two.'

'Does she and Whatshername still go to their wee sewing bee?'

'It's a woman's meeting.'

'That's right, a wee social.'

'I think they still go.'

'Do you know? she asked and stared at the television. She didn't speak till the programme was finished.

'I was talking to you, wasn't I?'

'It's all right.'

'It's all right for you, but what about me?' She turned to the wall. 'See what I mean, I'm all right for a wee while, then it's back again, worse than ever it was. What month is this?'

'August.'

'Some time before Christmas, or maybe it was Easter, I went to the doctor. I thought it was the pills, then I thought it was my head, then I didn't know what it was. Have I told you this before? I can never remember. I told him I wanted something for my memory. He laughed at me. "You can't get a pill to give you a new brain," he said. "I knew that before I came here," says I. "If you're having trouble with your present prescription, don't take it," says he. I'll cut a long story short because I can't remember it anyway; the pills that were supposed to calm me were making me more agitated. I had an awful job coming off them, but no one noticed because my mind's away. It isn't there any more. My memory left me.'

She looked at me and said good-night. That look; trying to explain something she didn't understand with the wisp of a smile trailing the corners of her mouth.

'It's my head,' she said. 'It's my head. Have you ever thought what it's like to lose your mind? And I'm worried about your father. He'll be sleeping in front of the fire in that room of his. He's not well and every time I mention it he just about snaps the head off me.'

'Do you want me to talk to him?'

'If you would, Phamie, I mean Cameron, I mean Debbie. Angus. Oh my God.'

I took a cup of tea into Dad's room. He was sleeping in front of the fire. 'Must have dropped off,' he said. He drank the tea and stared at the fire. I rose to go. Long silences were common between us.

'You know your mother's losing her mind?'

'She's worried about you.'

'It's her who needs looking after. She needs proper care and attention. She thinks I don't know, but she's been to the doctor and she's going to the hospital in a day or two.'

'She tells me you're more tired than usual.'

'Old age.' He said it glibly, the only explanation needed.

Cammy's room was empty. I took a book from the shelf and went downstairs.

'Is that you, Phamie?' Mother shouted as I passed her door.

'It's me.'

'Good. Come here a minute. I don't want you worrying about me. I'll get my memory back. I know I will. If it's the last thing I do, I'll get it back. You mark my words. Now put the light off and tell your father to come to bed.'

I sat reading in the living room till Phamie came home. 'How's things?'

She shook her head.

'Did you go to your meeting?'

'I left early.'

'Why?'

'A man.'

'That's great, Debbie.'

'No it isn't. I went to tell him I never want to see him again. People look at my face and think it tells them what I'm like inside. It doesn't,' she said. 'It doesn't and I wish it did.'

'Do you want to talk about it?'

'Not really.'

'Sorry.'

'Stop apologising. It isn't your fault. Why do men always apologise. He was the same. He kept apologising. "Would you like this?" he'd say; "Don't you want to go here or there?" so's I'd make the decisions for him. And if I'd say no, he'd start apologising. He kept coming over as nice and reasonable, kind, considerate, you know the sort, someone who doesn't exist, and all the time he was incapable of making a decision for himself. Not that it was all his fault. I don't suppose I'll ever have a proper relationship with a man.'

Greyness settles around the past. Time removes colour and all things become shades of the same thing; a little like pigeons who scurry away on pink toes or jump into the air just when you think you can touch them, or a line of crows on a fence, a sudden noise and they scatter like seeds in the air.

All I have of my past is stored in a friable memory. Things happen and as they happen you know you'll remember them. Never the big things, never the important events, but small and silly things, a glance, a smile or a touch. And because that's all you've got to go on, memories crowd together, become confused and merge into a bigger memory.

148

So this is a night and a morning. It could easily be a year and a day.

Debbie came into my room. She said, 'Night-night,' turned at the door and smiled.' I wouldn't mind sleeping with you,' she said.

And we were all night whispering. 'This is getting serious.'

'What would they say if we told them we want to get married?'

'At least I wouldn't have to change my name.'

And the next thing she said was that Cammy had forgotten his key. The doorbell was ringing. I went downstairs.

'Does Cameron MacPhail live here?'

'Yes.'

'Can we speak to him?'

'He isn't in.'

'How do you know, sir?'

'He wasn't here last night.'

'Would you mind if we had a look?'

'Who are you?'

'I am Detective Inspector Thomson and this is Detective Sergeant MacGuire.'

'It's half-past six in the morning.'

'It won't take a minute, sir.'

They looked in Cammy's wardrobe and under his bed.

'You the fuzz?' asked Debbie when they came downstairs.

'Sorry if we've troubled you.'

'What do you want him for?'

'I'm sorry, we cannot comment at this stage.'

'I'm not asking you to comment. I want to know what the hell you're doing here and why you're looking for my brother.'

'We're pursuing our inquiries.'

'And what happens if he comes back?'

'It's very unlikely he'll get back here without us knowing, sir.'

'What's this all about?'

149

'Sorry, miss, we can't say. You'll find out soon enough. Sorry to have troubled you.'

Birds were singing and the sun was bright. The street was deserted. They walked down Cuchullain Avenue and turned the corner out of sight.

'Fuck me blind,' said I.

'If you like,' said Debbie.

'What was that all about?'

'No idea, but I liked your offer.'

I was late for work. 'Your father didn't come to bed last night,' said Mum, wondering how to butter toast.

'He must have done,' said I, looking for a necktie.

'It's all right,' said Debbie. 'I'll take you to the hospital.'

'How do you know I'm going to hospital?'

'You asked me what the pink card was for; the appointment's at ten.'

After work I went round to Judy, who asked if I was seeing someone else.

'What makes you say that?'

'You're half-asleep.'

'I was wakened at half-past six this morning. The police were looking for Cammy.'

We had the place to ourselves. Her mother was working and her father was drinking.

'Apart from that, I don't feel too great. I think I've got the flu coming on.'

'There's a bug going round. I think you ought to go to bed.'

'You're right. I should go home.'

'That wasn't what I had in mind.'

And later by the fire watching the News (the Russians had invaded Czechoslovakia, Alexander Dubcek had disappeared), 'This is just like being married,' she said.

'I don't know. I've never been married.'

'You know what I mean.'

'No I don't.'

'What's wrong, Angus?'

'Nothing. That's not true; I've got things on my mind. I'm

150

worried about Cammy. I think he's in trouble. Well, I know he's in trouble, but I don't know what the trouble is.'

'I don't just mean tonight. It's been happening for a while. You used to say you wanted to get married, you said you wanted children and I thought you meant it.'

'I did mean it; but there are other things we ought to take into consideration.'

'Like what?'

'Our age, for one thing. I'm not really settled into my career. I might change. I could do something else. Banking isn't all that wonderful. I rather fancy doing something like medicine or architecture. I could still go to university. Anything, Judy. Anything.'

'Just because you want to do something else doesn't mean we can't get married. I would work. I'd support you. Dad says you don't want to marry me.'

'You know that isn't true.'

'No I don't. I've got to ask you to come to bed with me.'

'We haven't been making love –'

'Correct.'

'Because it hasn't been convenient.'

'What kind of word is that? You used to grope me on buses. You used to get me to sit opposite you and –'

'Judy.'

'Didn't you?'

'Uh-hu.'

'Was that convenient?'

'Convenient's the wrong word.'

'What's the right word, Angus?'

'There hasn't been an opportunity.'

'Do you remember what happened at Dave and Ann's party? You took me into a cupboard and –'

'I know.'

'Underneath the stairs. Anybody could have walked in. And what about the time I was cleaning the windows? I was talking to Mrs McIvor and you came up behind me.'

'You said you liked that.'

151

'I did. My complaint is that it hasn't happened for a while. And what about the time we went to Edinburgh? On the train. I was stuck in the lavatory for half an hour before you knocked three times on the door. Then there was the bother of someone waiting outside.'

If I imagined anything it was to compare myself with a musician who couldn't concentrate on the emotional content until he had mastered technique.

'What would happen if your old man caught us?'

'He didn't complain last time.'

And so on. When I got home, Phamie was sitting by the fire.

'How's Jude?'

'Pissed off with me.'

'What else is new.'

'I sometimes find it difficult adjusting to the permissive society I'm supposed to have generated.'

'You sound like Cammy. Something goes wrong and you blame society.'

'That's what Judy said. I think I need to lie on my own back for a change. Anyway, how did you get on?'

'The doctor was cheery. He wanted to take me to some dance or other. Can you imagine it?'

'You might have had a good time.'

'He was married.'

'How about Mum?'

'She'll never become a Granny-in-the-Corner; his phrase, not mine. He suggests she carries a notebook around to jot down whatever it is she can't remember. Mum asked him how she's supposed to remember the notebook; then she told him she'd forgotten how to write and that was the end of him. She's spent the whole evening making up labels to stick on coffee jars, sugar bowls and so on. Here.'

She handed me a gummed label. *This is milk. It comes from a cow and goes into everyone's tea except Angus but it goes into everyone's coffee which is made with hot water but can also be made with milk which can be drunk on its own hot or cold though it's better hot especially at bedtime mixed with chocolate.*

152

The door bell rang.

'Can we speak to Mr Angus MacPhail, please.'

'That's me.'

'It's Angus MacPhail senior we want.'

'What do you want him for?'

'We'd like a word, sir, if you don't mind.' Detective Inspector Thomson raised his voice, enough to make it chillier.

'He isn't in.'

'I feel I ought to tell you, sir. This is very serious. The house has been under surveillance for some time. In fact, it's surrounded as we speak. My men are all down the street. Detective Sergeant MacGuire is watching from the bedroom opposite and this is Detective Sergeant Boyle.'

'How do you do.'

'Detective Sergeant Boyle is very well, sir. He is also armed, as are all my men. I think we'd better come inside, if you don't mind. And I think you'd better get your father.'

'If the house has been under surveillance, how come you don't know where my brother is?'

We stood in the living room. 'We'll sit down, sir, if you don't mind. And we'd advise you to do the same. You're going to be seeing quite a lot of us over the next little while and in my experience it's always best if people in our position are at least civil to each other.'

'If you can't answer my more complicated questions, perhaps you can at least give me a clue as to what's going on.'

'It's about your brother, sir.'

'I guessed that.'

'He's been arrested and charged.'

'What with?'

'Bank robbery, sir. Quite a few of them. We know of fifteen, but suspect there are others.'

'Jesus Christ.'

And Phamie screamed.

She had found her father slumped in his arm chair. He'd had his first heart attack.

153

Eleven

Rain.

And the suburbs' finest hour.

If the soul of a nation is present in its literature, then consider *Great Expectations* without rain. Imagine *Wuthering Heights, King Lear, The Tempest* or *Tess of the D'Urbervilles* midst a flurry of sunshine; consider the opening words of *Jane Eyre*: 'There was no possibility of taking a walk that day.'

We have more euphemisms for rain than for lavatories.

Father was propped up in bed, two pillows behind him; an unopened book on his lap, he was staring out the window.

'Would you look at it,' he said. The forecast had said Changeable. 'Forms pretty patterns on the windows.' He sighed.

'What did he say?' I asked. Dr Patel came every day. He usually found an excuse to be passing.

'He said I'm depressed.'

'Yeah. He told me depression is a common accompaniment to heart disease.'

'Bet it cost them thousands to find that out and I could have told them for nothing. I didn't even need Dr Patel to tell me. I knew what it was before he came.'

'Can I get you anything?'

'A new body.'

He watched the rain slide down the window. I stood for a while, wishing there was something to say, unable to move through the silence. The longer I stood, the more awkward it became till I could neither stay nor go, but fled the room, angry at my incapabilities while he stared out the window.

Mother was sitting by the fire, her legs mottled with heat, playing with the loose threads of her apron. 'How is he?'

'He's fine, Mum. Sends his love.'

'Is his cold any better?'

'A little.'

'If I've told him once, I must have told him a hundred times not to go out without his scarf. And we haven't seen Cameron for a while. Has he gone hiking with his chums?'

'He'll be back tomorrow.'

'Good.' She switched on the television set and stared at the wall.

In the weeks after Cammy's arrest, as we slid through winter and into spring, my sister and I had a lot to explain to ourselves. We poked around, looking for clues, though we'd no idea what we needed.

Our lives were distorted beyond recognition. For weeks we had policemen scuttling over the house. They stripped us room by room, they lifted floorboards and prodded ceilings. They reduced the place to its walls and turned us into celebrities. They were very efficient and spoke with a clipped courtesy, especially when they refused to do the only thing we asked, which was to keep the press away.

Notes were pushed through the letterbox. The amounts offered for our collective story more than doubled what Cammy had been charged with stealing. Every newspaper carried stories about the dedicated professional who idolised Stalin, the loner who studied political theory, the suburban student who worked for a national revolution and so on. When they weren't sneering they were scared and Cammy was found guilty long before he appeared in court.

Dad seemed surprised at his ability to frighten us. Mum became more aware of herself. As her mind crumbled, she developed a sensitivity to our changing moods. Dad's attack, Cammy's arrest and the press stake-out confused her. Dr Patel suggested she go into hospital, which turned out to be worse. When she came home we were told she would resettle herself as our lives were restored to sanity. But she never regained anything she'd lost; rather, she became gentler, and the saddest things were the occasional flashes of her old self, which always gave us hope.

155

Phamie and I talked about everything. We needed each other. Meals became an important part of our day. Mother ate sitting by the fire, Father in his bedroom picked at his food and complained, but Phamie and I ate together, sometimes reading, listening to the radio or just mooching away at breakfast.

She was the first to realise the necessity of change. Three days after Cammy's arrest, while Dad was in intensive care and Mum's mind was being studied, Phamie phoned her guru Phan Huan Quat. She was on to Paris for half an hour, then brought camomile tea into the sitting room.

'You okay?'

And with the press cars lined outside, our house in darkness, blinds drawn and the telephone off the hook, Phamie sat in front of the fire rolling joints. The police were guarding our front and back doors. I didn't ask where the dope came from, nor how she'd hidden it. We lit one each and stared at the fire.

'The last straw came when he wanted me to change my name,' she said. 'I've got three names already and he wanted to call me Li. I told him that was it. No more names.'

'Are you going to get another guru?'

'Right now we need a doctor and a lawyer.' She paused, her head to one side. 'I think I've changed,' she said. 'How about you?'

So our days divided into a pattern. Phamie stayed at home while I went to work. The bank gave me time off and said they were sympathetic. The trouble started after the trial.

The first time I went to see them was to discuss Father with the Personnel Officer, a tall, thin man with shifty eyes. His hair was combed straight back across his head in an effort either to acquire or omit traces of a personality. He looked incapable of making a decision. A good front-man who coughed a lot.

'From what we hear, your father isn't going to be himself for quite some time and I'm sure this other business has been very trying. And your mother isn't too well either; dearie me.

I know you can hardly be bothered with this sort of thing just now, but there are a number of schemes available.'

He handed me a leaflet.

'Take a look at that and see how you feel. Your parents could go and live in the sunshine, Portugal, Spain, Italy, anywhere they liked really; or, there are places in England which they could rent on a timeshare basis, five, six weeks in the year if they want to. There are lots of timeshare schemes.'

He gave me another leaflet.

'I think it's something for you to consider.'

I left with a variety of alternatives, all offering retirement and continuing health. 'They're paying me off,' said Father. 'I'm unreliable now and so is my family.'

'Not at all, you're just depressed.'

'Yeah, it's the depression that does it.'

'It could be the start of a new life.'

'You sound like an insurance salesman. I used to have a life, Angus. Why should I want a new one? The old one suited me fine.'

'You know what I mean.'

'But you don't know what I mean. And neither do they. I don't think anyone knows what I mean, not even Dr Patel, though, Allah be praised, he has tried. I don't need this nonsense. I don't need a holiday in Spain. I need a new body. I don't need something which helps me pretend the old one's all right when I know it isn't. This one is tired. It needs a rest. It's used up, a bit like a motor car. They're not too great at first, need to run in, then they'll do for a few years. After that they need minor adjustments, but the killer's built into the system, planned obsolescence. Away you go and leave me in peace and take these silly forms with you.'

I brought the subject up again and he ignored me. I accused him of self-pity, resentment and sentimentality. 'Correct,' he said. 'All three and some more besides. Now, can I have a cup of tea, a little milk but no sugar, and a sticky bun, please.'

Weeks later, just before the trial and apropos of nothing, he said, 'It's this place, son. It grips you. If you're going, you've got to do it while you're young. I'm split down the middle, like everyone else around here. I am appalled at how trite, banal words and tunes can cause a patriotic sun to rise in my breast. Nowadays, it can even bring tears to my eyes, but that's the Valium. The place distresses me, the people annoy me and their subservience affronts me. I hate the way authoritarianism is drummed into every schoolchild, so we respect and even fear people who should be our servants, people like school-teachers, politicians, doctors, clerks at the labour exchange, shop assistants, bus conductresses for God's sake, to say nothing of the police or the law or anyone with an upper-class English accent, the people who ought to be chased within an inch of their lives, the people who sold us, continue to sell us, those who live off the backs of the poor, who blame their own ills and society's ills on people who cannot defend themselves and take their own lives as a yardstick as to how everyone else should live, the class who owe everything to the folk they despise. And more than any of that, I hate the God-forsaken church of whatever shade. The fact that it still exists in this country is an affront to us. These bastards helped our betters clear the glens, they banned colour and they banned music, they banned life, banned theatre and had us transported and they'd do it again if they thought we'd wear it, these ministers who apologise or try to contain, explain and thereby reduce to their own level a man like Robert Burns. What frightens me is that some folk would welcome it. They are beneath contempt and so are the apologists, of which we have many. But don't ask me to go, don't ask me to leave. I can't, can't do it. It's impossible. I love the place. And like any love that's worth anything I cannot tell you why it exists. I can tell you there's something in the way the light crosses the landscape, the way the hills change colour, the way the sky changes; or I could talk about the scenery. But it isn't one thing, it's many things; a compound, same as the hate. It forces me to acknowledge it and when I do that I am forced to stay. I love it the way you love a woman because of the wrinkles around her eyes. I'm not going. You'll have to bury me here.'

My father used to flick his hair from his forehead by throwing back his head. It was an unexpected movement, like the way he'd crack his knuckles or tap his teeth with his fingernails.

'Did you hear that God and Jesus were sitting on a cloud,' he said. 'They were having a smoke. They'd made the world and were wondering what to do. "I know what," said God, "we'll make Scotland." "Good idea, Da," said Jesus. So they planned it out. "We'll make it a lovely place," said God. "We'll give them hills and valleys, long glens for sheep and cattle, high mountains and lochs to vary the landscape, rivers filled with fish. We'll put coal beneath the ground to heat them, give them a varied climate and the best farmland to grow their crops." "Sounds great," said Jesus. "Everybody will want to live there." "No they won't," said God. "Everyone will leave. Wait till you see their neighbours."

'Listen, son. The English didn't do it to us. We did it to ourselves. We betrayed ourselves.'

'What will I do with the forms?'

'Whatever you like. I don't care.'

'And what am I going to do with you?'

'Leave me in peace.'

In time he became a peaceful man, padding around the house or reading in his armchair. As his ghosts departed he played chess, did a little carpentry, worked in his garden and continued to read. Twice a week he walked the mile and a half to the library where he started on the Fiction shelves at the letter A and worked along from there. He read philosophy, though I don't think he finished a book. Midway through, he'd sigh: 'I doubt if that man lives in the same world as I do,' he'd say, or, 'Well, that's one way of looking at it.' He'd snap the book shut and return it next day.

In summer he went for long walks and in winter he stayed in his study. As his appearance changed, he began to look younger. He ceremoniously gave his suits and ties to jumble sales, but kept a grey herring-bone tweed suit and a dark blue knitted wool tie. He wore an old fawn cardigan and baggy

159

corduroys which crumpled round his woollen slippers, always down at the toe and heel, which he wore outdoors. 'If it's good enough for Auden, it's good enough for me,' he said.

After the second heart attack his hair turned white. He didn't speak for six days. On the morning of the seventh day, he asked the nurse for his clothes and signed himself out of hospital. Dr Patel told us the attack was, 'Very minor. Nothing to worry about.'

'A minor heart attack,' said Dad. 'Now I've heard everything.'

Within a month he was back to normal and again he changed. His eyes became kinder, there was a glaze across them which almost lightened their colour. He seemed at peace, or at least resigned. He replanned the garden, hired young men to do the digging and planting, then sat with catalogues working out what was going where and when it would blossom. He spent hours weeding, scraping and turning the soil or raking the paths, which made his complexion red then brown.

For days he wouldn't shave and he eventually grew a beard. Mother didn't recognise him. She'd say, 'Good morning, sir,' or ask if he was the doctor, the gasman, the plumber or whoever she thought should be there. Once he told her who he was: a fortnight after he stopped shaving, his beard was white and full, his hair was long and he looked like a distinguished man of letters or at least a retired journalist.

'Good morning, sir,' said Mother. 'Who are you?'

'I am your husband.'

'How dare you. My husband's a far younger man than you. My husband has dark hair. He works in a bank and doesn't have a filthy old beard. When he comes home tonight I'm going to tell him a dirty old man tried to accost me in my own house today. We'll see how he likes that. If I were you, I'd go immediately. My husband has a nasty temper.'

After that he said he was whoever she thought he was, often asking, 'Who am I today, dear?'

'You are the man from the school board, though why

160

you're here I can't imagine. There are no nits in my children's hair.'

They developed a new intimacy and tenderness, often becoming openly affectionate, holding hands and touching, especially when he read to her. He'd fumble with his wire specs and read in a clear, loud voice, giving each character a different accent and displaying a theatrical sense of timing, especially when he read Sheridan Le Fanu, whom Mother loved. They read a lot of Dickens, most of Tolstoy, some Mark Twain, Ambrose Bierce, Thomas Hardy, Sir Walter Scott and everything by his favourite writer Robert Louis Stevenson. While they were reading *Kidnapped*, three, four times a day Mother would ask if it was time for her story. He was reading *Master of Ballantrae* when he died.

The last years seemed peaceful, yet there must have been a restlessness, an appalling loneliness about him. I could see how much he'd changed from the man who'd brought us up. Occasionally he contracted an old man's panic: 'Nothing much,' he'd say. 'A little gripe around the heart, that's all; the knowledge that you are physically unequal to whatever task is offered, too weak and far too tired.' Then he smiled apologetically, a smile we'd never seen before, a smile that made him old.

His desperation betrayed him when he lectured us, as though he had so much to pass on and so little time to do it, his time gathered like dust on a window-ledge.

'What difference does it make? None, providing you don't care about yourself, who you are, where you've come from or where you're going. It's a simple enough, honest emotion, which has been cheapened into sentiment. Ask an Englishman what difference it makes to him. If all you're talking about is national achievement, then you are no better off. You ally yourself with whatever you think is greatness and ignore the rest. That's the basis of Fascism. But if your nation has been conquered and then obliterated, all you're left with is an idea, a state of mind.

'And Scottishness is a state of mind,' he said. 'It comes from the fact that we are an occupied territory, and that, more than anything else, gives us an identity. We feel independent. We know we are different, but we are also dependent, which makes us assert our independence aggressively because it's a feeling, a spiritual feeling with no other outlet. And we are sufficiently unsure of ourselves to pretend neither the aggression nor the independence exists. We are a nation of extremists. Born losers. If we're pessimistic it's because we've been beaten so often, which makes our victories memorable. Because our history is little more than a survey of injustices, God knows how many old scores we've got waiting to be settled. Maybe every country feels the same. I've often wondered what it would be like to be a Pole for example, or a Czech, maybe even a Basque or a Georgian with their solipsistic nationalism. But *Dr Jekyll and Mr Hyde* was written by a Scot. And it doesn't mention history, but either ignores it or takes it for granted, which is ironic when you consider it's why the tourists come. Americans, Australians, Canadians, New Zealanders all come here because of our sense of history. They've none of their own. They destroyed it. Jesus. It must be nice to have only two hundred years of history to worry about.'

The beginning of March 1969, and the Apollo 9 mission. Television news showed the same set of pictures with a bleeping commentary. Russell Schweikart crawled from the command ship, through a 39-inch-wide docking tunnel into the lunar module. An American first. He was later joined by Colonel James McDivitt. They spent seven hours in the module and sent a live TV transmission back from space.

'God,' said Phamie. 'Who'd have believed it?'

During the occupation no attempts was made to conceal the fact that our letters were opened and obviously read. A policeman delivered our mail every second or third day, tied into a bundle with two red elastic bands. We had to sign a receipt book, witnessing the letters had arrived safely and absolving the police from all blame, just in case.

As we watched the spacemen flicker on television, I went through the week's letters. Nothing personal, except a small white envelope in a staggered hand and a folded sheet of middling-to-good foolscap with a drawing of a woodland knoll in springtime and a Victorian child picking armfuls of flowers, which weren't in the drawing. 'I can't phone you. Your number's engaged. Why don't you phone me?' was the message.

'You take me for granted,' she said.

'In what way?'

'A typical reply. Don't deal with what I'm saying; ask a question to give you time to think. For one thing you assume I'll always be here, for another you assume I will do whatever you want me to do. We hardly go out any more, I know there are special circumstances, but you could let me help with whatever's going on. I'm separate, Angus. All right, I know, I was out last week and two weeks before that.'

'I've seen you more than that.'

'Sure. You come round to complain. You tell me what's wrong with my life and what I can do about it; then you tell me what's wrong with your life and how you can't do anything about it because you're an orphan. Then you want to know why you were adopted when you were twelve years old. Angus, I'm supposed to be your girl-friend, not your analyst or a clairvoyant.'

'What's made you so bolshie?'

'Nothing.'

'Nothing?'

'Nothing much.'

'Where is he?'

'God knows.'

'Did he collect his wages?'

'At lunchtime and he hasn't been seen since.'

'What time is it now?'

'Ten past nine.'

'Where should I look?'

'Guess.'

163

Heenan's bar was as good as any. Judy's father stood by the door, singing a song with no words.

'Tell him to shut up,' shouted a barman.

Jimmy swayed, nursing a glass and a trickle of beer, his head on his chest.

'How's things, Jimmy?'

He didn't speak.

'Judith's worried about you.'

He tried to focus and dropped his head again.

'What do you say we go home?'

He couldn't co-ordinate speech, but nodded his head.

'You with him?'

Two barmen were standing between us and the door. Jimmy tried to lift his head.

'Get him to fuck out of here. He's been here all day. Time he was home. Look at the fucken state he's in.'

'I'm just taking him home.'

'Jesus Christ, he's pissed himself.'

Jimmy lifted his head. A barman hit him and the other kicked him on the way down, then with an arm each they used his head as a battering ram to open the swing doors.

'He's waiting.'

'You get him and yourself to fuck out of here. And tell him he's barred.'

Jimmy was sitting on the pavement, crying. His head was bleeding and he tried to stand. 'What's wrong?' he asked. 'What's the matter with me?'

The bar wouldn't let me use the phone, but the all-night Pakistani grocer made the call for me. An ambulanceman asked: 'Can he walk?'

'I think so.'

'If he gets violent, he's out.'

Alcoholics never admit to drinking from necessity; and their justifications are always dressed in clothes of fancy reasoning.

In the casualty department with other catastrophes gathered around the room, Jimmy stared at the floor. 'I'm not as bad as

164

some people,' he said. 'Some people can't leave the stuff alone. I can take it or leave it.'

'Has this happened often, Jimmy?'

'Never.'

'Well, the admissions nurse knew you. And the doctor. When I phoned home, Judith said, "Not again." And another doctor said it was nice to see you'd made it with someone other than a policeman.'

'They've mixed me up with someone else.'

'Judith's mum's gone to stay with her sister.'

'Aye. She's having a wee break.'

'She gave me this number.' I put a slip of paper into his top pocket: 041 332 3742.

'You next, Jimmy?' asked the nurse.

Judy was waiting. 'How did it go?' she asked.

'Fine,' said Jimmy, as though he'd been visiting a friend in hospital.

'How many stitches this time?'

'Four.'

'What happened?'

'I can't remember.'

'At least you weren't jailed. The last twice he's landed in jail. He thinks he's a hard man and starts throwing his weight around. He's got a face full of second prizes. And guess who has to go down and bail him out.'

'Make us a cup of tea, hen.'

'Make it yourself.'

'That's no way to talk to your father.'

'Don't give us it. If Angus wasn't here you'd be belting me around the place. Or Mum. Why do you think she's at Aunt Margaret's? And why did she want me to go with her. Look at yourself. Go on. Look. You're pathetic. You're not my father. You don't even look like him. You're just a man who lives here, who sponges off us, contributes nothing, swears and shouts and drinks too much.'

'Now you see what you're marrying,' said Jimmy, though he didn't look at me.

165

'Angus knows. So do all my friends. Why do you think I don't bring them here any more.'

'I'm going to bed.'

'You're on the couch tonight. That way I'll get some peace. I don't want to be bothered with your three o'clock tribunals and you won't be able to climb the stairs.'

As soon as the door to her room was shut she stretched her arms. 'Hold me,' she said. 'Jesus. Come here and hold me.'

'What's wrong?'

'I'm scared. I've never spoken to him like that before. I could only do it because you were here. I knew he wouldn't hit me. Now you know why I want to get out of here, why I want to get married.'

'I thought there was another reason.'

'Of course there is. But I've made my mind up, Angus. I want to get married. I want a home and I want a family. Every month when my period comes I think, What a shame. I'm not pregnant. Is there anything wrong with wanting these things?'

'It's all right, Jude. I know.'

'Sure. You know. But you're doing nothing about it. I'm always pressing you. It ought to be the other way round.'

Two hours later I was walking home in the rain. We'd made love, more a loss of energy than a climax. And we lay listening to the rain.

'I don't know what's going to happen to me,' she said. 'I don't want to be like Debbie and I don't want to be like my Mum. That group Debbie had was full of women who locked themselves in a room, smoked thousands of fags and could only relate to each other. I felt like telling them about him downstairs, what he's like, not only to me, but to Mum as well. I thought of taking Mum along. I asked her, but she wouldn't go. I'd hate to marry a man who drank with my father, never mind drank like him. I can't tell you how much his performances have cost me. Look at those books. I hardly read anything now; women's magazines and that's about it. I work in a shop and the job bores me. And why do I work there? Because of him, because of my wonderful father who has taken away any drive or ambition I might have had. A shop assistant is all I'm good for; pays me money and we all need that, or so my old man'll tell you. I've had to look at me. I've had to look at my life and I don't like what I see. So I need a break and I'm beginning to believe I need a new start. I want away. What's the point in reading anything other than daft romances when all you're going to be is a shop assistant or a housewife.'

Jimmy heard me on the stairs and opened the living room door. He was trembling. Every two or three seconds he scratched another part of his body.

'Can't stand this,' he said. 'I can't go on with this. Never again. This is the terror time. Fucken shakes. Look at them. Next you start seeing things. Or maybe you only think you see them or else you see them in the corner of your eye. That's worse. I used to think I could stop the shakes with will power, strength or something. Light us a fag, will you?'

I put a cigarette in his mouth. It trembled. 'Will power's no good for anything,' he said. 'If I try to stop the shakes they get worse. They go into your arms and your whole body gets it. Get us a drink, son. A drink will cure it.'

'It was drink that caused it.'

'Don't you start lecturing me as well. I phoned the number you gave me. Somebody's coming.'

A rat in a corner trembles because it wants to live. I walked home in the rain, thinking of *Bleak House* when the waters were out in Lincolnshire, how the world was created in water and flooded in *Mill On The Floss*.

I was almost asleep. Phamie came into my room, sat on the bed and we drank the camomile tea she'd brought.

'Debbie, will you tell me something?'

'Sure.'

'I want to know how I arrived here. I want to know why Mum and Dad wanted another child, especially a twelve-year-old boy who'd been brought up in a home.'

'I've no idea.'

'Don't you now?'

'No. But that reminds me, though I don't know why it should. I'm pregnant.'

I did not want to know this. It seemed no part of me, another kind of burden. And as my mind rejected it, a question was forming. 'You heard,' she said, knowing the question. She shrugged. 'I thought you might be pleased.'

'I am.'

'You might show it.'

'Whose is it?'

She smiled. 'Some guy's,' she said.

Twelve

Sunday, June 1:

I realise this Miranda affair, which is what things were before they became relationships, must end.

Perhaps one of us is coming to our senses. But how long can we be sensible?

The most obvious thing would be if she was transferred to another branch. It would be awful working with her after things had ceased to be what they once had been. But how could I agree to transfer her? So much for sense, doesn't last long around here, melts like snow off a dyke.

I am writing this down because I want to remember it. I want to look back in twenty years' time. In fact, I look forward to the possibility of forgetting this ever existed.

Now I'm late for church and Helen's calling.

Fuck.

I wish I knew why I was going. Douglas Strachan's invited us. And to make matters worse, I accepted.

Later. Evening.

All through the service, I thought of Miranda. Strachan came back here with Helen's parents. We ate roast beef and two veg and we did the *Sunday Post* Quiz, after which the talk was coy and cosy. I felt like an intruder in my own home. I don't think they excluded me. I rather suspect I excluded myself.

Monday, June 2:

I phoned. She answered.

'It's you.'

Hardly encouraging, especially when one remembers the responses I used to get.

'Can I see you at lunchtime?'

'No.'

'Why not?'

'Shopping.'

'But this is important.'

'What makes you think my shopping isn't important?'

But she agreed to see me, having made it sound like a concession, an interruption to an otherwise busy schedule, the way you alter your routine to visit a friend who's been rushed to hospital.

'I haven't got much time,' she said. 'What do you want?'

'Have you eaten? Do you want a drink? Or some coffee?'

'That's not what you want to see me about, is it?'

'Not really, but I thought that since we were here we might as well be sociable.'

'You're jealous again, aren't you?' she said.

'The book hasn't been going well.'

'The book hasn't been going at all. Not so much a novel, more a source of guilt. And, as your father said, guilt rhymes with kilt.'

'What does my father have to do with this?'

'Nothing, apart from the fact that you're trying to emulate him, trying to prove you're something other than his adopted son. Honestly, Angus. There are times when your head's made of glass, and not because it's fragile.'

'One of your more annoying habits is the constant ability to take a choice phrase of mine and repeat it back to me in wholly inappropriate circumstances. It's quite flattering, but rather tiresome.'

'In that case, you'll be happy to hear you won't need to put up with it much longer.'

'What do you mean?'

She handed me a 9x4–inch white envelope, bank stationery.

'I'd like you to pass this on to headquarters for me. I'd also like you to read it and to send an accompanying note, giving your approval and asking that the request be met.'

'I don't know what to say.'

170

'Say nothing. It's easiest. You've said too much already, said too much and done nothing. We can't go on like this.'

'If it's about Helen –'

'Who's Helen? It has nothing to do with Helen. It's you.'

'What have I done now?'

'Absolutely nothing; not what I expected you would do very much. I gave as much as I could and you took it, every last bit. You've no idea, Angus. No idea at all. You don't know what it's like for me. I've told you, but you choose to ignore it or else you reckon it will go away or that something will happen to change it. Well, nothing's going to happen unless you make it happen. I can't live with the fact that you're seeing me, that you say you love me, that I know I love you and yet you continue living with another woman. I can no longer put up with the fact that when you leave me you're going to sleep with someone else. No, don't interrupt; it isn't just that. It's the things you share with her that you do not and cannot share with me, like your life. I don't want to say much more because I'll probably start crying.'

We walked to the door, ignoring the waitress who stared because we hadn't brought a drink: 'Enjoy your stay?' she muttered from the corner of her mouth.

We blinked in the sunshine. I wanted it to rain. Nothing fitted: the sun and the summer dresses, the indolent walk of women did not match my mood; the rolled-up shirt-sleeves and the men's eyes, darting like finches, seemed too remote from Miranda and what she was saying.

'What about Brian?'

'You were talking to him when I came in this morning.'

'And you were jealous?'

'Is that why you flirt with him?'

'I don't flirt with him.'

'Then what do you do?'

'Nothing. Brian's just a guy who works in the same building as I do. We're forced to spend some time in each other's company, earning money. If I wanted any of the things you think makes Brian so attractive, I am perfectly capable of finding them for myself. I don't need you to do it for me. But the fact of the matter is that Brian's a pain in the neck. He thinks every woman he tries to charm should go weak at the knees and fall into his arms with promises of undying love. The first day he arrived, the very first day he got there he made a bee-line for me and was chased, so he's been coming back ever since.'

'I've noticed.'

'What I find insulting is that you think I'm incapable of resistance. You give me no credit of having a mind of my own and of having my mind made up. I could have a dozen Brians; don't want them.'

'Then why are you going out with him?'

'We're having a drink on Friday night. I'm not going out with him.'

'Then why have a drink with him?'

'I thought it would divert attention from you and I. And it would certainly stop him from pestering me.'

'He doesn't know that.'

'I don't care what he knows. I'll get rid of him.'

'How?'

'I'll put a packet of Tampax at the top of my handbag and make sure he sees it.'

She walked away from me, crossed the street and got into a taxi. When I got back to the bank a girl told me Miss Morrison wouldn't be in this afternoon. She wasn't feeling well. 'She hasn't been feeling well all morning, sir,' she said. Miranda's desk was cleared.

Her letters were perfumed. I wondered why women perfume their letters and decided it didn't matter. I liked it.

Her first letter was an official, straightforward request for a transfer. Her mother was ill and Miranda felt it would be best if she was transferred to a branch nearer home. The lie was supported by a letter from her doctor. And there was a note, perfumed and written on pink paper. The perfume had spread to the other letters.

My Dear Angus:

I want you to know that I love you and, as far as I can tell, always will. But it cannot remain a secretive, one-sided relationship. I've got to hide how I feel at the bank and I can't even phone you at home to tell you how I feel. You've got to phone me. If I told my family, they'd hit the roof and my friends would feel sorry for me. My life revolves around you. I don't mind because I love you, but there must be more than this one-sided movement. I know you don't feel it's one-sided, but that's because you're on the good side. You have often spoken about Helen and how you feel. I know everything that's wrong with your marriage but don't know why or how you stay and, unless a move comes spontaneously from you, I cannot push it. You obviously have no desire to leave Helen. In fact, I think you are rather comfortable with things as they are just now, so I suppose Helen is a sort of security blanket for you, which doesn't leave me in a very good position. I've tried to be available, to be here when you need or want me, to be here when you're ready, but I can't wait for ever.

I'd like you to approve my transfer. The doctor is a friend of the family. I told him there was trouble at work, people I don't get on with, and he wrote the letter. It was nice of him. I feel rotten lying about Mum, but don't know what else to say.

Please remember I love you and am doing this because I love you. The last thing I want to do is to trap you or to make you do something you don't want to do or will regret later. That would be awful.

You've made me feel happier and better and cleverer and stronger and lovelier than I've ever felt before or will again. Lots of other things too.

Love,
Miranda.

My office is small and carpeted, with a bland wallpaper, a swivel chair and an upright wooden construction for visitors. I have a large wooden desk and a couple of filing cabinets. I was given a couple of prints for the walls and that's about it. My office could belong to anyone and contains nothing of me or anyone who comes into it.

If I swing my chair round to the window I get a view of the outside world, or I can pull the blinds. When I first came here, I didn't want to look out the window. The view was depressing, crumbling tenements and human carelessness, round-shouldered men and women with hopeless faces, their children growing stale. Those were in the days when I thought reality came from a television set or a newspaper, when I thought there was at least a choice, even though they were choices we could not remember making.

I don't know where the people have gone, those who used to live here, but I don't suppose their lives will have improved, will be as renovated as the place they left. I expect they're still around somewhere, mingling now with others like themselves, out of the city and out of sight. For the area was renewed. I have forgotten when, but I surely recorded such changes in my surroundings in this or another Diary. First to go were the people and last to go were the rats, or maybe they only mingled, moved out of sight. The people left, or were forced to go, and the buildings crumbled. They hung in the air like rotting teeth, a war-torn landscape around them, disintegrating shops and nothing to replace what was gone. The district was cancelled, it became redundant. The environment was killed and the evidence removed. For weeks I could not work because of the bulldozers, cranes and lorries. It was a time of long lunches and drawn blinds.

Then a new shape emerged. The place was being tarted up; there were signs of familiarity, yet there was a newness and the youthfulness had little or nothing to do with the district we had known. They stone-cleaned the remaining buildings, landscaped the back-greens and scattered a few concrete pots crowded with dahlias, roses, daffodils and lavender and little mounds of stones in a concrete setting, new walls and concrete benches. They gave us a little patio with a bronze sculpture of

174

something stretching towards something else. It's symbolic. I'd rather have it there than not; as I'd rather have the place now, synthetic and shedding its built-in decay, than have it as it was before, ruined and forlorn.

Now we're frightfully up-market; I'm dealing with more loans and overdrafts than I ever imagined I would be allowed to deal with. There are little shops, full of pretension and just right for the area. There are even a couple of restaurants. Business has expanded and I regularly expect to be moved. The branch is too important for me to handle, unless they've forgotten Cammy and his little escapade and all that happened then. It's possible; but I believe business institutions have a collective and lasting memory. They never forget and, unless you do as they want, you will never survive their system.

From my window I can see the little patio, the people moving around the shops, the lads with their sleeves rolled up and the girls in their summer dresses, the young mothers chatting and pushing their prams back and forward, rising mid-sentence to recapture a wobbly child, the old men and women sitting in the sun beside the sales representatives making out their call sheets and calculating expenses.

The sun disappeared and the day darkened to a single memory, lambent and thrilling. I close my eyes and see it still: a wee boy in a red jersey trying to catch a pigeon with his fishing net. He gave up, watched the pigeons settle and peck, then, with a wild-eyed yell, he charged. On the screen of my eyelids I see him now: red jersey and wellies, arms in the air, head back and the fishing net slicing the air behind him. And the pigeons with their wings stretched towards him in an upward flight.

I phoned headquarters and spoke to Personnel. I told them Miranda wanted a transfer. 'We know,' said a voice of honey, oil and insincerity. 'She's just left. She has explained the position fully to us. And her doctor has also phoned. We were going to speak to you tomorrow. I don't foresee any difficulties.'

175

'I'd be sorry to lose her.'

'You're not suggesting we refuse the transfer?'

'Not at all. Of course not. I simply wanted you to know she is very efficient.'

'I'm sure she is.'

'And I was phoning to suggest she ought to have some sort of promotion and if it could be combined with the transfer that would be wonderful. I would be prepared to offer whatever references were needed in that area.' There was silence. 'But that is hardly my affair and I don't suppose it's yours either.'

'Quite.'

'And she is attractive, which means she'll probably get married and prefer having babies to becoming a banker.'

'We find such a preference is not uncommon in young women.'

Miranda's number was engaged. 'The receiver has been incorrectly replaced,' said the operator.

So I went to her house, waited half an hour, rang the bell and regretted it immediately.

'Angus.' She shook her head. 'Please go away.'

'I want to talk to you.'

'There's nothing to say.'

'I've approved your transfer.'

'Thanks very much.'

'I also suggested you should get some sort of promotion.'

'Goodbye Angus.'

'Miranda, I love you.'

She closed the door.

Half an hour later she opened the door and got into the car. 'Drive,' she said.

I do not know where we went. During life's big moments, the body insists on trivialising the event by doing something irrelevant, as if to remind you it is more important than any scheme you could dream up, mocking life and setting it into its own proportion. So you need a piss during your wedding ceremony, your nose itches as your child's head pops into the

176

world or you think you are going to sneeze the first time you make love.

Miranda sat with her head down, staring at her knees as I drove. And I wanted her. I wanted the silly sexual innuendoes which accompany love or come from love and are often as much a part of love as the words themselves. I wanted to look at her, wanted to see her legs, to look up her skirt and see what happened after that, as if I couldn't guess, but it isn't always the same thing that happens, depends on how she's feeling; sometimes she likes it and sometimes she doesn't, sometimes she gets into it and becomes quite inventive, other times you know she's doing you a favour, doing something you like because you like it and for no other reason, though I hoped it would operate some sort of emetic of the body, mind and spirit.

'I suppose you want to screw me,' she said.

> *Kirkton Road*
> *past shops on rt.*
> *filling station on left*
> *roundabout*
> *right*
> *first left*
> *second right*
> *Number 23*
> *blue door*

Pox take Don Calder, if it hasn't already done so. I wish him herpes.

He phoned yesterday. I was enjoying a quiet Sunday afternoon. The rain poured down while I, snug as a dormouse, recorded the fictional minutiae of my daily life as Helen regaled The Mother with details of my pestilential habits while The Father and Strachan watched *She Wore a Yellow Ribbon* on telly. I only answered the telephone because I thought it was Miranda.

Calder's opening gambit: 'Did I disturb you?'

His car is going in for a service on Thursday and could I give him a lift to the golf course for our little game, which has incidentally been brought forward because of the holidays? Why couldn't I say: 'Sorry, old boy, no can do. Wife's having a hysterectomy. Rush job. You know the drill. Here today and gone tomorrow.'

'Tell you what,' says the lardy putrescence, 'why don't you pick me up at the house. It's easy to find.'

That was at five-thirty. I had tea and toast and raspberry jam. Today he phones with directions and I am distraught.

Miranda hasn't phoned. I have looked at my so-called novel and find it reminds me of Don Calder. It needs rewriting and the thought of such an undertaking scares me more than the thought of Sweet Jesus coming down from glory to reign, never mind the method of his arrival. The truth is that I have lately preferred my Diary to my Novel. Can it be that I now find the present more interesting than the past. Perish the thought.

I am bored with the whole venture, have whirlies in the gut, jingling nerves and a brain like a lump of smokeless coke in a solid fuel central heating system, burner at Mark 6. It's all very well to dream of books, but the fucken things have to be written.

> *Replace light bulb*
> *Polish shoes*
> *Do dishes*

Miranda at least has the grace to phone when I am almost finished. There was something else to add, though I cannot remember what it was.

'I thought you wouldn't phone.'

'Sorry.'

'It's okay.'

'I couldn't get to the phone myself. I had to make an excuse to get out.'

'Will I see you tomorrow?'

'You can see me right now if you like.'

'And tomorrow?'

'Lunch?'

'Sure.'

'Listen, Angus. I was thinking. I can't phone you at the bank and you can't phone me once I go to wherever it is they're going to send me. I should find out where that is tomorrow. They've been awfully good and I feel such a fraud.'

'Take it. Take all the time off they give you. I've been through all that. During Cammy's trial, when my mother died and all that, I thought, all the time I thought, I must get back to work. If I'd known what they were going to do I'd have stayed off longer, I'd have faked a nervous breakdown. Anything. You take whatever's going.'

'I will, darling. Believe me.'

'I don't mean it that way.'

'Hoped you might. But listen, how can I contact you?'

'We'll find a way.'

'I love you.'

'Must go. Helen's car.'

'Lunchtime?'

'Same time, same place.'

When Helen walked in, I was typing the above. 'You've been busy,' she said.

Helen calls. Must rush. Do as I am bidden. If I'm lucky, I may get an hour in the attic tonight. She's always tired after a visit to The Mother. What did they discuss when they saw each other yesterday? Hush. Paranoia, be still.

I don't believe this. She wants to know why I haven't replaced the light bulb in the hall, why I haven't done the dishes.

'Coming, dear.'

The difference between love and herpes is that herpes lasts forever.

Tuesday, June 3:

D. H. Lawrence weather.

179

Earlier this evening, around seven o'clock, I was in the attic. Things are pretty well organised up there. I have a table, a chair and a reading lamp. I have a kettle, coffee, mug and trimmings. I have a jam jar stuffed with pencils, a cardboard filing system, a notebook and a tray. I have three cardboard boxes, gum labels, folders and a marker. I have security and peace.

Until Helen disturbs me. 'We have a visitor,' she said, her head bobbing out of the trapdoor as she balanced on the Parkway ladder. 'He's from the church.'

Our visitor looked like Crippen, or the way I imagined Crippen when my mother used his name. For years I thought it was a Scots verb whose English equivalent was creeping.

'Would you like a cup of tea?' asked Helen.

'No thanks,' said I.

'I didn't mean you.'

'Who did you mean?'

'Our guest.'

'And can't I have a cup of tea?'

Crippen didn't stay long, which left us to our own company. 'We're always arguing,' I said.

'No, we're not.'

Me and my Diarism. Why do I record these conversations so faithfully; why bare my humiliation for posterity? My case rests upon the sure and certain knowledge that those who form an opinion of me from reading this will not believe it happened, that The Diary is a form of fiction.

And like a child who has discovered the joy of being naughty, I ran to phone Miranda. It has become much more clandestine. The arrangement is that she goes to a phone box at a pre-arranged time and rings the phone box I'm in, usually at eleven o'clock every night. If anything goes wrong, if something unexpected crops up, we ring the other's home phone twice.

'Brian phoned tonight,' she said.

'And what did he want?'

'Guess.'

'So what's happening?'

'Nothing.'

Walking home it occurred to me that I have been spared the usual costs of adultery. Restaurant bills, taxi fares, flowers, clothes, presents to patch up a quarrel, hotel rooms and theatre tickets which cement the affair have all been denied for the most part.

And when I got home Helen was making cocoa. I approached from behind. 'Don't,' she said. Nothing unusual in that.

'Why not?'

'I don't feel nice. I'm all sweaty.'

'I know. I love it.'

'I'm going to have a bath,' she said.

'I'll go in first. I need a slash.' I said it because I know she hates the word.

I spent an hour or two in the attic, though I am no longer sure why I am working, far less what I am supposed to be doing or what I am looking for, raking through boxes and folders, reflecting how prices have risen and times have changed.

Another fragment, I think of a letter, done on the old Underwood:

rather than English literature which draws a characteristic strength from its treatment of the human as a social being, its attempts to unravel the threads of society and from the way it depicts the conflicts that arise from individual desires and social demands; in other words, adultery in Dollis Hill.

The trouble seems to stem from the fact that when writers better themselves, their main theme becomes their own betterment, or a variant of Aladdin and his Wonderful Lamp, the story of Moses or Cinderella. It is essentially a middle-class view of life where the need to better oneself is seen as the need to become middle-class, to ignore or reject working-class values and traditions.

No wonder my first great identification was with the Americans, who not only manage to cover the range of their society, but almost always assume their reader is at least as intelligent and as sensitive as themselves, especially Steinbeck, whom I actively encouraged my children to read because he seems

I do not remember my father giving me anything to read, far less a book by an American writer. He told me Dickens was a hack, Lawrence at least understood passion though it frightened him, but that this century's greatest English writer was P. G. Wodehouse. Americans, he said, had removed purity from the language. To view the novel as a vehicle for class warfare, he said, was to ignore its other possibilities.

Dad and his letters, me and my Diary; me and my middle-class novel about adultery.

Wednesday, June 4:

This morning, sitting on the lavatory, reflecting on the sadness which has afflicted this country and would always be with us –

The above has been cancelled, consigned to the dustbin of redundant memories; fucked.

Another row disturbed my concentration, spoiled the flow and sent God-alone-knows what gem whirling off, undeveloped, into the jungle of raggedy-arsed dreams. I will not even do the row the honour of recording its progenesis, subject, development or even content. Let it also be consigned. Or added to the woodpile to be used as fuel.

Tuesday, June 5:

Above the stone fireplace is a picture of a flower lying on a stone step. We sat drinking instant coffee.

'That picture is very sad,' said Calder. 'Every time I look at that picture, I think it's very, very sad.'

On the way to the golf course he indicated our company of sportsmen would be one less. Andy Simpson, a nice man who always spoke in terms of his career, would not be joining us. He's been moved to another branch.

'You know how it is,' said Calder. 'After a thing like that the company always feels it's better to give him a fresh start. Not that we take sides one way or another. After all, it isn't Andy's fault if his marriage doesn't work out. Who can tell these days, marriage is such a lottery. How's Helen? Still teaching? That's good. Morag says she doesn't know what she'd do without her job. It's good for her to have an outside interest, now that the kids are getting on a bit.'

Rain stopped play. After nine holes, we had lunch. I often feel that, insofar as it exists at all, our national diet has been designed to make us healthy, able to work and praise God. Food is for eating, not enjoying. Stew and tatties, herring and mince are food. Veals and sauces, wines and dressings are gluttonous frippery. But things are changing. We ate consommé, quiche and salad, trifle, brie and biscuits, coffee and after-dinner mints.

I tried to steer the conversation towards the conspiracy of crafty bastards who make us buy things we do not need: after-shave lotion, underarm deodorant and after-dinner mints. But my fellowship of sporting bankers are confirmed consumers and spoke of investment prospects.

Andy Simpson was mentioned with the second bottle of wine. Then they praised Margaret Thatcher (a round-shouldered woman, currently Prime Minister) pausing to reflect on the lack of opposition she has encountered since our Socialist leaders have chosen to tear themselves apart over the purity of their cause and the solemnity of their devotion, aided by an Alliance of power-hungry nice people who seem intent on keeping the Tories in power.

Then, since it seemed relevant, I gave a small monologue on how different it was in our day, and we've all passed a lot of water under the bridge since then; how the Sixties raised the image to national importance and brought forth a cult of youth and adolescence so that nowadays it's all over by the time you're twenty, except that those hardest-hit by our economic recession are those under twenty. Heads nodded. Someone mentioned political awareness and Don Calder

183

enthused about strong leadership. The general consensus appeared to be that the blame lay with those under twenty-one; tough luck being born at such a rotten time.

'How's things, Angus?' asked a sportsman, craning his neck, ashamed to be seen having a piss.

'Surviving,' said I. It's the catchword of the Eighties.

Driving Calder back to his domain, I mentioned I was losing my only competent member of staff, Miranda Morrison by name. And not for the first time I was reminded of the intense pleasure man derives from talking about someone he is having an affair with as though she was a casual acquaintance.

Miranda's mother is ill, said I, and she wants to work at a branch nearer home, though I am sure Head Office would suit her fine. I was sorry to see her go, but didn't feel I could stop her. Come to think of it, Central Branch, where Calder works, is nearer; better train service. Yes, her application went in a couple of days ago. She hadn't mentioned it, but I felt sure she would be splendidly suited to computing. She was certainly bright enough and could be easily trained. Apart from anything else, she was very pretty.

I don't know why I did it, though it has more than once crossed my mind that with Miranda in such a position, it would be pleasantly easy, not to say justifiable, for her to remove a large amount of money from one side of a computer screen to another bearing our joint names. And we could live happily ever after.

I didn't go in for coffee. Helen was expecting me.

When I left Calder, I retraced the route I followed last time. I've thought about it since I heard on Woman's Hour that *déjà vu* is no more than a breakdown in communication between the brain and the eye. I was convinced that if I drove around the same area I wouldn't see Judy again. The odds against it were too great. I was mistaken.

It was around six o'clock. I phoned Helen who wasn't in. I bought a cup of coffee-flavoured tepid water and sat by the café window, watching the world pass me by.

Judy passed by, her hair on top of her head, a black T-shirt, red jacket, floral-patterned skirt that touched her knees, black tights and delicate black court shoes. She had a tote bag over her left shoulder.

I banged my knees on the café table. The proprietor checked I'd paid the bill and smiled sarcastically when he saw me run.

By the bus stop, opposite the library, I touched her arm. 'Judy.'

She turned, half-expectantly. 'I'm in a hurry,' she said.

'It's me. Angus.'

'I'm sorry, but I don't think I know you.' She raised her left arm and waved. I caught the glint of a wedding ring.

'Of course you do. I'm Angus MacPhail.'

I hoped it was surprise, but knew it was ignorance. Neither my name nor appearance registered. 'Debbie's brother. Surely you remember Debbie. In fact, I don't know how you don't remember me.'

'This is my husband,' she said.

He was taller than me, dark-haired and good-looking in a conventional way, cloned from the pages of women's magazines.

'Something wrong?' he asked.

'I don't know,' she said.

I said, 'I don't think I've made a mistake.'

Judy looked at her husband. 'I think you've made a mistake,' he said.

'Wait a minute, your wife's name is Judy?'

'Uh-hu.'

'Judy. It's me. Angus.'

'Do you know this guy?'

'No.' She turned away. Her husband smiled. There was a touch of mockery, maybe even pity: 'Bye,' he said.

He put his arm around her and they walked away from me. She was talking. He turned twice to see me still standing there.

I don't know how long I sat in the car. Eventually I turned the ignition. The engine coughed a bit, then it wheezed. Car needs a service, I thought.

185

Helen didn't come in till after nine. 'Didn't I tell you?' she said. 'I had an appointment.' She had a bath and went to bed.

I went to the pub and left early to phone Miranda, after buying a half-bottle of whisky which is now an empty addition to our rubbish bin. Why does booze always betray you: I wanted to get drunk but couldn't, wanted to forget but kept remembering.

There is a building on Inverness High Street opposite the Town Hall. A dozen or so Biblical texts have been carved into the stone wall, twenty feet above a chemist's shop.

HABAKKUK 2:15 – Woe unto him that giveth his neighbour strong drink, that puttest thy bottle to him, and makest him drunken also.

REVELATIONS 3:16 – So then because thou art lukewarm, and neither hot nor cold, I will spue thee out of my mouth.

REVELATIONS 21:8 – But the fearful, and unbelieving, and the abominable, and murderers, and whoremongers, and sorcerers, and idolators, and all liars, shall have their part in the lake which burneth with fire and brimstone, which is the second death.

1 CORINTHIANS 6:9–10 – Be not deceived: neither fornicators, nor idolators, nor adulterers, nor effeminate, nor abusers of themselves with mankind, nor thieves, nor covetous, nor drunkards, nor revilers, nor extortioners, shall inherit the Kingdom of God.

That's me ruled out. So what else do you want to know? Bonnie Scotland, I adore thee, almost as much as the notion that people offer each other strong drink because they want company in hell. Or our reputation as a tolerant nation.

You'll join me in a wee refreshment?

Part Three

GROUCHO: The party in the third part will be known as the
          party in the third part.
                                    A Night At The Opera

Thirteen

ORIGINS:

'It's okay,' said Phamie. 'The baby isn't yours.'

'Are you sure?'

'Positive.'

'I don't know whether to feel happy or sad.'

'Who does.' It wasn't a question.

Depression came with an amalgamated confusion of emotions so powerful as to leave us paralysed, powerless to act. A sense of maturity, or at least endured experience, came with the smell of autumn.

'Prison,' said Cammy, 'concentrates the mind wonderfully.' He appeared to be least affected and constantly spoke of the trial, of what he was going to say and do. He didn't like his lawyer, but was happy to stick with him at least until the show was rolling. When we saw him we believed he had alternatives, or pretended to believe it for his sake.

We were sorry when the police left. We'd got to know them quite well and their presence gave us a uniform release valve. They were efficient, mannerly and detached, and though they expressed no opinions, their manner did it for them.

'Thank you for your co-operation,' said Inspector Thomson when the last of his men had gone. 'I hope we haven't been too much trouble.'

'Not too much,' said Father. 'Just enough.'

Apart from turning us over, there was a continuum of statements. They knew I'd been taken to a party meeting, knew what had happened and beyond corroboration the matter was never raised again. When they seemed convinced that the sum of our parts added up, that we obviously knew Cammy's political opinions but nothing about the extent of his activities, the questions stopped. When we compared our statements it appeared the police knew what they wanted and looked to us for corroboration.

Dr Patel told them about Mother, but still they questioned her. God knows what she told them.

'I told them Cameron was a very good baby,' she said, 'in spite of the fact that he got jaundice just after he was born. It never made him grumpy though. Croup was his trouble. He was an awful boy for the croup.'

Left to our own resources the mists descended, evolving from white, through grey and blue to black.

BANK:

A panel of four men kept me waiting for an hour in a marbled hall that smelled of polish with only the *Bankers' Journal* and a stiff-necked secretary for company.

She wore a heavy brassière that showed through her rayon blouse like a bandage. The only noise was the scratch of nylon as she crossed and recrossed her legs. 'The gentlemen will see you now,' was all she said.

One man asked the questions. The others listened. No one took notes. I remember the room, the view through the window, the Hornel painting, the long table, heavy curtains and the echo of my voice when I spoke, sitting on a chair that was made to be admired. I remember feeling I didn't care, that I shouldn't be there, that no matter what happened I would carry this day around like a stone. And for the first time in my life, before anyone spoke, I craved revenge.

'We've asked you to come and see us because of this business with your adopted brother. Sorry, you were adopted. That's right, isn't it?'

'I've always thought of Cameron as my brother.'

'Quite. I don't really know what the proper term is, so let's just say you're related. Now, he seems to have got himself into rather a bit of bother, and the Bank is involved insofar as some of our money has been taken. Most of it has been recovered, but there is still the matter of the impending trial and we'll need to wait for the outcome of that.

'In the meantime, let me say that we are convinced, and the police have confirmed this, off the record, of course, that you are in no way involved or even implicated. But you are a bank employee and we have to look at everything, particularly your future with the company should you decide to stay with us after these unfortunate events have reached their conclusion.

'Again, I'd like to say that we have been very well satisfied with your work up to now, as we were indeed with your adopted father. Both of you have shown a remarkable aptitude for banking and, if asked, we would have said you were, as far as we were concerned, more the child of Angus MacPhail than his natural son has proven to be. But that shows how wrong we can be sometimes. Nothing is certain, not even in banking. Isn't that right, gentlemen?' The others smiled. 'Now, Angus; why don't you tell us how you feel about this sorry business?'

I don't remember what I said. A trickle of sweat ran down my back.

'I think that just about covers it, gentlemen, don't you; unless anyone has anything they'd like to ask? Right then. We think it would be best, Angus, if you were relieved from your duties with us for, say, the next four months. By this time the court proceedings ought to be concluded. You will obviously be needed at home beforehand and I am quite certain you'll want some time to consider your future when things are over. We will get in touch with you once we know what is happening with your brother, and we can have a further chat then. In the meantime, we don't want you to suffer financially, since we're sure there will be some distress in other areas. The bank will continue to pay your salary as usual, though there will be a slight adjustment since you aren't actually working; it should work out at around three-quarters pay. Tax and National Insurance will, of course, be deducted and we will continue our commitment in that direction, as well as our contributions to the company's pension and insurance schemes.

'If there's no further business, I think we can let you go.

191

There's no need to go back to your branch today, unless there's anything you want to collect, of course. There isn't? Good. That's fine, Angus. Thank you very much, and thanks for coming in. I'm glad we've had this chat. Good day and good luck.'

I actually thanked them. My shoes squeaked across the marble floor as I left the building and walked into the midsummer and autumn of nineteen hundred and sixty-nine.

JUDY:

Every statement I made came back like the reflection in a spoon; distorted, fattened and absurd.

'I want you to show me things,' she said.

'What kind of things?'

'Books; I want to learn about books.'

'There's nothing to know. You've either read a book or you haven't. If you've read it and enjoyed it, that means it's a good book.'

'Then why do you say some of the books I read are trash? If I like it and my opinion's as good as anyone else's, what difference does it make?'

'The stuff you read is trash because it romanticises and sentimentalises decent, human emotions. It's trash because it's second-best. But you know the difference, don't you?'

'What if I don't care?'

Judy smoked the way a young girl smokes, a little too feverishly, with too much obvious enjoyment and at the same time too much casualness, looking at the cigarette when she took a draw, holding it with the tips of her fingers.

'I smoke because I want to. I enjoy it and will stop smoking when I want to and not when you reckon I ought to. I smoke dope when I can get it and that has nothing to do with smoking tobacco. I smoke dope to get stoned and smoke tobacco for everything else.'

'All I said was that smoking is bad for you.'

'Will you stop picking on me. It's not my fault the bank don't like you, that your old lady's doolally, your old man's

192

not much better, your sister's pregnant and your brother's in jail. Not a nice deal. But it isn't my fault, so stop picking on me. I know how you feel. Believe me, I'd swop places with you any day. Say the word.'

And was it that time or another; was it then or some other time around then, some time in the summer, her eyes electric and nostrils flaring: 'I don't know a single thing about you, Angus. I don't know the books you read, the music you like, anything. I don't know a single thing about what you like and what you don't like. I've tried to find out, but I'm either too stupid to learn or you just won't tell me.

'I've tried to learn things for you, but I haven't learned all that much, so I don't know anything, except that I love you. I know that. But it isn't enough, is it?

'You don't love me; I know you don't love me, but you're so bloody selfish that deep down, where it matters, nothing can reach you. You pretend to be open and innocent and all the time you don't even care because you can't think of anybody but yourself. On to the next adventure, the next affair. Dress it up and make excuses, pretend it's a big experience when all the time it's just a ride, which is all you're ever going to get because you are too involved with yourself to accept what another human being has to offer. She'll be inadequate, won't give you enough because no one can. Poor old you, innocent and look what happened. You've had your cake and eaten it.'

I had grown morose. Too much was going on for me to be concerned about the fact that even my voice seemed to upset her. What love there was became feverish or lacking in passion. It developed an intensity that was unemotional yet persistent, forcing me to concentrate on the act.

'Why is it important?' she asked.

It was what was left, but it too had become distorted. I wanted to increase the intensity, to force up the tension, to screw the nerves a little tighter. I started doing things I'd never done before. Her breasts and shoulders, arms and neck were marked where I had bitten and sucked until the skin became blue and green, red and yellow; they looked like scabs, sores, raw and open, angry reminders against the white and pallid skin.

It was as if we'd missed the point, as if we'd gone past it, thrown it away or lost it. Now we were making love to recapture love, its feeling or effect.

'Why aren't you tender?' she asked.

All I can remember is that we either argued, went to bed or both. I used her to make me feel better, and what I was doing made me worse.

When the end came it wasn't what I expected. There were no promises, no tears and no regrets. 'Fuck off,' she said. 'And don't come back.'

I walked home, through the bitter scent of summer dust pitted with raindrops.

Sunday, 20 July 1969. Everyone was watching television. 'Come in,' said Mother. 'Everyone's watching the man in the moon.'

CAMMY:

The trial was a formality. We only needed to know the sentence.

Father and I went to court every day and ate lunch without speaking. Phamie came when she felt like it, which wasn't often. Apart from anything else, she did not like the possibility of being photographed.

Reports of the trial were in every newspaper:

MacPhail interrupted the counsel and spoke for half an hour. Lord MacTavish said such a speech was unusual at this stage, but agreed to met Macphail carry on.
MacPhail said: 'We live in a violent society and have become accustomed to the rule of the gun.'
He said there was nothing wrong with taking money from banks for revolutionary purposes.
And added that Stalin, one of his heroes, had done so to further the cause of the Russian Revolution.
MacPhail said banks had too much money and that they were undemocratic institutions.

194

He said he knew nothing about shareholders or their rights.
Daily Moon 18 September

That clipping is typical. Apart from the fact that half an hour is a long time to say what was reported, the quotes are taken out of context from a speech about investment. Cammy always maintained that to defeat an enemy you must understand his methods.

Every newspaper mentioned how Father had retired from bank service and I had been temporarily suspended. I was cited as a witness, but never called.

The prosecution began with a daily procession of bank clerks who told the court masked raiders had threatened them, how much was taken and what a dreadful experience it was. Then there was a clutch of policemen who confirmed each other's statements.

Cammy had been arrested after a surveillance. The police had been tipped off when the Bottom End landlady found the money. She turned up in a fur coat, sparkling and slurring her speech. Her evidence was not as colourful as I'd hoped it would be. She mostly confined herself to single-sentence answers, except when Cammy's counsel asked where her sudden wealth had come from and suggested she had allowed some of the cash to remain within reach.

'Do you mean I pochled it?'

'I cannot produce the word, let alone understand it,' said Lord MacTavish, suddenly alert.

'It means took by stealth, m'lud.'

'Then why didn't the witness say that?'

'I did say it, it's just that you didnae understand it.'

'And was that what you meant?'

'There seems to be rather a direct change in the witness's circumstances, m'lud.'

'Indeed?'

'If you mean this coat,' she said, 'then let me tell yous it belonged to my late husband's mother and if you'd've gone through what I had to go through to get it you wouldn't grudge me the coat, nor anything like it. And what would yous've said if I'd've turned up here in my old apron and frock? What would I have been called then? You should feel black, burning shame. Yous can send the police back round to my house and they can search it again from top to bottom if they like, for I can well assure yous that they'll find nothing irregular there, except him, Uncle Joe, the workers' friend.'

She pointed to an old man in a black beret, the one who'd asked me to leave the meeting. This was the only time I saw him in court. He was the party's spokesman. They had issued a statement dissociating themselves from Cammy's adventurist policies. They said he had been entirely self-motivated and none of the money had gone to party funds. They did not offer an explanation as to how the landlady had alerted the police after finding the money in her house, tamely suggesting no one knew it was there, that Cameron knew the house well enough to hide it, saying all would be made clear by the defence. In the meantime, Cameron exonerated his comrades of all blame, took full responsibility, had done everything himself and regretted nothing. They got off scot-free.

'I understood it wasn't the likes of me who was on trial this afternoon,' said the landlady. 'God knows, I'm only a poor widow woman who's had no one in the world to support or comfort her for more than twenty years.'

She had merely rented the room to the old man. He brought strangers to her door. They met once a week, sometimes twice, their meetings were in secret and she wouldn't recognise any of them again if she met them in her soup, except Cammy, of course.

The prosecution had opened with the suggestion that Cammy had taken me to Bottom End and had wanted me to join the party because I worked in a bank. Cammy's lawyer mentioned this in his opening statement, asking why Cammy hadn't therefore also invited his father. Cammy, he said, was not a terrorist, a vicious and obsessive politico, a Svengali, a Fagin or a Bader-Meinhoff scion. Counsel, a tall, thin, flamboyant man who resembled a cartoon undertaker, pointed a bony finger at Cammy. 'This man,' he said, 'has become a metaphor for the politics of our time.'

'I thought Bader-Meinhoff were two people,' interrupted Lord MacTavish.

'Quite so, m'lud.'

And Lord MacTavish sighed a deep sigh.

'I will show,' said the lawyer without pausing for breath. 'I will show that in the nineteenth century Cameron MacPhail would have been regarded as little more than a crank, or at best a religious zealot. Lenin, whom MacPhail professes to follow, Lenin abandoned his greatest loves, chess, music and literature, he abandoned these things to follow his calling and devote himself to the matter in hand, to bring to the revolution the same fervour a religious devotee would have brought to converting the masses for Christ fifty years earlier. He was, m'lud, a religious maniac for his time.'

Cammy, on the other hand, was out of his time. He was an innocent who had been used by others, abused by the people he trusted, who had played upon his simplistic and narrowed view of society, who had exploited his beliefs for their own personal gain. And now they had betrayed him. He was absolutely typical, a product of the lower middle classes who was therefore subject to their social diseases, envy, greed and resentment. He wanted and could not have, therefore he set about trying to change society to suit his desires. A human story often told, with tragic consequences. MacPhail had been snubbed and therefore wanted to get his own back. His father and brother worked in a bank. Had MacPhail himself secretly desired such a life? Had he applied and been refused without telling anyone? We can but speculate, but such speculation is not without precedent and is never fruitless.

MacPhail had been a student, had sought to be educated. Was education the answer, or was he merely seeking a way of feeding his own resentments through education? Education is never the answer for this type of personal dilemma. Adolf Hitler had led the best-educated nation in the world to moral, social, economic, spiritual and physical ruin. Education is therefore not the answer and could, in this instance, be seen as the problem. For what did Cammy have to show for his folly? The world, at least, had a new art form from Hitler's greater folly, for he had virtually invented *son et lumière*. But what about Germany?

'I hope this is leading somewhere,' said Lord MacTavish.

'MacPhail, m'lud, is at best an ill-educated innocent. And he is a true innocent, for he believes in the purity of his cause with a fervour that is at once both spiritual and deeply religious.'

Cammy sacked his lawyer and conducted his own defence. He called no witness, cross-examined no one, but tried to tell the court what he believed in, with a tendency for longish speeches, which Lord MacTavish interrupted.

He was sentenced to thirty years imprisonment.

JIMMY:

Christopher Columbus was an alcoholic. When he set out he didn't know where he was going, when he got there he didn't know where he was, when he came back he didn't know where he had been and he did it all on someone else's money.

So said Jimmy MacDonald, Judy's father, who looked younger and healthier.

'I stopped drinking, that's what happened,' he said. 'I stopped because I wanted to. Everybody knew I should stop, but it only happened and can only happen when I wanted it to happen.

'I could never work out what was wrong. I didn't want to be the way I was and thought I ought to be able to control it. But the only way I could control it was to stop it. See, I thought I was all right till I got the taste of it, but I could never work out when that happened. Then I learned, the first one gave me the taste and after that I was compelled to carry on. No choice. Like blood to a tiger. That's what alcoholism is, son, it's compulsive. Now tell me, what do you know about compulsion?'

It was after the trial. I'd gone to see Judy because I thought I

198

needed her. I still think I needed her. I missed her and missed how she had made me feel. I missed everything, even the arguments, but most of all I missed the warmth.

'You're something of a celebrity,' said Jimmy. 'Of course, you've been quite famous around here for some time. Judy's going out with a bloke who introduced himself to her because someone said she'd known you. Great, isn't it, life's little ironies. Anyway, she isn't in. They've gone to a cheese and wine party, something to do with his work, which means they'll come back here drunk and constipated. I was supposed to have gone with them but I decided no one, including me, was going to say anything I wanted to hear.

'So, what can we do for you? I thought you'd given her the push, or was it the other way around?'

I told him there were one or two things I wanted back, a few books.

'Not a great reader, my Judy. But I'll tell her you want the stuff and suggest she gets it to you. You could take the books away with you right now, except that I'm not too sure she'd want you in her room. No offence, but you do understand what I'm getting at?

'I know my boozing affected my family. I didn't look after them as well as I should have done and the fact that they never knew how to expect me, when to expect me or what to expect from me, made things a wee bit uneasy. No girl likes to have her drunken father slobbering all over the place when she's entertaining friends, especially boy-friends. That sort of behaviour can make her more than slightly self-conscious and tends to lead towards her accepting second-best. I've recently realised that Judy became more lethargic, less interested in reading and studying generally, less interested in living, when my drinking got bad. And the worse it got the more introverted she became: not that it was ever good; it was never quite normal. I was not what you would call a social drinker. I drank for effect.

'And the point I am making is that I intend to make up for these things now I'm off the sauce. I'm quite happy about you not coming around any more. The trial had nothing to do with it. I don't think you and Judy were well enough matched. You were on the make as far as she was concerned. Let's say she was older; not much, I know, a year or two perhaps, but enough to make it noticeable.

'Let me tell you something; when I sobered up I found I had to give up some of the people I thought were my best mates. I used to see them in the pub and I wondered how they were doing, though they never bothered about me, because they never came near me; I could have been dead. So I went to see them, to prove I was alive. And guess what; they didn't want to see me, or rather they'd didn't want to see me sober, because the spotlight was off me and on them. All the crazy things they did were being spoken about and though they might have been bad before, they were never as bad as Jimmy MacDonald, but Jimmy MacDonald had sobered up, so why couldn't they do the same. They wanted me pissed.

'But all my friends weren't in pubs. There were others, people who saw me in a certain light, who looked at me in a certain way and didn't like the changes. Strange as it may seem, the people I live with weren't too happy at first. My wife was used to treating me like a baby. So when I sobered up and started wanting to pay the bills and accept my responsibilities, she got a bit upset because she felt her role was being eroded. And Judy was not at all happy about the fact that I started telling her what time to come in, no men in the dormitories and stuff like that.

'I also found, and this is the good bit, there were people who didn't want to know me drunk, but who wanted to know me sober, next-door neighbours and the like, people who were used to treating me like an elephant, who had patted my head and fed me buns, now treated me like a human being. So in order to stay sober I had to change my company, change my habits and change my way of life. I even had to change my thinking. That's a bit more difficult, so the process is slower. But there's help, you don't have to do it alone and you feel better, more able to tackle such things. There's a lot that used to be important which is no longer important, and some things I never thought were important have become very important.

'Am I making sense, son? There are people who make friends and stay friendly all their lives. But you and I aren't like that, are we? And I don't think my Judy's like that either. I don't think it would be good for her to see her old friends. She's trying to build a new life for herself and needs a bit of time to sort things out. Maybe in a little while, when the heat's off, it might be nice for you to have a wee chat, but for now you both need to meet new people, to make some new friends. You won't find it difficult to stagger on to the next friendship, will you?

'I'll tell her you called and I'll also make sure you get your stuff back. Okay.'

Two days later a man with a squeezed nose brought three cardboard boxes to the door. 'Jimmy MacDonald sent them round,' he said.

WENDY:

I met her that night.

'I've just broken up with my boy-friend,' she said.

ODYSSEYS AND ENDINGS:

Death has become our new obscenity.

There used to be a place for grief in our society. Mourning was public; we wore black for a month or two, then a black diamond sewn to the right sleeve of our coats or jackets, we doffed our caps when a cortège passed and our parents stood silent by the roadside.

Those were the days when pornography was in the writings, drawings, photographs or films designed to promote sexual excitement. The word is a nineteenth-century creation from two Greek words: *porne*, a harlot, and *graphein*, to write. The nineteenth century was obsessed with sex, and children, who had been brought up to be ashamed of their bodies and to suppress their sexual feelings, were also told they would die, that death was all around us, present every day and a glorious part of life. For many it was the emblem of hope, the promise of relief, a great equaliser. Things would be better then. Children's fiction thrived on it; a natural ending.

But sexual pornography has been released into society's collective and individual consciousness. It keeps the wheels of industry turning because it sells things, which has almost made it thoroughly respectable, and even though it is largely male-orientated, its appeal is universal. No one can ignore it and no one bothers about pornography.

Death has taken its place in the closet. We do not talk about death. We burn the bodies and scatter the ashes to remove the evidence. Tears are not encouraged, grief is dismissed and distrusted. Mourning embarrasses us.

Our landscapes have changed and James Joyce is largely responsible. Today's world is smaller; our events happen on a global scale. Jet airplanes have made everywhere accessible and television has opened the oyster. No matter where you live, the streets of New York are familiar. Homer wrote the *Odyssey* and Joyce wrote *Ulysses*. Since *Ulysses* we cannot travel the way Homer travelled, so we travel inside ourselves. Our odysseys are in the mind.

And today's strangers are in the mind, sometimes surfacing in our dreams and linking somewhere at the back of beyond. We kill a spider, it becomes gigantic and returns to seek revenge in much the same way as Calgacus might have gathered his army or Cuchullain his strength. Few of our strangers are people.

We no longer know who our strangers are. They could be sharks or snakes; they could be fire, air or water; they could be the man next door or they could be ourselves. We don't even need to dream them. Cinema will do it for us. Our fantasies, fears and phobias appear on the screen larger than life, so we can indulge or suppress them; emulsified pornography in place of filth.

When pornography was secret it flourished in our minds.

Now it flourishes in the cinema. Nightmares are redundant. We don't need to do a thing, except get scared.

They used to scare us with vampires, ghouls, ghosts and all that walking-death zombie crap. Today they frighten us with the very act of destruction, with whatever turns people into ghouls or ghosts, whatever makes them violently extinct.

In the past the truth could always console us. Ghosts, ghouls, vampires, Frankenstein, that whole bit is made up, it does not exist. But people do hang around street corners with carving knives. We read about such murders in newspapers and see the horrors excessed on television news, which has been chosen for us. We do not see all the news. We see entertainment disguised as information. We see the selected news.

The carving knives and meat cleavers, their reportage and disguise has alienated us further from the inevitability of dying, from the many and varied ways of death. Joggers and health-food munchers also die, but our present culture is based on youth and the young don't die, or if they do they were good, maybe even innocent.

We need to bring back grief, to use our own release systems, to have no more skeletons in the cupboard.

MOTHER, FATHER, FAMILY:

She died on a Tuesday afternoon, just after two o'clock.

When Phamie phoned the bank, I felt a sense of relief. Her illness had been so awful, had removed her personality and left us with such a travesty of the woman we had known that death came in friendship, even though she might not have known she was suffering or what she had become.

I don't intend a blow-by-blow account of her illness, the effects on us or its wastage. It isn't necessary. The end was neither slow nor merciful. She died.

My father sat staring out the window. It was spring. The garden had bunches of daffodils, colourless tulips and green nonsense all around us. He shook his head. 'I wish you'd been here,' he said.

It was only when I saw my sister crying, the rounded shaking shoulders and the red-rimmed eyes; it was then I realised I would never see my mother again.

Grief came like fear. It settled inside my chest and stayed there. I carry it around like a stone. And suddenly I had so much to tell her, suddenly there was so much to say, so much to do; no request was too great, no service too slight. My grief was for my inadequacies as well as her death, for my failure as well as my loss.

I remembered how we used to laugh because we thought she was a stupid old woman and with the insensitive assurance of youth never thought she was ill. I remembered how she used to tear pages from books, neatly dissect scraps from newspapers or magazines and stuff them into the ventilation bars of the gas fire; how she would ask the same question over and over, stop mid-sentence and shake her head; how she was lost outside the house, a frightened child who often wet herself, cried herself to sleep or played with the nearest toy, fumbling with paper or the nearest material; how she used to think she was a girl again, eight years old and late for school; how she sang hymns:

Shun evil companions, bad language disdain,
God's name hold in reverence, nor take it in vain.
Be thoughtful and earnest, kind hearted and true,
Look ever to Jesus, He will carry you through.

I remembered and could not cry, aching with a grief I could not name, for the common grief we cannot understand. I did not cry then and have not cried since, though every day I think I might. And what wouldn't I give to have a cup of tea with my mother right now.

'It's a pity you never really knew her,' said my father.

'Don't Dad,' said Phamie.

'You don't mind, do you Angus?'

'Of course not.' I did not know what I was supposed to be objecting to. 'I think it's good. I think we ought to talk about her.'

Phamie pursed her lips and gave her head a single shake. It was as close as she came to disapproval. She was feeding her new son, Caspar. 'At last I've got a man who needs me,' she said.

The baby confused Mother. 'Whose wee baby's that?' she asked every day. 'Shouldn't you take it back to its mother?'

'It's my baby,' said Phamie. 'He's your grandson. His name is Caspar.'

'Don't be silly,' said Mother. 'You couldn't possibly have a baby. You're just a girl and not even married.'

'You seem to have taken it worse than any of us,' said Father.

'I've no idea how badly you've taken it.'

'There isn't much point to this conversation,' said Phamie. 'I know what you're going to say, Dad, and I think you should leave it alone.'

We were at home on the evening of Mother's funeral. Cammy had been allowed out under escort and seeing Cammy always upset Father. He had changed since the trial, especially in his attitude towards Cammy and to Cammy's politics.

'For the sake of Gentle Jesus and the furtherance of His Kingdom here on earth, the church has always been on the side of the strong,' he told the minister who took the funeral service. 'I would therefore be especially happy if you could dispense with the irrelevancies of comfort. I do not wish to hear some anodyne about a better life hereafter, nor do I want to know about suffering here on earth, especially if you are going to suggest it has a purpose. You are here to provide the service my wife would have wanted were she able to choose. But she was incapable of choosing. And since the flowers on the grave belong to the living, we'll have none of them either.'

The service was clear, without sermon and all the more moving in its simplicity. Its timelessness reminded me that the funeral was another excuse for Father to shout at life.

'Don't,' said Phamie. 'Please, Dad. Don't.'

'Don't what?'

205

'Don't carry on like this. It won't do anyone any good. Not even you.'

'My son is in jail because he is an idealist, a simple-minded idealist, the judge said. He is a bank robber who was let out for his mother's funeral under escort, with a couple of brosers to intimidate him and remind us of what he did. Let me remind you, they brought him to the graveside in a van, let him out, stood beside him tugging his sleeves and when the service was over he was taken away. Cameron MacPhail was allowed no time to mourn with his family. He wasn't even allowed to speak to them. Yet he did not rob banks for greed. He kept none of the money. He did not do it for personal gain. He is much more dangerous, because he was politically motivated. Think about it, Phamie. Think about it and tell me how I should feel.'

'I don't think you should take it out on Angus.'

'Why don't you make the tea?'

'Make it yourself. Caspar needs his feed.'

'In that case, it's beans on toast.'

There was something tragic about him. He didn't know what to do and it embarrassed him. He refused all help, yet had to think about how to open the can and simply turned the gas up full. I lowered the flame when he was cutting bread. His conversation was intermittent. Father making the tea took a great deal of effort and concentration. When he finished he expected praise.

'I don't know why I can't do this,' he said. 'It used to look simple enough. Lack of practice, I suppose. Maybe it's something women are inherently better at, like having babies. Maybe there are things which can best be divided into men's work and women's work.'

'The best chefs are men,' said I.

'This is no time to talk about chefs,' he said. 'Anyway, women haven't had the opportunity, or so my daughter tells me. Do you think the laws of the centuries are changing, Angus? Do you think we are finally getting shot of the

Calvinist work ethic, or are we losing the work ethic because we are losing work? My class were told that work is all we're good for, and now we are being told we're not even good enough for that.'

It was the first time I'd heard him refer to himself as working-class.

'This meal is miraculous for its execution, if nothing else,' said Phamie.

'It may be bad but it hasn't been executed yet,' said the old man. 'I was saying earlier, Angus. It's a pity you never really knew your mother.'

He didn't look at Phamie, who had stopped chewing and stared; as though he were a naughty boy who, having been told not to jump in puddles, makes sure you're watching and with all his force jumps into the largest, muddiest puddle he can find.

'Her mind has been going for some time,' he said. 'We had suspected it for long enough and, of course, there came a day when we knew, when we were absolutely certain our worst fears had been realised. Mummy's mind was walking away from her at such a rate we couldn't catch it. And what made matters worse was that the kids were growing up. She needed something to keep her mind occupied and since the happiest time of her life had been when the children were young, she figured the perfect solution to this problem was to have a child. She would feel needed and wanted someone to care for. The trouble was that she was getting on a bit; change of life and all that. The mind was willing but the flesh was weak. Anyway, babies demand too much attention. She needed some time for herself. So we hit on the idea of an older baby and, rather than have to go through that whole conceiving bit, we adopted you. Shame; it never really worked. As we all know, she lost her mind anyway.'

And every day for the rest of his life, he growled at the world. I moved to the city and found the place where my wife and I started our marriage. A week after I'd gone, Phamie phoned and came to see me.

207

'He loves you,' she said.

'He has a funny way of showing it.'

'It's him and his generation. The only way you can show affection is by insulting someone. Your best friend is an old bugger. But every day he asks how you are. Do you remember how Mum used to reckon that if you didn't speak when you answered the telephone, it wouldn't cost you? He's the same. He reckons that if he says nothing it will go away and if you say nothing it means you've forgotten. No charge. But he's paid. I know he's paid. Listen, he's the same with Caspar; worse. "The bastard child is crying," he says. But every day I find him staring at the baby when it's sleeping. And he never misses a feed. Even in the middle of the night, he gets up to make me a cup of tea. But he always says the baby wakened him and he couldn't get back to sleep. Angus, there are two empty bedrooms in his house and he's sleeping on his own. It must be hellish.'

In time it became the occasional Sunday lunch with Father, Phamie, Casper, Helen and me. He spoke to my wife as if she was mentally defective. 'Horrible old man,' she said.

'It isn't you, it's me he's getting at.'

'What do you mean?'

'He reckons I would never have married if I'd stayed at home.'

'So here we are,' she sighed. 'Trapped by our parents.'

'Do you feel trapped?' I asked Phamie.

'Not particularly. Do you think I'm trapped?'

'I think you could be.'

'A typically noncommital answer. I get out two or three times a week. I go to my conscious-raising classes and my dream therapy group. I see people and even though life isn't perfect, it's all right.'

Phamie got more attractive as she grew older. She lost a lot of her gawkiness, her sharp edges rounded and her eyes turned grey. For all the time I'd known her she had worn her hair in a shock of dark, wavy curls. She had her hair cut after the funeral, it lost its wildness and Phamie looked more like

208

Mother than herself. It was difficult to imagine her spirit was as free as it had been. She looked different and dressed the way magazines suggested someone of her age ought to dress. The first thing to go was the patchouli oil which had preceded her entrances with a ghostly joy. All was swopped for the click of high heels, fashionable sweaters, short skirts and she looked like the other young mothers when she took Caspar to the playgroup or attended the clinic when she was expecting Melanie, who arrived a year after Caspar.

Both were recognisably Phamie's children. I tried to imagine their father from the evidence of his children, but could only imagine Mother looking like that when she was Phamie's age.

Phamie looked after Father in much the same way as Mother had done. She gradually changed the surroundings, decorating the house with brighter colours, pastel walls and Liberty curtains, recovering the chairs and sofas and turning the house into an extension of her room. Father appeared not to mind. He moved into my old bedroom, the smallest in the house, and Phamie moved into the old master-bedroom. Melanie had Phamie's room and Caspar took over Cammy's place with Mister Men wallpaper and a Superman carpet. Father's study remained intact until after his death.

Perhaps it was my marriage ('I'm sorry, Angus. No matter what I do I still think of her as your wife, not as a member of the family') but Phamie became more secretive, less willing to relate stories about herself, less willing to confide.

'I think I'm pregnant again,' she said one Sunday afternoon while we were washing dishes. Father and Melanie were asleep and my wife was reading to Caspar.

'What are you going to do?' I tried not to sound anxious.

'Wait and see. What else can I do? There's no way I could have an abortion. I couldn't do it, that's all. And I don't know how Father would take to another little stranger crawling around the place.'

'He seems to have taken to Caspar and Melanie.'

'He's got no choice. I'm sorry, that didn't come out the way I meant it. You know what I mean.'

'How did it happen? I'm sorry, that didn't come out the way I meant it either.'

She smiled. 'I'm not on the pill, if that's what you mean. I gave it up when I got unnatural highs and lows and my tits swelled up. I was into a relationship at the time, so I thought it would be okay. Caspar was a mistake.'

'And what happened to the relationship?'

'Couldn't leave his kids.'

'And this time?'

'A housewarming party up the road. Don't tell me. I already know. It's no fun, Angus. Try being a woman for a day. And try being a woman on her own. A woman with no man and a couple of kids is fair game. Men are such liars. And I believe them, till suddenly there's a wife and four kids they've forgotten to mention. But I've found out how to get rid of a man: tell him you're pregnant. Trouble is, you know me, a couple of drinks, a smoke of dope and I get horny. Nowadays suburban parties are like the parties I used to go to, except all the swingers are married and I'm on first-name terms with their commitments.'

Next time I asked, she smiled. 'Where's the snow that fell last year? I think I ought to do something to celebrate, but how do you celebrate a false alarm?'

'I suppose it would be silly to suggest you try for a more permanent relationship.'

'It isn't silly of you to suggest it, but it would be damned silly if I was to do it. I tried it. Remember George? How about him? Remember his parting gift?'

'That was a long time ago.'

'Seems like yesterday to me. I'm not saying everyone's like him, in fact the others have been regular people. But I don't think I'll ever get over it. Something like that scars you for life, no pun intended.'

The sun through the window caught the auburn tints of her hair and she leaned on the draining board and spoke in a calm, matter-of-fact way, as if she was relating a story of Caspar's curiosity or Melanie's wit. It was the day Father read his Masonic speech.

He went every Friday. I was surprised to learn where he was going and that Masonic membership wasn't open to all. He called it the Club.

He sat in the kitchen with a bundle of papers, drinking Earl Grey tea; the ring of the cup, saucer and spoon was a counterpoint to his reading.

'I thought you'd like to hear this wee speech I'm giving to the Club on Friday night. They've asked me to do something, though I'm not sure this was what they had in mind. I've gathered it together rather hastily. It's more in the way of an exploration, though as I was writing it my ideas became clearer. I had no idea I thought this. I only found out when I wrote it.

'It isn't original, maybe it isn't even right. I've almost certainly omitted some important points and have probably included things which have little or no bearing on the matter in hand, whatever it is. There are people who could do this much better than me and some have already done so; in fact, I may have inadvertently culled the whole substance, or part of it, from them. But this is the way I see it, a personal view, nothing more or less than that. The talk is called *L'Ecosse Oubliée*:

'We all have a view of the country we live in. We have views on what it is, what it means to us and how it's been treated. And our views are quite right, absolutely correct, because our country, Scotland, is now a landscape of the mind, a dream territory, mixed up with ourselves and our past.

'We are dealing with a mythology. I am not interested in where the myth began or how it developed. Where does any myth begin? And who cares? It isn't important, because our myth has become so powerful that we are living with the results.

'It has something to do with the way we see history. Our history is the history of a single class who are guilty about their past and have developed a mythology to hide it. But one mythology begets another. Myths creep around; they know no boundaries, fester in the imagination, take root in the soul and flutter. Our past is awful, so we invent a nice one. This is

211

neither new nor unique. It has happened elsewhere. Every country does it. We are not the only dreamers in the world, but a national industry has been built on our dreams, or rather the dreams we've been given. Fact and fiction do not exist. There is neither left nor right nor wrong. Only the myth is true. And we have accepted both the dream and the means of dreaming.'

His shoulders were rounded, his beard needed trimming and there was a hole in the right elbow of his cardigan. His shirt didn't have a collar and he fastened both legs of his braces on to a single button. He seemed to have shrunk with age, or rather he seemed to have been squashed. He was smaller and fatter. His eyes watered and he wiped them, smiling with embarrassment as though to assure us it wasn't tears. His hair needed combing and he wasn't yet used to his false teeth. He went for days without them, but obviously wanted the speech to sound right, so he was wearing the teeth. The letters S and F sounded the same, often fading to a whistle, and his smile looked like a snarl.

In his crackling, old man's voice, occasionally wagging a finger, looking at the wall as he addressed his imaginary audience: 'We have been obliterated,' he said. 'Scotland does not exist, except in the mind. Our reality is the Scottish Tourist Board.'

It was necessary, he said, to understand that Scottish language and culture were more than regional variants of English. They had distinct and separate beginnings. But what was generally accepted as Scottish popular culture began life outside Scotland and was fostered with significant political implications.

Our popular culture is not our folk culture. Our folk culture has become redundant. Our popular songs do not portray the industrialised Lowlands where four-fifths of the population lives; rather they sentimentalise around a timeless, primitive, tribal culture which was deliberately and bitterly smashed. And we've been given a panoply of symbols to assert the mythology.

212

Nowadays, kilts are rare, even on the streets of Edinburgh. They are mostly worn by visiting tourists, pseudo-Nationalists or upper-class Scots with English accents. The so-called tartans were invented by the textile trade during the Industrial Revolution. Yet when Sir Harry Lauder wore the kilt as a stage costume, he was immediately identified with Scotland. Why?

Because of the Army. The kilt began life as a military uniform. Our best export, apart from our civilians, has always been our soldiers. The Romans built walls to keep us out and by the nineteenth century we were the most formidable fighting force in the world. So when Lauder wore the symbol of imperial militaristic zeal to sing his nostalgic nonsense, quasi-love songs and sentimental drivel to expatriate Scots in America and the Empire, he was exporting a grossly senti-mentalised view of our rural past which has been used to anaesthetise workers against their industrial present. He sang of a Scotland which had been ruthlessly cleared, where houses were burned, people forcibly exported and replaced by game, deer and sheep.

But the kilt is only part of a whole symbolic array which separately or collectively signifies Scotland: tartan, bagpipes, thistles, saltires, even the very landscape, a landscape which is usually shown without people. Strip away the symbolism and what's left? Not much, except the irrelevant game of tracing it.

Sign systems have a high level of redundancy, but one element can bring a whole ensemble into play. Mythical representations do not float free in any society. They perform a social function and predispose us to perceive the world in a particular way. And whose interests do they serve? How many myths have we created and how many have we simply fostered? Sir Walter Scott is usually blamed for causing the rot, but he was a hard-working novelist who cannot be blamed for what others have done to his work. We don't need another symbol for failure when we're so unsure of ourselves that if you strip away the symbols there's nothing left. We are half in love with the cheap, the tawdry and the second-rate; we flirt with failure while our myths and prejudices poleaxe success; we foster the myths that kill us, drunkenness, meanness, hooliganism and so on.

Alcoholism is known to be evidence of a spiritual sickness and Scotland has the highest incidence of alcoholism in Europe. We search for an identity in alcohol which we ought to find in our society and in ourselves, which is also what the American Indians do; we are Europe's Red Indians. And our need for independence is also spiritual. We need to find ourselves. We don't have a centre. Our past has been removed, has become our folklore, our mythology, the symbol of a broken dream we are still dreaming. We need to return to reality. Not the reality of the computer or the television set, but the reality of how the cradle of the Industrial Revolution could be constructed as a dream kingdom where a military uniform is our national dress, where our popular culture is sentimentalised nostalgia for a rustic never-never land where conflict was minimalised and terror became a source of honour. We need to understand how that happened.

Planned obsolescence. Ultimately everyone lets everything become forgotten. And we have forgotten our history. Once the past is no longer a threat it can become romanticised, so now they're doing to John MacLean what was previously done to Robert Burns. And we don't remember. Our history has been rewritten, cosmeticised into character and failure.

It's no use blaming the English. The same thing's happened to them. Look what romantic history has done to Henry VIII, one of the most disgusting degenerates who ever drew breath; Merrie England, Tudor romance, Good Queen Bess and the pirate Francis Drake. And Gold help the Irish; they're still fighting a war propelled by American dollars donated to a place where people say Begorrah, a jaunting car landscape of the mind, just as Blodwyn in the Valley and Dylan Thomas in heaven contribute to the Welsh economy. This God-forsaken country is populated by people who have no respect for themselves, who have accepted second-best and allowed themselves to become no more than a satellite state. We are to America what Czechoslovakia, Hungary or Poland is to the Soviet Union.

Our very language has become our folklore and our real folklore has degenerated into pub entertainment. The essence of folklore is change. If it doesn't change it must be artificially preserved, like the Iron Curtain stuff. We have accepted symbolic preservation along with everything else and the next phase is death. When a nation forgets its history, reinterprets its history to serve the needs of others, or, worse still, believes the myths they've created, that nation disappears. And we disappeared long ago.

History no longer happens on a level we can influence, never mind change. History happens somewhere else. It's a weekly event. It happens on a world scale for the benefit of the television camera. And while we were diverted by American or Soviet imperialism, Scotland was being obliterated. No one bothered. The voices of protest were portrayed as cranks. It's the most important issue around today. Solve that one and everything else will fall into place. Because it happened stealthily, over a long period, because we were taught it in schools and accepted it with mother's milk, the real memory has been obliterated. We pretend the reality is different or we pretend it hasn't happened. But all that's left is the name. Scotland does not exist.

'That ought to do them,' he said, 'though I doubt if they'll understand it, never mind agree.' He went back to his study.

'Do you know what my granny told me,' he said, turning at the door. 'She told me God banished the man in the moon for chopping wood on the sabbath.'

We didn't ask how the speech went. I told my wife about it on the way home. 'Horrible old man,' she said. 'Absolutely horrible.'

'He's wasting away,' said Phamie. 'All he does is sit in his room. I think he's writing things, but I don't know what he's writing. It's such a shame. He ought to be enjoying his old age.'

215

'Seems to me he's having a great time.'

'You don't have to live with him,' she said.

The changes in my life seemed unimportant to him. He treated me as a failed experiment. 'At least you're not in jail,' he said. 'But if I know my bankers, a middle-of-the-road air of respectable decorum is what's called for; in other words, they'll pretend to forget all about you. And it's the pretence that's worst. But they'll be watching. Believe me.'

'Was that what happened to you?'

'I don't know and I don't care. I wasn't cut out for banking. I was interested in other things and they knew it.'

The bank officials sent for me. I turned up at eleven o'clock as requested and waited in the polished marble hall for over an hour. I thought how in other circumstances the sound of the secretary's stockings would be exciting.

'Well, Angus, things don't look too good, do they?' the same official said after he'd welcomed me, apologised for the delay, enquired for my health and my parents' health. I don't remember what I said, but I noticed my accent was rougher than their accents, or felt rougher. My father had always said the Scots were made to feel inferior about their accents, that the sound of a middle-class anglicised accent either put them in their place or infuriated them.

Someone said, 'It's in everyone's interests to let the whole affair die down. We realise this will be more difficult for you than for the rest of us, nevertheless we think you should try. We're sure you will agree that the bank has been very cooperative, we have tried to help in whatever ways we can.

'So we've decided to send you to one of our smaller branches for the time being, just till things are settled. And, of course, it goes without saying that this in no way affects your future with the company.'

I looked at him and knew he was lying. He knew that I knew but didn't falter. He said his piece as though he was reading a script. What they'd done to my father, they were doing to me. Father had refused to play their career game and my crime was that he'd adopted me. Cammy was an excuse. I have carried that injustice to work every morning.

Father died on 2 March 1979, a sharp and chilly Friday afternoon, the day after an insubstantial Devolution Act had offered us no choice in a referendum where they didn't need to rig the ballot because they'd rigged the rules. More voted Yes than No, but more than either didn't vote at all, and, by the rules of the ballot, those who did not vote counted as Noes. So, in spite of the fact that two and a half million Scots voted to produce a majority of over seventy-seven thousand, there was no devolution, making this the only recorded case in world history where apathy translated a substantial majority.

Cammy was allowed out for the funeral. His escorts stepped forward when he did and picked up the cords of Father's coffin. 'Please,' I said. They looked at me, insulted and ashamed. 'I don't want you to touch them.'

'I knew your Dad,' said a small man, picking up a cord. Cammy held the head cord and I had the feet. Phamie refused a cord. People neither Cammy, Phamie nor I had ever met held the other cords, which would, I think, have pleased our father. He liked a bit of a mystery.

'I can't throw out his clothes,' Phamie said two months after the funeral. So we went through the things together.

Strange how death gives ordinary scraps an emotional charge or a significance beyond understanding. In the hip-pocket of his shapeless, green corduroy trousers I found a slip of paper, a garden list of fourteen items, plants, shrubs and seeds. Only two were legible, the others crossed off. The things my father never got were *Raspberry Canes* and *Blue Violas*. I have the list folded inside my wallet and carry it with me.

'You could take some of this stuff,' she said. 'It would fit you. It's no good keeping anything for Cammy.' I smiled and shook my head.

She handed me a pair of shoes he'd hardly worn. 'Take them,' she said. 'They're a nice pair of brogues.'

217

I left the shoes and never saw them again. Shoes are the worst; they hold the shape of the feet, are moulded and polished by the wearer, a little evidence of vanity.

I took a tie I'd never seen him wear; and I haven't worn it either.

Fourteen

Sunday, June 15:

A bird was trapped in the chimney, between the dining room gas-fire and the narrow pot at the top. It fluttered like a salacious whisper.

I phoned the Gas Board's emergency number. 'Is it an emergency?' they asked, then suggested I close the door to keep the noise out. I told him I'd tried that. 'Okay,' he said. 'Be there in an hour.'

They arrived six hours later while I listened to the paltry flappings behind the fire. In fifteen minutes everything was disconnected and a bundle of eyes and feathers lay in the corner, covered in soot.

'He's okay,' said the man from the Gas Board. 'He'll go when he's ready.'

We sat drinking coffee watching the bird sitting as if it was dead on its feet. Then it shook, hopped and flew out the window.

Helen left this morning.

Monday, June 16:

She came back last night at eleven o'clock. I heard the front door click just as I was thinking about walking to the phone box for Miranda's call.

'Hello,' I shouted.

Helen did not answer. She went into the kitchen. I picked up the telephone, dialled Miranda's number, let it ring twice and replaced the receiver.

'Who were you phoning?' asked Helen, standing by the kitchen door with a mug of chocolate.

'I've been trying to phone Don Calder all night. He isn't in.'

She walked past me, into the sitting room. 'Strange that you should want to phone Don Calder.'

'It's about the golf.'

She sat on a chair, crossed her legs and smiled. 'There are various ways of saying this,' she said, 'but I think the straight way is best.'

My stomach chilled and I immediately knew what I hadn't bothered to notice, immediately saw what now is obvious. She pulled back the curtains, but I didn't want to look. She assumed I knew more than I did and took my lack of interest in her movements as lack of concern for her, assumed I couldn't care less.

'I obviously can't take all my stuff tonight,' she said, 'but I'll come back for it. If you don't mind I'll take it away bit by bit. I don't need much. You can keep the furniture, but I would like you to think about selling the house. That way we'll both get some money. I don't really need it; Douglas is retiring next month and will obviously have a good pension, certainly enough to keep us both, but I would like a little something to fall back on. No one likes to be totally dependent on someone else.'

She had two suitcases packed, phoned and he came round. He sat in the car. She opened the curtain and waved, gathered her stuff and off she went. 'See you,' she said.

Friday, June 20:

Take it, said God. Take everything. You can take whatever you want. Then pay for it.

Sunday, June 22:

Phoned Miranda. We met in a lay-by.

'What is it this time?' she asked.

'There's no point in you moving in.'

'I thought we'd decided that. I don't want to move in to the house Helen's left. I want to move into our house.'

'But we can't get a place until I sell the one I've got.'

'Don't, darling; don't upset yourself. I can wait. I'll wait as

220

long as it takes; I love you, Angus. Hey, are you listening; I said I love you.'

'Yeah, I know.'

'And do you love me?'

'Sure.'

'You don't sound sure.'

'I'm sure.'

'You used to tell me all the time and now I've got to ask you. It's okay, I know you're under a lot of strain, trying to keep your head above water. But I'm on your side, I really am, darling. And if something's bothering you I want you to tell me?'

'It isn't something, it's everything.'

'Tell me.'

'The book's ground to a halt.'

'But that's fairly common, isn't it? Everyone knows about writer's block.'

'But there's nowhere for the book to go. There's nothing else that can happen. There isn't an ending, in fact there isn't even a story, never was.'

'Maybe you should give it a rest, try something else.'

'Such as?'

'I don't know; stories, a play, another novel, anything. Leave the book alone for a while, then go back to it. I know you; you're obsessive, and I love you for it, but maybe you ought to distance yourself, that way, when you go back to it, you'll see it more clearly.'

'Whatever else I do, it won't be another novel. The history of the novel is a history of pretence, black people pretending to be white, Scots pretending they are English, working-class pretending they're middle-class and middle-class pretending they're upper-class.

'Angus.'

'It's true. Fiction is so pessimistic, which obviously has the effect of making people like me feel powerless, which is what it's supposed to do. We've been told we're powerless and now we feel powerless. The bourgeoisie have taken over everything.'

221

'I think you need a cuddle.'

'No, listen to me. They even won the war, did you know that?'

'Who did?'

'The bourgeoisie, who do you think? Churchill won the war. He had a little help from his generals and their officers, but the soldiers merely did what they were told, the men and women who did the fighting and died for fuck-all simply responded to good leadership. So how can you compete with that, how can you come to terms with, far less survive in, a system where everything is subjected to revision or reassessment and that revision is adopted and fed back as propaganda.'

'What does this have to do with your novel?'

'Nothing: except that we have become dinosaurs in our own lifetime. We have neither history nor meaning. Who needs novels when there's computers and video games to entertain us.'

'Aren't you even writing your Diary?'

'What's the point? Experience doesn't transmit itself to the page. To write your own history is not enough. You have to fictionalise.'

'Have you told anyone how you feel?'

'I'm telling you.'

'How about seeing your doctor?'

'I don't need Valium.'

'I did say I thought you needed a cuddle.'

'Sometimes you remind me of a favourite line of my father's. He used to quote a bit from Chekhov about girls with bare shoulders and high ideals.'

'Come here.'

'I'm okay.'

'Then come here anyway.'

Oh, body and shame. She would have tempted Saint Ignatius Loyola, never mind me.

We lay in a bundle, Miranda and I. 'I wonder if I'm pregnant,' she whispered.

She told me she thinks that every time and worries till her

222

period comes. Then she's upset because she isn't pregnant. Which reminded me of another time.

'I thought you said women should only use men for screwing?'

'Did I say that?'

Driving home I imagined every filling station, lit up and empty, was a vehicle from outer space, alien and tranquil.

Friday, June 27:

3 a.m. A hoolity night.

The central heating is off and I sit like Raskolnikov with a blanket round my shoulders, my student cap hanging by the door. A shiver rushes through me so I switch on the gas fire. If gas fires had been around in Raskolnikov's time, he couldn't have afforded it, yet it's strange how Russian novels take the climate for granted. Many are cauld but few are frozen.

Can't sleep. Met Miranda in a different lay-by. We snuggled up like hamsters, lost in a summery tremble.

Earlier I spoke to Helen's mother, who hadn't seen her daughter for ages, she said, absolute ages. 'I don't know what to think. Human nature, I suppose.'

'Why is it that when something lousy happens it's blamed on human nature?'

'If I see Helen I'll tell her you phoned.'

'I want to make some arrangements for her to collect the stuff she's left.'

And an hour later the phone rang: Helen. 'I'm coming over.'

'When?'

'Seven o'clock.'

'What's the rush?' she asked, sitting in front of me.

'I want things settled as soon as possible.'

'You always were a bit too persistent for me.'

'Don't you mean horny?'

'It would be nice if I didn't have to suffer your hang-dog expression and self-pitying nasal whine.'

'Now that we've gone through that part of the proceedings, do you want a cup of tea?'

'Coffee would be nice.'

'I don't want to make anything you might enjoy. Coffee wasn't offered.'

Over tea and digestive biscuits she told me none of the staff seemed to have noticed that Helen and the Heidie were kipping up. 'I suppose they're so used to seeing us working together by now that they see it as a natural extension of our relationship.' The neighbours had also taken kindly to her moving in.

'And how do you feel about sleeping on a dead woman's bed?'

'We have single beds.'

'And I suppose the neighbours think you're a widow?'

'Why are you pretending to be hurt? I suppose you imagined our marriage would peter off like one of those American movies where the husband falls for a younger woman and leaves his wife, who is very distraught. Gradually, through therapy, she finds herself, then makes the big leap and sleeps with Another Man. And just when she's pondering the fact that this new prospect is so different from her husband, he's more sensitive, likes music, is interested in new things, like Mexican art which he wants to share with her, hubby phones. They have lunch and all is fine till it's time to part when, suddenly, he wants her back. She runs off and fumbles around till, confused and bewildered, she arrives at His Place, the New Man's Manhattan apartment. They have a martini and dance off down the avenue of a New York sunset.'

'Christ, you even come off best in your imagined movies.'

'You're pretending to be angry. But I imagine you're as relieved as I am. It leaves the way for you to bring your own clandestine relationship into the open.'

'Sorry, you're not getting away with that. All you're doing is trying to relieve your own guilt by imagining I'm in the same boat as yourself.'

224

'Angus, I know there's someone. And I know it because I can smell her.'

When she left, I phoned Miranda.

'Who were you phoning?' asked Helen. I had just replaced the receiver when the phone rang.

'Someone was phoning me. Wrong number.'

'I'm going to miss your lying, Angus. *Trés amusant*. Your level of invention is rather good. You ought to write a book. Anyway, you will have noticed we got nothing sorted out. The fact of the matter is that you can keep everything except my clothes.'

'I thought all this was agreed when you left.'

'But I've changed my mind slightly. There are one or two Lladro and Capo Delmonte pieces I'd like to take, if you don't mind. And apart from that the rest is yours. Douglas and I have decided we don't want anything from our previous marriages. We're going to start afresh. He's giving his stuff to a jumble sale. I'll collect my things next week. And I'd like a divorce, Angus. We haven't spoken about it and I am sorry to have to tell you over the telephone, but it would be best; that way we all know where we stand, don't you agree?'

If Father's assertions are true and we live our lives at an imaginary level and have become our own imaginary creations, can it be that reality is not to be endured?

All night, writing this and before, I've had a sense of weariness, reminding me of the time before the trial when I couldn't go to work. I left the house on time, caught the bus and all that, but when I saw the bank I could not go inside.

> Come Autumn, sae pensive in yellow and grey,
> And soothe me wi' tidings o' Nature's decay!
> The dark, dreary Winter and wild-driving snaw
> Alane can delight me – now Nanie's awa.

A bluebottle is trapped in the room; it bumps and buzzes into everything, rests for a couple of minutes and watches me while I feel foolish with my rolled newspaper, especially since it's killing itself anyway.

Monday, July 7:
Helen collected her stuff and was positively expansive: she gets the divorce, I get what's left.

'And what happens if I don't want a divorce?'

'I can't comment on that, Angus, since I've never known what you've wanted, but your pride will prevent you from doing anything other than divorcing me, especially since you are the injured party.'

Another thing I don't like about Helen is that she insists on pronouncing my name as two distinct syllables: male and female, yin and yang, Ann and Gus.

And today I bought a silver repro art nouveau frame into which the picture fits perfectly. I have coloured that picture inside my head. The hat is a darkish green, the colour of leaves, grass and all growing things. The coat is dark blue with a palish blue blouse, two of the tones of the sea and sky. Her shoes are black.

This lady has haunted me since Greenbank House and her identity is as ambiguous as her face squinting into the sun; sometimes it's a smile, or a quizzical ripple that fades to a frown. On the sideboard her moods match mine and now I could not live without this small silver-framed and dumpy woman I never met.

Monday, July 14:
The first weekday of our holiday fortnight, four-fifths of the city's population have been removed to Spain and it's raining. I write to the noise of rain on the double glazing, which means I'm unable to hang out my washing which means I'm behind with my ironing.

'You must be giving the wife some regular boffing,' said Calder at our golf outing last week. 'That shirt looks great. Did she starch your collar? Jesus. That's service.'

My contempt for this toadeous bladder of lard has reached

such grandeur as to make it difficult to write his name. He leers and asks if I'm missing Miranda, tells me how good she looks and thanks me weekly for 'putting me on to her, old boy'.

Miranda says he is always trying to introduce a sexual element into their conversations and doesn't know how much longer she can stand his attentions. 'I left you because I couldn't stand the secrecy and now I can't stand the alternative,' she said tonight. 'I don't know why you can't tell him to lay off.'

'If the bank knew my marriage was over they'd shift me sideways, into some administrative position. Every year my salary would be increased by not very much and I would be asked if I was sure my future lay with the company, especially when they considered how good they had been to me during my brother's trial and so on. I've told you this.'

'Ever thought of leaving?'

'You mean picking up the pension and wandering off. I'm going to have to do that anyway. It's a matter of time.'

'And what would you do?'

'Don't know.'

'I got a phone call. A friend of mine, Susan, is working in London. She's offered me a job beside her, nothing to do with banking, sales executive with an advertising agency.'

'The high life.'

'It's very well paid, Angus, and I know I could do the job. It would be a new start for us. I couldn't go without you and if you tell me not to go I won't do it.'

'Let's not talk about it now.'

'I know, darling. I only mentioned it, that's all. Think about it and let me know. Will you do that?'

'Sure.'

'You know, this place could be quite nice if you painted it and got rid of some of this furniture. What you need is a couple of sofas, nice deep sofas with soft furnishings, lots of little lamps around the place and decent curtains. Liberty, Laura Ashley, that sort of thing. And plain walls done in pastel colours with lots of pictures. I quite fancy having a go at this place. Would you let me?'

227

'Hardly seems worth it if I'm going to sell it.'

'All right then, our place, can I decorate our place?'

'You mean the London town-house?'

'Anywhere, darling. Anywhere. I'd live anywhere with you.'

That was earlier, this is now; 1.25 a.m. and she's just left. *Revelations 22:12.*

Thursday, July 17:

Phamie came over last night.

Last night was Thursday. This is Friday morning. Hot chocolate, dressing gown, slippers, gas fire and Diary.

I felt quite touched that my step-sister should have abandoned her night off, paid a baby-sitter and forsaken all pleasure to devote herself to my misfortune.

'Whatever's wrong, you're looking well on it,' she said, surveying the room. 'Christ Almighty, look at it. Helen's gone; I can tell. This place is so bloody tidy, like a Wimpey showhouse, nothing's out of place, everything's really neat and prissy. Bet the carpet hasn't been hoovered though. It's all show, Angus. Even from the outside the place has a sour air of masculine gloom. And I'll bet the bathroom's hilarious.'

Her presence changed the room. She took off her coat, lit a cigarette and made a pot of tea. 'Tell me about it,' she said. There were seven fag-ends in the ashtray when I finished. 'Don't tell me,' she said. 'I know. I smoke too much. It's because I'm a woman. More women smoke than men because they need it.

'So what's the score with Helen? I know you've told me, but I wasn't listening. I was wondering if Tracy was back. Melanie has this imaginary friend called Tracy and last night she told me Tracy wasn't here. She's gone to live in her own house. That was why she couldn't sleep. She was worried in case she'd never see her again. So, repeat it for me slowly; what's your problem?'

When I repeated much of what I'd said, she sighed. 'I always found Helen a bit of a cold fish, but that's my bias showing. I

228

think you'd be very hard to live with. You're so bloody silent and individual. It's that home you were brought up in, all that isolation. No mother. So, who's the new woman and when can I meet her?'

'First you tell me the place is gloomy, then you want to know who the new woman is.'

'Sure. The two are not mutually exclusive. I know you've got someone. But you don't have to tell me. It's okay. I understand.'

She spoke about the kids and how they wouldn't get a holiday this year. She was hoping to get away for a week or two, but Melanie was enjoying the garden and Casper loved being off school, playing with his friends and running around on his bike. Then, suddenly, she asked, 'When was the last time you saw Cammy?'

I promised to visit when things were settled. It was difficult since he'd been moved from the top-security nick.

'He's all we've got,' she said. 'There's you and me and him and that's it. The MacPhails.'

'I've given up trying to be a MacPhail.'

But visiting Cammy's a chore. He's changed, his politics have hardened, yet in other ways he's closer to us than ever. He has pictures of Caspar and Melanie in his cell and writes to them every week.

Helen was never keen on prison visits: '*Trés dépressant*,' she said. I tried to apologise, but Cammy understood better than me. 'It must be awful for her,' he said. 'Why should she come? She doesn't know me. And it's a long way for you to come on your own.'

'I think you should try to see him,' Phamie said. 'Make the effort. I know he'd appreciate it.'

Visiting Cammy has become my penance for being adopted. I go to Perth once a month without knowing what I've done to deserve the penance.

Which reminds me. Phamie brought up three sheets of paper. 'For you,' she said. 'I found it in a drawer. God knows how it got there.'

Not one find, but two. A scribbly note was saved alongside the piece itself, trapped in the paperclip between the first couple of pages. I've no idea when this was written or where it was sent.

which of course you are welcome to use, though I don't seem able to write anything serious this weather. Not that humour necessarily evinces a lack of seriousness, for, as you are well

A BLAST FROM THE NORTH (From Our Scottish Correspondent) or SOME THOUGHTS CONCERNING THE QUANTITIES OF OOSE GENERATED BY TROUSER TURN-UPS AND THE EFFECT IT HAS ON THE MENTAL HEALTH OF THE COMMUNITY, WITH PARTICULAR REGARD TO THE LOWER ORDERS:
by Angus Macphail

Oose (u:s) *n. Scot. dialect.* dust; fluff. [of unknown origin] *Collins English Dictionary*

It will hardly have escaped even the most desultory observer's attention that there is a vast amount of so-called unemployment in the northern reaches of this country at present. It is also a well-known fact that most of the so-called unemployed are scroungers – cut-purses, felons and footpads who will neither work nor want.

Since wealth is divinely apportioned by our Maker and the process can neither be helped nor hindered by human interference, and since poverty is also a major contributor to unemployment of the body, mind and spirit, we must also assume that unemployment is divinely apportioned. As St Paul said to the Ephesians, 'The Lord giveth and the Lord taketh away,' which has often been interpreted as one of the Saint's more ambiguous statements, as a pathogen for unbelievers or a tool for the righteous, but, surely, in this instance, his meaning is clear for all to see.

Be that as it may, laziness is not, and never has been,

apportioned from above. And while I contend there may very well be a few needy and deserving cases where hardship can be seen to have been caused by unemployment, by far the vast majority of those currently yclept unemployed are no more than lazy and indolent loafers.

Neither can laziness be proved to be congenital, so what then is the cause of this massive increase in laziness on a scale unknown in the annals of the civilised Western world. I think I can offer pointers towards a solution.

Trouser oose, no more or less. That is the culprit. It is caused by men having turn-ups in their trousers.

Since the unemployed have to walk in search of employment, sometimes for great distances, even miles at a time, oose is generated by the movement of their feet, the dust on the roads and the traffic in general. The oose will gather in the trouser turn-up and when there is a sufficient quantity it will rise into the atmosphere and the stroller will absorb the noxious substance by inhalation through the nostril. After the oose has been inhaled, it is my contention that it circulates inside the head causing severe damage to the brain, so that after a long period of unemployment, much walking and inhalation, the oose in the brain causes laziness.

Dust will clog up any sort of works. The veracity of this thesis need not be tested further than a random observation of what oose does to a vacuum cleaner. If it does that to a machine, think of the damage it could cause the human brain.

It is therefore obvious that full employment can be achieved by forcing the poor to have their trouser turn-ups removed, thereby doing away with that dangerous and flamboyant area where the source of the problem congregates. There is no good reason for the cuff of a ruffian's trouser to be turned up. It is mere frippery, caused by vanity and an improper sense of proportion regarding their status and as such should not be encouraged.

Further, who knows what illnesses could be cured by removing trouser turn-ups. If a surfeit of oose in the head causes laziness, it is not beyond the bounds of possibility that it is also the main cause of mental illness. It is my contention that we could save vast amounts of money on the National Health Service by having trouser turn-ups removed, together with the oose that congregates there. We would cure, or at the very least improve, the mental health of a vast majority of the poor community, needy and otherwise, for once this noxious dust is circulating it will not, indeed is incapable of, discriminating between a needy, deserving unemployed person and one of the other sort. Removal of trouser oose will cause many of the so-called mental health establishments to be closed down, the patients sent home and the properties returned to their former and, in my opinion, rightful owners, who may then restore them to the whole community as housing complexes, restaurants or even *Les Palais de Dance*.

Therefore, by ridding society of trouse oose we would, at a stroke, improve mental health, cure laziness, return our country to full employment and herald a return to gracious living.

This theory, by no means revolutionary or untypical, came to me this morning when I cleaned the oose from my own trouser turn-ups, which causes me finally to reiterate the old adage that, if each of us had a care to our personal appearance, society as a whole would improve immeasurably.

My father's last written piece. Let's call it that. Undated, so we can't be sure. But near enough.

Saturday, July 19:
It's actually Sunday morning.

Saturday is wash day, which means there's a pile of ironing tomorrow. I also make a chicken casserole which we ate in the living room, sitting on the floor, watching telly. Miranda refused to do my ironing.

She tells me Calder is besotten. He tries to touch and rub

232

himself against her, contrives himself beside her in a crowd and accidentally squeezes her tits. His attentions are recognised and resented by every other woman in the department, though no one would have him in a gift. I thought she was able to deal with this, but now I am not so sure. Anyway, first things first.

We were watching the golf when I told her. I had to tell someone, just as I know I will have to put it down on paper sometime, write it out properly, convert it into a story, a poem or something. Diarisation is not enough. The incident in itself is nothing, though quite touching in a pathetic sort of way; it's the implications.

Rather as you'd pick a scab to make it heal, I've been trying to see this Judy again. I could not believe she did not know me and wondered why she was so adamantly forgetful.

Yesterday's golf was enjoyable because we were again rained off and spent the afternoon in the bar. And some of the euphoria continued into the car. I switched on the radio as the opening smash and flutes of Chabrier's *March Joyeuse* conducted by Beecham erupted, followed by the *Coppelia* Prelude.

Such joy unmasked when I saw her, sitting in the swingpark wearing a brown suede jacket, jeans and a pale pink angora jumper, her hair like strands of mist.

I smiled and waved. She turned away, gathered the child, strapped him in the pushchair, glided the pram round the corner and that was that.

I sat in the café for almost an hour. Only when I was too embarrassed to stay did I move, only when the prospect of more coffee was too appalling did I go.

Walking towards the car I heard someone call my name. I stopped and looked around, saw no one I recognised and carried on. Then again I thought I heard my name. I turned and a stranger came towards me out of the crowd.

The ghost of a face lay in her face. 'Don't you recognise me?' I smiled.

'Who'd have believed it?' she said. We smiled at each other, she with irony and I with embarrassment. She shook her head. This woman was shabbily dressed and middle-aged. She wore no make-up. Her hair was limp and tied at the back, her shoulders rounded and her hands were red.

'Angus,' she said. 'Angus MacPhail. You said you'd remember me for ever. I'm Judy O'Brien and used to be Judy Macdonald.'

She told me I hadn't changed all that much, older like everyone else, a few grey hairs and going bald. How was the family, Debbie and Cammy? Her mother was dead, but her father was still around, off the drink and full of new enthusiasms. Which way was I going? She was off to meet her daughter and did I have time to come along?

We walked together through the crowds and saw her daughter wheeling a pushchair.

'What's the use?' said Judy. 'They never learn. I think she's made the same mistakes as me.'

Judy's daughter looked at me slyly, giggling as we were introduced. 'This is the man I told you about,' she said. 'This is the man who thought I was you.'

'God help you,' said Judy.

She was two years older and a grandmother. Her daughter was mother to the woman, the way Judy stayed in my memory, fresh and hopeful as she was in the best of times.

Miranda smiled. 'That's life,' she said. 'Time's winged chariot.'

And later she phoned: 'I'm sorry to have to phone you. It's just that when I tried to talk, you were preoccupied with other things and I don't like to intrude when you're like that. Well, it sometimes seems as if I'm intruding.

'Angus, I've never enjoyed the secrecy and I hate it now, not just because of Calder but because I don't see any reason for it. I know you've tried to explain, but I still don't see why you can't tell them, why you can't at least tell Calder to lay off. You don't need to tell him everything. Just tell him you're seeing me and he'll get the message. I can't stand it and I can't stand him. I don't want to go to London, darling. I love you,

234

more than you'll ever know; I love you and I want to be with you. But if it isn't going to happen I'll need a clean break. So tell me. I don't mean to force your hand, but I applied for that job, the one Susan told me about, and I've been offered an interview. All you have to do is tell me not to go. Not now; no, don't do it now. Think about it and tell me what you want. Let me know. If you say nothing I'll know what you mean and I won't mention it ever again. Honest. I'm sorry to phone. Forgive me? Thanks. Night-night, darling. Sleep well.'

Sunday, July 20:
    Went for a drink at lunchtime.
    Not a good idea.
    Met a man who spoke with a very pronounced Highland accent, a professional man having a lunchtime drink with his son, who spoke with the same accent. We got to talking about the Gaelic, which the father spoke, but not the son, who only knew what little he'd picked up, having been raised in the city. The father never bothered teaching the lad, reckoning he'd never need it. Indeed, the father had decided never to use it again.
    The first time the son heard his father speaking Gaelic he got a fright. The old man was talking in his sleep. He bought me a drink and admitted he always dreams in Gaelic.
    I'm not going back to that pub. It depresses me.

Monday, July 21:
    A recycled envelope arrived this morning, my address written on brown sticky tape which obliterated my sister's name and address.

You know where.
Don't know when.

Dearest Step-Brother:
    Clearing out a drawer this Saturday morning I found this between the sheets of newspaper. The goddam stuff keeps cropping up. Thought you'd better have it. What do you do

with these pieces anyway? I've read some and they don't make sense to me. I don't suppose they made sense to the Old Man either. Perhaps if there were more we could do something with them. Sorry about tearing it up and all that, long ago I mean. The idea of seeing Dad's handwriting when he was dead freaked me out.

So come up and see me sometime!

Love and kisses.

Euphemia   XXX

The last of the Underwood. The carbon copy of a letter.

just as occasionally one can see a silver birch, an ash or even an elm growing from a rock, or the way bramble, ground elder or dandelions can push their way through the tarmac. It's another perspective on a nation whose unwritten motto is: They didnae beat us by much.

The intentions were good enough, but far too late to be any use. We've been dragged into the twentieth century; we don't want to be here so we've left our minds in another time which never existed. Old men in kilts occupy the bodies of children and work computers.

Consider how a job can become an insult: hawker, tinker, fishwife, scavenger and so on. We do not consider the merits of the task, only the defects, however marginal, however real or imaginary, and attribute them to the whole profession.

That happens all over the world, but this violent landscape and fickle climate, the tension of monuments to the past, all around us and growing, appearing from the mist and rain like mute and lovely ghosts; those who took us by force and have kept us with force, those we defied with silence, those we misunderstood, laughed at, detested or understood only too well, those we obeyed and felt superior to, those who left us with a country which is enigmatic and unintelligible, confined and uncontainable, proud yet sluttish; they all formed us, made our character and ourselves, conditioned by events outside our control as well as a terrifying insularity of the mind. I call it Scotland; you may call it someplace else, England, Japan, Czechoslovakia, USA, we could be anywhere.

I am now and throughout my adult life have always been obsessed by this country and its peoples. My crime is that I wanted it all and, more than anything, wanted to tell it all, the good and the not so good, to redress the balance, to take it away from the simpletons who have restricted us, narrowed our vision, saw us for what they could get. Too late I realised that one cannot tell it all and even if one could one mustn't. For everyone must make their own discoveries, everyone must make their own private journey to where they belong. You can ignore it, but that is a deliberate act of belonging somewhere else. You could, on the other hand, choose all of it, little or nothing, but we must make our own mistakes, find our own loves.

There are no universal truths, only our own truths. There are no absolutes, especially about a country or its people; there is only a way of seeing. To limit our understanding we fail to understand our limits. We must not restrict our discoveries and cannot confine a place to our opinion of it.

Realising what I have tried to do, I must tell you I've failed, as everyone who tries will fail. It is impossible. Publish this book and you will make me a laughing stock because some smart-arsed casuist will say, 'This is not how it is, rather it is this way.' He'll tell us how he sees it and of course will be quite right, failing to mention I am also right. He will tell his opinion as I have told mine. It is not a matter of right or wrong, simply of choice.

Our education system has made us believe history happened elsewhere. We were taught English history, or British history. Scottish history is for the tourists. We are the only country in the world who are not taught our own history. And if you do not believe we are a country then you have not read the Treaty of Union. Being taught that history happened elsewhere means we have no belief in

237

ourselves and are automatically educated into having an inferiority complex, believing nothing important happens here because nothing important has happened here and nothing important will happen because we do not know what has happened.

I do not mean this to apply to me, though I am obviously as eligible as others deem me. Therefore, I must again ask that you return my manuscript. I realise I am quite late in asking. There will obviously be financial difficulties, contractual clauses and God knows what else to be met. I will meet them, because I cannot now change my mind.

Thank you for your interest. You have no idea what a joy it has been for me to realise that life has not been useless and my worst fears were groundless. Your faith in this book has made me very happy and more than I dared dream of, yet enough to make the project worthwhile.

After two heart attacks, I ask myself questions I have asked all my life and the answers seem ever more remote.

Where is my life? And when will I live it?

It seems I have spent so much time away from the things that are important. The penalty I paid for scribbling was too great. Because of my obsession I have deprived myself of the sight of my wife and children. Yet I had no choice and would do the same again. The joy is in doing and nothing else. I was condemned long ago, condemned to observe life rather than live it, to take notes rather than participate.

You cannot make my life a failure. If I publish, that book will become the yardstick others will measure me by. I have asked my daughter to burn it, to make a pyre after my death. When I go it goes too.

A page and a bit, torn across the bottom. Please don't find any more. Please, Phamie, burn it, again and again and again if need be. Unless you find the name of the publisher.

The Comeback

An old man I knew used to fight in the booths. Stripped to the waist for three rounds, he'd take on anybody. He beat a man with a yellow face and watery eyes who brought up blood before he fell; for this he got a fiver and the title at ten shillings a fight.

He stayed to beat hungry men who were fighting a dream. Heavy men did not fight him; it was understood, he had his work and they had theirs.

The Boss said the fair was moving and did the champ want to come for more money?

But with two nights to go a bald, sad face came into the ring. He clinched and whispered: 'My wife is sick. Lie down. Please. I need the money. My wife will die. Please. Lie down.'

Eventually the champ got fed up listening. He was about to tell the guy to get on with the fight, when a kidney punch in the third made him wince. Then there was an uppercut and a left cross.

The new champ got a fiver. Next night he was taking on all comers. But the Boss wouldn't let him fight the old champ. Bad for business, he said.

The fair came back at the end of summer and the old champ got a fight on the second night.

'Remember me?' he said in the clinch.

'Uh-hu.'

'How's your wife?'

'She's fine, thanks.'

The old champ was KO'd in the second round.

Sixteen

Saturday, October 11:
   The Comeback returned today. My forty-third rejection slip.
   Perhaps we ought to introduce rejection slips into our everyday practice, as the first step towards making life more like fiction. We meet someone, don't like them and hand them a rejection slip.

> I regret I am unable to continue
> our association. Thank you for
> your future co-operation.
>   Angus MacPhail

Helen's in Majorca. Left this morning.
   She and the paramour, Douglas Strachan, came round last night, extolling the joys of early retirement, eating my canapés and sausage rolls, drinking my wine and holding hands; a pretty sickening display from a couple of geriatrics.
   Everything has been amiably agreed, though I did affect the huff for a wee while, allowing it to flow into the delta of Better Man Won. No hard feelings and divorce going through.
   'And how do you think things will go at the bank?' Douglas asked as if he cared, stroking his moustache and lifting his eyebrows.
   'Don't know,' said I. But I do know because it's already happened. I'm seeing the committee.
   Tonight's fiasco should never have occurred, though I always knew it might. It's Helen's idea of a nice time. We socialise and pretend to hide our feelings instead of handing out rejection slips.
   '*Au revoir*, darling,' she said and offered me a powdered

cheek. I shook hands with her, nodding to Douglas and said goodbye. Cards at Christmas for a couple of years, then nothing.

She thinks she's being decisive, having left me for Douglas. And I know differently, but which of us is right? Both accounts are true or have truth in them. What she remembers and what I remember are perfectly correct, even though neither happened. It's called Freedom of Choice.

Friday, December 5:

A letter from Miranda arrived today.

She's been to the National Theatre, to a concert and a show. She's taken a walk along the Embankment, stood on Hyde Park Corner on Sunday with weekday afternoons in the Tate and National Galleries. *Trés civilisé*, as Helen would say.

And she's settled into her shared flat. The job's going fine and she's seeing someone. Best to tell me herself, rather than have me hear it from someone else. Whom?

Terribly sorry. Soon I'll see it was for the best. Hope all is well. Take care.

Take care: it's the new catchphrase of the eighties. People say it so often, you know they don't mean it. Or am I being cynical? Has television given us a sense of neighbourliness? 'And remember, be careful out there.'

And so on. PS says Miranda: There are National Front slogans everywhere. *If they're black, send them back!*

Who wants to live in a country where people learn nothing?

Sunday, December 7:

Phamie phoned: 'How's it going?' she asked.

I told her.

'Are you sure you're doing the right thing?' was her second question.

I told her about the committee because she asked.

'Sorry you're going,' they said. 'Quite understand, of course. The reason we've called you in is to find out if there's anything we can do. You've been with us all your working life and we're going to miss you.'

241

No one mentioned why I was there. No one mentioned what caused the commotion: rumours of a liaison with a girl who no longer works at the bank. No one mentioned Miranda crying or the suspected breakdown, Calder's comfort. No one mentioned the previous chats.

They lie so blandly, like politicians. Even the word liar is too brash; too honest. We need something softer, with more syllables. Two-syllabled words can be harsh. They lie nicely, with care, aplomb and a little dignity. As soon as they say they're sorry, you know they're lying.

Okay, I know: politicians are easy targets. But if a politician said, 'Vote for me so's I can do what I like,' no one would vote for him. Or her. Yet that's what happens. Similarly, if a banker said, 'All I care about is money,' no one would give him any. Or her. Yet that's what happens.

'And what are you going to do now?'

Into business for myself, said I. Becoming a shopkeeper. Always fancied it. Now's the time. Must strike out. Things are tough. Bold approach called for. Service industries all the rage.

'Well,' said someone. 'If you ever need the services of a bank you know where to come.'

Tuesday, December 8:

I phoned my sister.

'Guess what?' she said. 'Casper wants an Action Man for Christmas. I'm really really upset about it. I don't know whether to give it to him or not. All his friends have one, so he wants one too. Yesterday he asked who John Lennon was, and when do you want your Christmas present?'

'At Christmas.'

'I thought I might bring it round.'

I opened it as soon as she got here. Wrapped in green paper, with red and white hollies, the label shows a Pickwickian figure making merry: *To Angus: Merry Christmas With Love From Debbie, Caspar and Melanie XXX.*

It's a Victorian text, framed in a deep red wood with a

golden filigree lining every corner. The text has a border of intertwined roses, acorns and ivy:

> JESUS CHRIST
> *is Master of this home.*
> *The silent listener to*
> *every conversation –*
> *The invisible guest*
> *at every meal.*

She has a rare sense of humour, my sister.

'Angus,' she said. 'It's daft, you and I living apart. Where are you going to go? You've sold your house and Cuchullain Avenue is very empty. We need a man around the place, so what do you say?'

'Phamie, I think I love you.'

'Well, that's a start.'

So I wandered around for the last time tonight, up the hill past deepest suburbia. The new couple are settling in and I ghosted around, watching while they stared at their television set. The woman, who looks like Rembrandt, was knitting. She sang to the Coco Pops advert while her husband read the paper.

I turned up my collar and walked back to the hotel, catching my reflection in the foyer. I've been here for a couple of nights, so they're used to me. No one budged when I stared at myself in the swinging door glass. I looked like my father, Angus MacPhail; as though he was watching me.

I told them I was leaving, would gather my stuff in the morning and have the room cleared by eleven o'clock.